"You are beyond m

Oliver continued, "You and awakened desires. I don't want this to tumble around our ears, and if we became closer and something went wrong between us, we would both suffer. Friends are hard to find. Good friends are rare."

"True. No friend has ever made me feel like you do." She put her fingers over his and took his hand from her jaw, but clasped it to keep her balance. She tiptoed, steadied herself and put a kiss on his cheek. "Good night."

Addison gave her the light, and she stepped inside. As the door closed, she heard his voice.

"'Night, Sophia."

The sound of her name on his lips caused a renewed longing. Bursts of feeling that almost took her to her knees.

She put her hand to her forehead. She may have made a mistake, but she would so like to continue with the error.

Author Note

Most characters I've written have seemed alive to me, and the little boy Stubby is foremost among them.

Stubby was instrumental in my first published novel, *Safe in the Earl's Arms*, and in my second, *A Captain and a Rogue*. I hated to leave him behind because I loved writing about his joy for life and his rebel spirit.

Now I've brought him back for a brief appearance in this book and his own happily-ever-after. I hope the former seafaring cabin boy touches your imagination as much as he did mine.

HARLEQUIN®
HISTORICAL™

Recycling programs
for this product may
not exist in your area.

ISBN-13: 978-1-335-40762-7

Tempting a Reformed Rake

Copyright © 2022 by Elizabeth Tyner

For questions and comments about the quality of this book,
please contact us at CustomerService@Harlequin.com.

Harlequin Enterprises ULC
22 Adelaide St. West, 41st Floor
Toronto, Ontario M5H 4E3, Canada
www.Harlequin.com

Printed in U.S.A.

LIZ TYNER

Tempting a Reformed Rake

HARLEQUIN
HISTORICAL

Liz Tyner lives with her husband on an Oklahoma acreage she imagines is similar to the ones in the children's book *Where the Wild Things Are*. Her lifestyle is a blend of old and new, and is sometimes comparable to the way people lived long ago. Liz is a member of various writing groups and has been writing since childhood. For more about her, visit liztyner.com.

Books by Liz Tyner

Harlequin Historical

The Notorious Countess
The Runaway Governess
The Wallflower Duchess
Redeeming the Roguish Rake
Saying I Do to the Scoundrel
To Win a Wallflower
It's Marriage or Ruin
Compromised into Marriage
A Cinderella for the Viscount
Tempting a Reformed Rake

English Rogues and Grecian Goddesses

Safe in the Earl's Arms
A Captain and a Rogue
Forbidden to the Duke

Visit the Author Profile page
at Harlequin.com.

Dedicated to Suzy—
one of the *best* librarians in an occupation
that attracts wonderful people.

Chapter One

The Smoking Boar was like any other dockside tavern in England, except it smelled like rancid cow hides and had patrons who didn't notice.

Oliver Addison stopped in front of the scarred owner, a man whose eyelids gave him the façade of perpetual sleepiness, but appearances deceived. He'd left more scars on men than could have covered his own body twice over.

'Why did you send for me?' Addison asked.

'This man here needs to speak with you.' The owner gave a sluggish nod to Addison's right. 'He asked for you by name.'

Addison rotated, expecting to see a man. Instead, a fresh-faced boy, with shoulder-length reddish hair and wearing a seafaring coat, waited. The boy sat on a lopsided chair, a table in front of him and another chair opposite leaning the other way. He scrutinised Addison. The owner and the two other patrons did the same.

The lad held out a hand. Empty. Addison acted on the offered gesture.

'I'm Stubby. My friend, Mr Broomer, sent me here

to ask for you. He works at Cap'n Ben's house while Cap'n Ben's at sea and Broomer keeps an ear to what's happenin', so he knew you could help me.' The boy grasped his mug. 'He's heard of you being here to make certain you get all the shipments you're expecting for them peers and the banker. Says you understand both sides of the law better'n most and folks can trust you.'

'True.'

'I'm lookin' for family. And he says you know every woman of bad morals in London.'

Addison barely moved his lips. 'Maybe half.' A person's past had a long memory. The boy's age would be somewhere near shaving. Brown eyes, not his own blue. Addison raised a brow, half expecting to be informed he was a father. The boy reminded him of a younger version of himself, but not in likeness.

'I want you to help me find my mother. She worked for Mad Kate. And I can't find a Mad Kate.'

'That's all?' Addison put a hand on the chair back, surprised to feel a glimmer of disappointment that the lad hadn't claimed to be his son. He'd always tried to be spared that sort of moment and now he almost wished he hadn't.

'That's a lot when you ain't got folks.'

'I understand.'

A silence rested between them while Addison contemplated where he'd heard the name the youngster asked about. 'Mad Kate married and is now Mrs Wilson.'

'So Mrs Wilson ain't a workin' lady no more?' The boy took a drink from his mug and didn't blink.

'Mr Wilson left with another woman a month later,

but Kate liked being Mrs Wilson, she just didn't like Mr Wilson.'

'Where can I find her?'

'That's no place for a lad.' Addison gripped the chair harder.

The boy stood, puffed out his chest, then drained his mug. 'I've sailed around the Cape. I've been at sea most of my life. I'm shorter and younger than you, but I ain't no baby. I'll find Mrs Wilson myself.' He rose and displayed a man's swagger in the bony frame.

'I'll take you there.' Addison didn't move. He'd been a strutting youth once. 'I've a vehicle outside.'

The boy sniffed, and wiped his mouth with his sleeve. 'I'd appreciate it. Otherwise, I was gonna ask my friend, the Earl of Warrington—' he raised his chin so high he appeared taller and older '…and he would help me find her. But he's in the country and I decided I'd like to know sooner rather than later.'

He grabbed the front of his seafaring frock coat and tightened his hands on the lapel. If he'd had a visible chest, it would have been thrust out. 'I'll send *my* carriage driver on his way and go with you. I got use of Cap'n Ben's carriage while the *Ascalon* is at sea.'

Addison took in a breath. 'You're that cabin boy? The one who sailed on *Ascalon*? The ship that returned with the Grecian beauties and the Earl wed one of the women.' All of London had spoken of it for a time.

Stubby's chin wobbled in agreement and he touched his shirt collar. 'I left my cravat on the ship.'

Addison snorted.

'I don't need no neckcloth to make me sportin'.' He studied Addison's neck. 'But not everybody is fine in a cravat.'

'You could use a haircut.' Addison moved his head in acknowledgement of the verbal joust about the cravat and gave a superior nod to the long hair.

The lad shook his head, his reddish mane brushing well over his collar. 'The ladies like it. Ain't ever cutting these locks short.' He winked. 'Women behold my hair, offer to cut it for me and notice I need fattenin' up.' He rubbed his stomach. 'I won't ever be hungry.'

'Perhaps I should grow mine longer,' Addison said.

The lad examined him, one hundred years of confidence and attitude in that thin body. 'I'd imagine it'd be a waste o' time.'

Outside what Mrs Wilson called her establishment for only the best of impure ladies—and worst of morals—Addison stopped. 'You're not following me in there.'

The lad's jaw tightened. He glanced at the door, stared up at Addison, studied a high window and widened his stance. 'I want to find my mother. She might be searchin' for me and I don't have no relatives. I want some of my own. Every family I got belongs to somebody else first.'

Raucous female laughter filtered through the wood.

'But I be glad to wait for you.' The boy examined the sky. 'It's too nice a day to be inside. I'll wait here. I got to know if Delilah is here.'

Addison kept his smile hidden and walked inside, relieved that the boy wasn't following.

Once beyond the door, a male servant showed him to Mrs Wilson's office. She sat, her wig on the stand behind her desk. The false hair reached taller than her head. An additional wig lay flat on the table at her side, like a flattened animal that had had the life squeezed from it. Wisps of grey hair escaped her peach-sized bun and her features were scrubbed clean of cosmetics.

'Robby mentioned you've a special request,' she said. 'What can we do for you?'

'I'm searching for Delilah. A woman who worked for you at your old place.'

'Delilah?' She scratched her cheek. 'Delilah?' She paused, thinking, and picked up the wig on the desk and put it on. 'With auburn hair? Prettiest colour I ever seen. Had a little boy with her and she knew there'd be sailin' folks around. She found him a place to apprentice on a ship. That one?'

'That would be her.'

She adjusted her wig, tucking in the strands. 'As soon as we found a place for the little redhead, she was gone the next day. Don't know what happened to her.'

'What was her last name?'

'August. But it was the month of August. If it had been June, that might have changed her name.'

'Where can I find her?'

'Can't help you.'

He indicated the ledger on her desk. 'Perhaps you could check notes you made in the past and find out where she went.'

She snorted. 'I don't keep records like that. It doesn't do anyone any good.'

Addison nodded, thanked the woman, gave her his name in case she recalled anything helpful, told her where she could find him, and hesitated before he left. 'You'll be paid.'

Tired grey eyes studied him. 'Doesn't matter how much. Still can't help you.'

'Her son's trying to find her.'

'Well, it would be nice to reunite the child with his mother. You know how we place strong emphasis on families here.' A grin, then she slapped the book on her desk closed.

He'd have to inform the lad that he'd reached a dead end in his search, but that was better than having to tell the boy his mother had died. Besides, now Stubby could always have an image of an angelic woman who had had his best interests at heart.

His boots snapped on the wooden floor as he left and he paused before opening the door and stepping outside. He'd be destroying Stubby's hope of relatives. That gave him an uneasy feeling in the pit of his stomach.

He moved into the sunshine and a woman with a small portmanteau spoke with the boy—she did seem to be admiring his hair.

Then his attention locked on her. A thick shawl was clutched firmly around her, long enough that the fringe on it hung to her knees and swayed in the breeze. Evening sunshine trickling over her hair, giving her the air of purity and respectability and maybe hints of a bygone era.

He didn't move. Studying an illusion. An illusion he'd never seen before.

When she gazed directly at him, one flick of her double-thick lashes and he knew he didn't want her to step inside Kate's place. His body stirred, but he shoved his desires away, forcing himself to concentrate on the problem in front of him.

A woman with the appearance of goodness in front of Mrs Wilson's could fill a tally sheet with mischief if she wished.

The boy grinned, his attention diverted from the female, and he took two running steps towards Addison. 'Did you find her? My mother? Is she here?'

Addison felt a kick in his own gut when he saw the hope in the expression. But life spared no man its realities and the boy was about to be thrust with an alarming jolt into manhood.

'She left a long time ago. She didn't leave any way to contact her.'

Stubby deflated as if someone had given him a kick in the midsection as well. His shoulders almost collapsed in on themselves.

'I'm sorry.' Addison heard the sympathy in his voice.

Stubby's jaw poked out as if he were biting his tongue. It was hard for a lad to cry in front of a man.

'Well... You take your ports where you can find them,' he said, then brushed a hand over his eye before turning to the woman behind him. 'But I found a sister. Her name is—' Stubby peered at her, waiting.

'Sophia,' she inserted. 'Sophia Marland.' She met Addison's eyes and took a step away.

Stubby grinned, standing proud again. 'I have a sister.'

Addison corrected the boy. 'She's not your sister.'

'Oh, yes, she is.' Stubby swaggered again. 'She said she'd be happy to be my family and I'm takin' her with me. She said she's fallen on rough times and was stoppin' here because somebody inside might help.' He took Addison by the arm and moved so they weren't facing the woman and he spoke softly. 'I know she's not really my sister, but she needs somebody respectable like me to take care of her. She needs a brother for a chaperon.

She's either my sister or my ward and I want a sister more'n a ward.'

'You can't. I don't think you quite understand...' Addison softened his voice, sparing a fleeting appraisal of the woman.

'Yes, I do. She ain't got no way to support herself.'

The woman stood, biting her lip, watching Addison. He wasn't going to let the woman take advantage of the boy. Likely she'd have had a family of six parents if it would put a pence in her palm.

'She's between jobs. Like me.' Stubby rushed to continue. 'And her hair's a nice colour, but it ain't goin' to keep her fed.'

'I'm sure she's between—jobs—but—'

Stubby held his arm in an L shape and made a fist, patting the muscle. 'I'm man enough to care for a sister.' He swung his arm in, snapped his fingers and said, 'I can have a position for her in no time. I ain't no feather. I'm strong as nails.'

Addison might not have seen the woman's shudder but for the fringe on her shawl and the soft tendrils of hair framing her eyes.

'I have a job for you,' he said to Stubby, against his better judgement. 'Where I live. I have something for you.'

'You have work for her?' The boy crossed his arms and raised a brow.

He spoke softly. 'We'll leave her with Mrs Wilson. She'll be happy to take her in.' The old lightskirt would, too. The young woman reflected innocence he was sure she didn't have. No one could be that pure and he knew it was an illusion created by the soft sweep of her lashes.

Then her lips destroyed her angelic mirage and made a man hungry.

He studied her and had to steel himself to keep his imagination from revisiting a place that did him no favours.

'Oh, please, mister—you know of a job for me? A real job?' The eyes begged.

'No.' He shook his head one swift shake.

She swallowed as if she'd been slapped, and something stabbed inside him. The lightskirt was skilled. He felt like a traitor to the crown.

'Don't worry about it.' Stubby smiled, stepping closer to her. 'I tell you, I have friends in big homes. I—' He looked askance at Addison. 'I can find you work in the same place as I live 'til we make our own way. And you and me can be family.'

'You can really find me employment? The respectable kind?' she asked the lad. 'I've not eaten today—'

Her desperation resounded somewhere deep inside Addison. The woman was reduced to putting her hopes in a lad.

'Oh, yes.' Stubby put his hand flat against his chest. 'I've sailed around the Cape and most everybody livin' where I sleep be seafarin' and will be happy to see you. I'll vouch for you as you're my sister.' Stubby held out his arm for her to take, lifting the elbow high. 'You can go with me.'

Her eyes darted from one to the other.

With his left hand, Stubby clasped at his lapel again. 'We eat every day, rain or shine, and you get used to the rooms bein' still.'

She took his elbow.

'Thank you.'

The two started to leave.

'No,' Addison commanded. The sound thundered into the air, stopping both in their tracks and he stepped closer. 'You—' he glared at her '—will not be leaving with him.'

Stubby smiled at the woman. 'I'm between him and you, so you can run. That place Addison came out of has a front and most likely a back door. You can go in the front and out the back. You can find me at the big house, about six streets over by the statue. On the wall by the doors, there's two crossed oars, but they're stone and won't do anybody any good. Broomer...' he eyed Addison '...will let you in. And he's near taller than the oars and even bigger than this one. Tell him you've got an appointment with Mister Stubby.'

The woman's lips thinned and she studied Addison harder than any cleric had.

In the next instant, she darted for the brothel, but Addison sidestepped and caught her arm in one lunge. He held her firm. Dark, liquid eyes questioned him, the lashes transforming something inside him from steel to powder. His heart thundered in his ears and he forgot what he was going to say. It wasn't, 'Come with me. I'll find you work.' It wasn't what he was going to say, but he said it anyway.

Her arm relaxed.

'I can vouch for him,' Stubby said from behind Addison. 'He's not much to look at with hair that brown colour, but he used to be a duke's son when he was my size, but he growed right out of the family when his mama died and now he ain't got a papa 'cause they don't get along. That's what the man at the tavern said. If my papa had been a duke, I would have kept him.'

Addison dropped her arm. He opened his mouth to tell them both to go to the devil and he could see from her expression that she knew he was about to send them away.

'I can cook. Clean. Do the floors.' The woman's speech was rushed. 'For food and cast-offs. You don't have to pay me.'

Something rustled inside him where a heart should have been. He couldn't let anyone go hungry to the streets.

If all she needed was a roof over her head, he could provide that until she got itchy feet and took off for a bauble someone would wave in front of her to catch her attention. Likely she'd be gone within the week when she found out how staid and mundane his household was. Mrs Crisp didn't put up with much. In fact, he would never have made it as a member of her staff.

The boy and the woman needed each other. Discards hoping for a family. He was thankful he didn't hold a thimbleful of that inside him any more and he'd made damn sure he would never again require his father's assistance as he once had.

He'd sent a message to the Duke that morning. If it meant searching out Oldston personally to get an audience with His Grace, he would, and if he never saw the man again, it wouldn't matter.

Addison's thoughts were diverted when another man walked by and perused the woman.

She put her head down.

No. Likely nothing good would come of having the two under his roof, but he doubted it would last long. He would have to watch them to ensure he wasn't bringing trouble into his life, but if he did, the best constable in

London lived nearby and he'd have no heartbreak summoning the man. His existence had to remain upstanding at all costs.

'One thing you both must understand,' he commanded, his view locked with the woman's gaze. 'I require little interruption under my roof. I have duties and I cannot be distracted with commotions. If you can agree to that, I will allow you both a chance to prove you're worthy of employment.'

The boy was already running to the carriage, but the woman was frozen in place, eyes wide, reminding him of a terrified animal.

'I'll—you'll not even know I'm there.'

He'd seen a drawing of a deer once, a doe, and decided she reminded him of the untamed innocence. Not only the uncertainty in her wide eyes, but the sleekness he was certain hid under the billowing shawl.

'I'm sure. But you will be paid the same as the others I employ.'

Addison silently swore at himself, thinking he'd have to limit his late-night forays into the kitchen. But, no, he rarely saw anyone except Cook when he finished his paperwork and decided to stretch his legs. He was hardly aware of the others, yet he didn't think it would be the same with this woman.

The sound of a throat clearing interrupted his reverie. The boy was holding the door of the vehicle open, soldier straight, but it would have been more impressive if he'd not given a little cough to point out he was working.

The child cocked his head. 'Mr Addison, you mind if we go by Broomer's to let him know I got employment so he don't worry none when I don't show up tonight? Broomer should pay…or you can take it outta my wages.'

'I will do so.' He barely opened his mouth to speak.

From habit, Addison took the woman's arm to escort her into the cab, the softness under the bulky overgarment in his grasp reminding him that he held a woman and the swirl of skirts putting an exclamation mark on it.

Too late, he recalled she was to be a servant, but he refused to do her the disservice of dropping her arm.

He assisted her into the carriage. The boy clambered in after them.

Addison reassessed his earlier disappointment about not having children, thankful not to be the father of a child who managed to bring home a woman from outside a brothel. And a son of his would likely do just such a thing.

Chapter Two

The first thing Sophia noticed when she stepped into the carriage was the green book on the backward-facing seat. It had no title. The man didn't seem the type to keep a journal. When she studied the worn cover, she decided it was a ledger. Possibly to keep accounts of all his funds.

The man moved to sit beside her and the boy clambered in, lifted the book, caught the man's gaze on him and dropped it.

She tried to ignore her awareness of the gentleman at her side, but it would have been like trying to disregard a smouldering volcano. Her senses demanded she regard him.

When he moved, she got a whiff of his shaving soap and the interior of the vehicle had captured the scent and hung on to it.

He was comfortable in the conveyance, yet she'd seen gentler grimaces on men before they started fighting and he wasn't even angry. It was his singular appearance. The darkness of his hair and eyelashes. His eyes were cold beneath dark brows. A pleasant enough blue but the expression in them unrelenting.

The boy, Stubby, if she'd heard right, wasn't afraid of him though. She wondered how they'd met and why the man had taken time from his day to help the lad he didn't seem particularly fond of.

The man hadn't slung a fist at him when Stubby had remarked on the man's appearance or his separation from his family. But the man was in his own world, from his aristocratic nose to his boot heels. She'd never thought she would be so grateful for a near-child's bravery, but still, the spitfire reassured her.

'You got any babies?' the boy asked.

She shook her head, surprised.

'Neither do I. Least, none that I know of.'

The man's head stilled and his eyes narrowed. 'None that you know of?' Each syllable spoken directly and with force.

His teeth were strong, otherwise they would have chipped off at that moment and she would have heard the sound of shattering. He glanced at her as if to say she was responsible for the situation.

'That's what my friend, Cap'n Ben, always said and it's true for me, too. Ain't got none that I know of.'

'I am relieved,' the man said and, for an instance, the darkness in his eyes faded. He retained the stone stature, but he added, 'Same here.' And the day somehow seemed lighter. She felt that deep inside he was laughing, but nothing was showing on his face to indicate humour.

'Well, maybe—' the boy started speaking.

Sophia's mind raced. She didn't want to give him a

chance to voice his thoughts, whatever direction they were going in.

'It's a lovely evening, isn't it?' she asked, speaking over the top of his next utterance.

'A perfect day.'

'Getting dark. Like always,' the boy said. 'Kinda disappointin', finding out my mother didn't leave no chance of me findin' her, though. Kinda makes me feel like she might'a forgot about me.'

The man lifted a brow when he observed her, as if asking how she was going to get out of that faux pas.

'I'm sorry,' she said, chagrined after being so insensitive. 'I'm sure she didn't forget about you. The name of the ship would have been hard for her to remember and she might not have known when it was in port. I'm sure she meant to stay in touch.'

The little bony shoulder twitched up. 'Not that finding a sister didn't make up for it,' he said.

'Thank you,' she said, pleased that the boy had secured a post for her. Hopefully, she would have plenty to eat soon. Her mouth watered.

'If your name would've been Delilah…' the boy mused, lost in his perusal of his boots. 'Not that Sophia's not a nice name.' He examined Addison. 'Ain't it? A nice name?'

Addison didn't answer.

'You shouldn't ask such questions of your employer,' Sophia inserted.

'She's correct,' Addison said, his lips moving the barest amount. 'A name takes on the characteristics of the owner.'

Sophia bit the inside of her lip. Her husband had always called her Ophelia, which had been endearing at first, but then a bit of a nuisance. It was as if he wanted her to be someone else and she wasn't sure if he wanted her to be the woman in love, an actress, or the victim.

''Pose you're saying it's a nice name.'

'That couldn't be determined on such a short interval of acquaintance.'

'I could.' The boy shrugged.

'Sophia is a suitable name,' Addison agreed.

They settled, oddly reminding Sophia of a family, yet she'd never taken more than a few rides in her childhood with both her parents.

'You have any other family—-?' the boy asked the woman.

Gripping the bag tightly in her lap, she nodded. 'Yes.'

Addison surveyed straight ahead.

'A family like mine?' the boy asked, brows raised. 'Borrowed?'

'Small. The ones in my heart have troubles of their own.' She raised her chin and glanced from the corner of her eye at Addison.

'Is one of the family members a husband?' Addison asked.

She squared her body like the child did. 'I'm a widow.'

Stubby nodded, saddened. 'It's harder to keep family than I would have thought, especially 'cause I don't even know any of 'em's full names. My mama used to sing to me and she told me she'd find me when the *Ascalon* was in port, but I guess she never heard.' He leaned his head back against the seat. 'I would have estimated blood family to be something special, but I guess I'll never find out.' Air whooshed from his lungs in a sigh.

Then the lad questioned Addison. 'You have a family? Other'n that papa who didn't marry your mama but give her a lot of jewels? Is he still alive? Is your mama?'

'I have enough family to suit me. Subject closed,' Addison answered, peppering the boy with a look designed to shut his mouth.

'What does subject closed mean?'

'We're not to discuss it any more.'

'Family, or subject closed?'

'Both.' A trace of a warning growl leaked into his statement.

The boy didn't blink, but he puffed out one cheek. 'I be glad I have my cabin boy skills to fall back on, 'cause this man might not be the best in the world to work for.' Stubby grunted and then appraised Sophia. 'We should let you speak to my friend Broomer. He runs a house owned by the Earl and Cap'n Ben and sent me to Addison. Said Mr Addison knows most everybody and the rich folks trust him with helpin' 'em buy things to make 'em more money.'

She closed her lips and patted her index finger against them.

The boy flounced around in his seat, perused the vehicle top, the window, the carriage roof again and kept his eyes upwards.

She feared Mr Addison would stop and send her and the boy on their way. She didn't dare study his face, fearing what she might discover, yet she couldn't sense the restlessness in Addison which would have alerted her to his losing his temper.

But she perceived that Stubby was forming a question that would be best left unsaid. 'What were your duties on ship?' she asked, thinking it would be the safest topic to divert him.

She didn't want him upsetting Mr Addison.

* * *

Addison half ignored the child as the boy spoke about sailing knots and ropes, a topic which would never be a favourite.

'I hope you don't 'spect me to wash the floors,' the child interrupted himself. 'Broomer does sometimes and, if I hide, all the neighbours has been told they got to send me home.'

'If you are to work under my roof, you will do as I say,' Addison said.

'I suppose,' the boy said. 'Peas being what they are.'

Addison observed him directly, a silent but emphatic command for the boy to stop talking.

Stubby raised his brows. 'You wouldn't like them every day on a ship either.'

'At least you had food,' the lady whispered.

'I suppose,' the lad said, 'if peas count as food.' He slumped back into the seat, propped his elbow on the side of the carriage and peered out the window. 'You could call them that, but not real honestly.'

'You will both find I have certain rules,' Addison continued. 'No additional family members brought to my house without prior approval. No late nights. No frequenting taverns or brothels. Start to work as soon as you rise. Chores before all else. Do as the housekeeper and butler say.'

The lad opened his mouth.

Addison glared.

'That sounds reasonable and acceptable.' The woman spoke before the lad could question the requirements.

Stubby smiled, but it was a little too pure. 'It sounds reasonable to me.' He peered at the woman. 'Guess you'd best not be finding you a new husband soon. Don't think there's a place for him with us.'

'I don't expect to.' She tensed before she gave a quick glance at the window, then she reassured Stubby—or herself. 'I've been married. Better to have a little brother than a husband any day of the week. If he's quiet.'

Stubby stretched wide, twisted his head and beheld her from the corner of his eye. 'You think I need a haircut?'

'I think you're perfect,' she said. 'Except I bet you can't be silent the rest of the carriage ride.'

'You win.' Then he observed Addison. 'He needs his hair a lot longer.' His attention shifted back to her. 'You any good with scissors?'

'My hair is fine,' Addison bit out the statement.

'Of course it is,' she said. Again, the bright smile.

The boy's brows rose as if that were so much balderdash. Then the imp's mouth pinched and his eyes narrowed. 'Was that a place where we went where a lot of lightskirts live?' he asked Addison.

'Yes.'

'You go there a lot?'

He felt her body tensing again beside him.

'That is an impertinent question.'

'So I s'pose you do.'

Addison tried to chastise the lad by giving him a glare, but apparently a life around sailors had made the lad fearless.

'When Mr Wilson left, he took Mrs Wilson's funds with him. She hired a constable I know to fetch the money back. I have helped her invest funds others have spent there. None of my own. Not. A. Pence. It is my business to know the financial matters of London.' Ad-

dison's glower challenged the lad not to question him
again.

'Hush…' the lady whispered to the boy. 'Please…'

Addison wanted to reassure her that she needn't
worry about the boy's speech, but he did need to learn
manners around ladies.

'This is a lovely carriage ride.' She rushed the phrase.
'A well-equipped vehicle. It is thrilling to see the streets
from this view.' She stared out of the window. 'Thrilling. Is that vehicle the Prince Regent's?' she asked.

The boy's attention followed her gaze, but Addison
recognised the diversion for what it was—and the false
bravado in her voice. Besides, the vehicle she noted
barely had four wheels.

If they had been hurling towards the edge of a precipice and were nearing a tumble to their deaths, she
would have spoken just as cheerily when asking if—
perhaps—the coach should slow.

Somehow her voice pierced into Addison. Her in-
ability to say anything else but an agreement, otherwise believing she might suffer for it.

She believed she was going over the cliff and she was
hanging on to the ledge with all her might.

Before their wheels fully stopped in front of the steps
with oars framing the entrance, the boy jumped out,
running to the door to find his friend.

The man didn't move. Neither did the air inside the
vehicle. The darkening sky took the last hint of sunshine
and she was thankful for her wrap, but it didn't decrease
the distance between herself and the pillar at her side.

'Do not invite any callers into my residence.' The
man's command sliced through the silence, making

her aware that they sat so close the fibres of her shawl pressed against her arm and the warmth of his coat sleeve penetrated the cloth.

'I will not. I wouldn't be having callers wherever I live.'

His scepticism appeared the same as she imagined the boy's would have if she'd told him peas were tasty.

'I know I was outside Mrs Wilson's, but I—' She didn't think it best to tell him she had family there. 'I was seeking assistance.'

Again, he showed disbelief.

'I pass no judgement on your life. But under my roof you must live always as if you have a rector advising you of every movement you make.'

'You are welcome to pass judgement.' She interlaced her fingers. 'If I wished to work at Mrs Wilson's, I could have found work there earlier. Mrs Wilson mentioned it to me before, but I declined.'

'Working at my home will not be easy.' The quiet brush of fabric against fabric again, and the variation in the sound of his voice, alerted her to his watching her.

'It's not always wise to choose what's easy,' she said, firming her chin. 'It may turn out to be the opposite.'

He laughed. But the sound was for himself. 'I found that out. A lesson I haven't forgotten. At one point, the situation reversed itself and what may have seemed the difficult path became the only option I could accept. Do you agree that you will live a most respectable life while you are in my employ?' His voice relaxed.

'Most certainly.'

The answer must have appeased him because he changed course in his discussion. 'Mrs Crisp, my housekeeper, and Cook do not get on well, so take care not to be caught in any disagreement with them.' His comments seemed intended to reassure.

'I've lived in a home where people don't get on well,' she said. 'I was married for three years.'

'Not a love match?'

'Not for long.' She kept her voice bland, wishing she could see his eyes to gauge his reactions, but instead she concentrated on his voice and his steadiness.

'Love is for the innocent. Not adults.'

'Or people who don't want to work at Mrs Wilson's.' She spoke softly, not wanting him to see her statement as disagreement with his.

'True.'

'Not that she's a bad sort,' she added.

His laughter was silent, more of a movement of chest than a sound. 'In her profession, it probably doesn't hurt to be a bad sort.'

The silence was too quiet, or his breaths too measured. 'And you have not worked for her in the past?'

'No.' She could tell he listened to her voice as intently as she listened to his. 'I haven't.'

She heard the door shut and saw the boy running to re-join them.

'It's so dangerous for a woman.' She spoke quickly before the child could hear them.

'Yes,' he agreed.

The carriage door opened and the boy jumped inside. 'Broomer wasn't there, but I told Peg and he said he'd pass the message along.'

He gave the boy enough notice to appease him, but she could tell he had retreated into his own memories. He lifted the ledger from the seat across from him and thumbed through the book.

When the boy asked him what he read, Addison spoke about purchases and cargoes and sailing times and costs and profits.

She was invisible, or so she sensed, until the boy said something about how you couldn't hide from work on a ship so you might as well not try. That was another thing about ships he didn't like.

Addison tossed the ledger back on to the seat, then his head turned enough to spare her a smile, known only between them.

Awareness burst inside her, shocking her with its strength. She'd cared for her husband once, but he'd never made her catch her breath. She forced her eyes to remain on the window and reflected it might have been safer for her to have stayed at Mrs Wilson's. This Duke's son might not have inherited his father's name or estate, but he'd inherited something she'd not seen in anyone else.

Perhaps it was his confidence, and his size. But whatever it was—she would not want him to smile fully at her.

Sophia didn't think butlers were supposed to have such a shock when their master brought home new employees.

'Tell Mrs Crisp I've hired someone to assist her.'

'But... Mr Addison.' The butler latched the door and contemplated his master. 'Usually Mrs Crisp or I handle the additions. It is how you wished it.'

Sophia gripped her portmanteau and perceived that the servant was much braver than she.

Mr Addison barely acknowledged he had heard the comment and his clasp didn't tighten on the green ledger. He perused the cover briefly and his voice became softer. 'Tell Mrs Crisp I've hired someone. To assist her.'

The butler nodded, but the gesture too slow to be complete acceptance. 'I'll show her to Mrs Crisp.'

'Wait,' Addison commanded, his voice halting the man. 'Bring Mrs Crisp to us.'

Silent communication flashed between them and the butler immediately left.

The boy's mouth opened and Addison shot him a glance which quieted him.

Addison opened the volume as they waited. He didn't appear angry, but she wouldn't have wanted to be Mrs Crisp or the butler. She didn't wish to disturb the silence and even the youngster seemed to sense Addison's power and command.

A few moments later, a woman, eyes downcast, stepped into the room. The butler followed.

'This is Sophia, who will be assisting you,' Addison said, closing his book.

She didn't know what to do. Suddenly, the other two were staring at her and the little boy waited, letting the adults deal with the tension.

'And this is another new staff member, Stubby August,' Addison continued.

'August?' Stubby asked, a frown causing his brow to pucker. 'That be my last name?'

Addison nodded. 'Just like she's your sister.'

'August,' Stubby repeated. 'Don't know if I like it. Where'd you pick it up at? At that lightskirt place where Sophia was goin'?' He hooked a thumb her direction.

Mrs Crisp gasped.

Addison hadn't changed expression, but he'd shaken his head and let the book rest at his side.

'There isn't room...in the servants' quarters...for two,' Mrs Crisp muttered.

'Surely, Mrs Crisp, a woman of your abilities would be able to find a place for the two additional workers.'

'I suppose, she can, *for now,* stay with the scullery girl and the *boy* can stay in the attic. But I admit my surprise as you have previously left all the underservant hiring decisions to me. I do not know how this will— I see no hope in this.'

'That arrangement sounds adequate, Mrs Crisp, assuming your room, in my house, does not become vacant.'

The comment rolled from his mouth, but somehow gave her the impression of each of them standing on a frozen pond, with Addison having the ability to shatter the ice for everyone but himself and to send the staff plunging into cold water.

'I cannot abide such a disruption in my well-constructed duties.' The older woman's thin jaw moved forward.

Sophia cringed at the woman's bravery, or foolhardiness—waiting, because even though she barely knew Addison, she could sense his reaction.

'If you are sure, then I will provide a letter of reference for you.' Spoken easier than most people would have wished felicitations.

'I will be packed and will leave in the morning.' Air snorted from her chest. She stalked away, her shoes clattering more than hooves on cobblestones.

Sophia hardly breathed, fearing she would be held accountable. She gripped her portmanteau closer, afraid to dart for the door. She had nowhere to run.

'If Mrs Crisp is to leave, then I cannot stay.' The butler's voice rolled smoother than hot treacle. 'She has become dear to me.'

'That will be two letters of reference. Have the carriage driver take you where you wish tomorrow, but I will need the vehicle returned before midday.'

'Of course,' the butler said. 'I will leave the rest of my responsibilities in the hands of the capable two you've hired.'

No one moved for a second.

Addison didn't retort, commanding more with his silence than most men could with a shout.

The butler left in the direction of Mrs Crisp.

'Well—' Addison spared the barest gaze their way '—I suppose that will make it easier to find a room for both of you.' He spoke to Sophia. 'I would suggest you not move into Mrs Crisp's room until she has vacated it and you will need to find a space for Mr August later.'

The little head nodded. 'I can be your butler. I worked my way up to cabin boy from nothing at all and I seen how Mr Broomer handles the door.'

'We will see. I expect you both to make the transition into the household seamlessly and continue in the tradition of Mrs Crisp and the manservant, or else I will not even see to a letter of reference.'

'That will suit,' she answered, swallowing, amazed she wasn't on her way once again to Mrs Wilson's.

He took a second longer than necessary to speak again. 'Cook is visiting family and won't be back until late in the night. You will find something to eat in her kitchen, but I suggest you leave it tidy.'

He took a lit lamp from the table by the door and handed it to her. 'Seamless,' he repeated. 'I will be able to manage in the darkness tonight, but take care to make sure this is extinguished when you fall asleep.'

She stared up into his azure depths and wondered if a friendly gauntlet had somehow been dispatched. She took the lamp—accepting.

With the briefest nod, he left, striding up the stairs, each silent step precise and unwavering, and, she supposed, no different than he moved any other evening of the week.

'I really don't know that much about opening a door for folks,' Stubby whispered. 'But I guess I can visit Mr Broomer for any questions I have.' He glanced around. 'Where do you think we should sleep tonight? Don't matter none to me. I can sleep on this floor. On hot nights, I slept on the deck.'

'As you're perhaps to be trained as the new butler, I don't think you should sleep on the floor in the entryway,' she whispered. 'Perhaps we can find the kitchen, though. That would be a nice place to sleep, what with all the smells of cooking left behind. As my first duty, I believe it would be important to see what foodstuffs are on hand.'

'Maybe they have some confections they could share.'

'Perhaps.' She took a step in the direction of the butler and Mrs Crisp. Then she paused and listened for footsteps fading away. She heard none.

She couldn't see Addison, but she was certain he'd heard their conversation.

But then her stomach ached for a bite to eat and she didn't care any more. There was food in that kitchen and she was going to find it. Right now, nothing mattered to her more than a meal.

The man beyond the stairs was a concern for another day.

But she hesitated, waiting, aware. She couldn't see him, yet she could feel his presence, not only in the rooms over her head but all around her, just as she had in the carriage.

She savoured the moment, feeling safer than she had in years, and not certain why—but she didn't loosen her grip on her bag.

Chapter Three

'Saints be.'

Sophia jerked awake. There was an overlarge woman with a lit lamp high above her and holding the light as if she might fling it at Sophia.

This was more of an awakening than she expected. She lifted her head slowly from the portmanteau pillow.

'You need to get out,' the woman said. 'Now. We don't let no street wanderers in here.'

'I'm the new maid.' Sophia kept the lamp in her vision. If the light was flung her way, she'd have to move quickly. She gathered herself to jump aside. 'Mr Addison hired me last night.'

'A likely story.' The woman caused the flame to flicker and Sophia couldn't take her eyes from it. It was as much a weapon as any knife.

'Get up slow now,' the woman commanded. 'Go to the door and I'll let you off with a warning.'

'Mr Addison hired me.' She searched her mind for more information that would attest to her right to be there. 'Mrs Crisp is leaving.'

'Like thunder she is.'

'Truly.'

'Sophia's telling the truth.' Stubby rose from the spot he'd found for himself beside the door.

The woman jumped, startled. She whirled around, the flame beneath the globe flickering erratically. 'There's two of you?'

'Mr Oliver Addison, master of this house, hired both of us. I be the butler. That means you answer to Sophia or me. Not sure which.'

'You little mite. You aren't big enough to talk so.' She glared at him, but lowered the lamp.

'I've sailed around the Cape,' he said 'And I'm as big as I need to be.'

With her left hand, the woman shook a finger at him. 'You're going to sail right out of my kitchen if you don't leave now.'

Sophia stood. 'Please. If the butler and Mrs Crisp haven't left, talk with them and you'll find out that Mr Addison has given us employment. Temporarily,' she added, understanding instinctively that it would pacify the older woman. 'Please check with them.'

'Do not touch anything while I'm gone.' The cook backed to the door, shutting it as if she were locking them in.

'I wish she would have left the lamp.' Sophia rose, trying to fingercomb her bun back into place, still thankful of the feast she'd had before sleeping. If she had to leave, the detour had been worth it.

'She didn't notice my hair,' Stubby mused. 'I reckon we won't get on well.'

'Promise me you'll keep silent.' Sophia had to convince the boy not to cause trouble. 'That's what brothers do.'

'Not any I've ever seen.' Then his nose wrinkled and he glanced around. 'I ain't never been good at quietness. And his is a nice place, but it ain't got no seafarin' ways. I bet you can't find a harpoon anywhere. And I know Broomer's missin' me something fierce. He's like that. And I can't see myself wearin' a butler's garb. I be givin' notice and findin' my own way out.' He took a step to depart. 'You leavin' with me?'

She stood, debating whether to go with him, fearing he had imagined the job he'd mentioned to her when he'd decided to make her his sister. 'I can't. A maid is a fine post. And I don't know if I'd fit in with a seafaring household.'

He nodded. 'You can follow me later if you change your mind. You stayin' don't mean we ain't family, though.'

At the door he paused, waiting. 'Swear on a pirate's oath you'll visit your little brother.'

'Of course, you're family now.'

With that, he grinned and ran out the doorway.

She wished he'd stayed, but she understood his need to leave and she needed employment.

The man, Addison, had taken them in. He'd not clouted the little rapscallion for speaking his mind and she knew he'd admired the lad's spirit even though he'd grumbled at it. But he wouldn't accept any disagreement with his wishes.

She'd spent her whole life trying to make other people happy and would likely spend the rest of it the same way, so she would take her chances. The kitchen was incredible and smelled of a confectionary shop.

She took in her surroundings. The home was a good

place to secrete herself away. She'd avoided notice the last few years and planned to continue to do so.

Being a maid was the best she could hope for. A servant hardly seemed a person to others, but more a fixture, and, without thinking, she'd given the man her real name—not that it mattered. The newspaper had fastened on to the false one.

Something in Addison's voice had warned her that he would not accept untruths. She couldn't blame him for that.

The door opened again, interrupting her ruminations.

From the shadows framing the rotund figure, she knew it was the cook.

The woman glanced around, searching.

'The lad's gone,' Sophia said and felt his loss.

'For the best.' The woman chuckled. 'Mrs Crisp has packed up, and her sweetie, the butler, is leaving, too.' They heard footsteps and strident tones in the hallway.

The cook shrugged. 'Don't think Crisp is going to be telling me goodbye. Won't hurt my feelings none.'

She put the lamp near the two empty plates stacked with the utensils on top, but soiled. 'You made yourself at home in my kitchen last night.'

Sophia tensed. 'Our pay included meals and we did not wish to disturb anyone's rest.'

'Well, don't be disturbing my kitchen or you won't get no rest. I'll have the scullery girl show you around. But you do not take anything in my kitchen without my permission. Even crumbs.'

All the imaginings of decadent foods disappeared from Sophia's mind, replaced by a plate ladled full of peas.

Well, as the boy had said, you take your ports where you can find them.

The cook appraised Sophia in the dim light. 'I believe you'll need some time to pull yourself together.'

A young girl walked into the room holding a bucket of water, eyes half-shut with sleep until she saw Sophia and she stopped moving, staring.

'Addison hired this woman and Crisp is leaving,' Cook said. 'Or has already left.'

The girl broke into a smile and did a little jig. 'Crispy is leaving? I hope she takes Ina with her.'

'Broke my heart as well. But her niece is staying. And this is Sophia.' The cook pointed a ladle to the door. 'I suppose she will get Crisp's room for the time being. Show her to it and give her some of the water.'

The girl nodded, poured some of the water in a pan on the stove before doing as directed, and left the way she came, waving an arm for Sophia to follow.

The hallway was dim, but the scullery girl took her to the empty room, left water for her and stood in the doorway a few moments, chattering about her beau. Then she gave a wave and smile before leaving.

Sophia put her portmanteau on the bed and righted a chair sitting askew in the centre of the room, then shook her head, amazed, for the time being, to even have a room.

She lifted the pillow from the floor. Smoothed out the covering, which appeared to have a footprint in the middle of it, and turned it over before placing it on the bed.

What she knew about cleaning in a large residence wouldn't fill the smallest mustard tin, but she understood hard work and knew she had plenty to do if she was to keep Addison from having upheaval in his routine.

Before she even had a chance to open her bag, the door opened and a woman about her own age stalked into the room, scrutinising her. 'I'm Ina. You're needed. Addison sent for you. He's in the dining room.' Then she disappeared, pulling the door shut with a hair less force than a slam.

Dread plunged into Sophia's stomach. She should have eaten more the night before. If Addison tossed her out, she'd leave through the servants' entrance and she'd ask the cook if she might have a bite of food to take with her.

Mr Addison had let go of the butler and Mrs Crisp who'd questioned him. But he'd also instructed Stubby and Sophia not to disrupt Cook's kitchen. She could not fault the man for his priorities.

He'd spoken kindly to the carriage driver when they'd alighted and the exchange had been easy and familiar between both of them. Neither her husband nor her father would have spoken so kindly to a hired coachman.

She sighed as she ran to find out where the dining room was. For someone who'd had so many fortunate events in her life, though certainly lately some not so happy ones, she'd not managed to do well.

She hoped she had a new life now. She so wanted to put her past behind her. Living in Mr Addison's house would make her feel safer than she'd ever been and she would work hard to live up to his expectations.

She would make certain he never found out about her being accused of murdering her husband.

Chapter Four

Addison sat at the table. In front of him, but to the side, sat a large platter with one roll, its aroma filling the room. He took the Bath bun, hardly tasting the sweetened flavour as he ruminated on what he should do.

A storm had blown through his life. And he'd brought it inside. He'd not needed anyone to tell him what a mistake it could be. A warning wisp had sounded, but he'd slammed it down, attributing it to an awareness of the desires a woman could stir in him, knowing that even long and longer hours of work didn't always douse them.

The little ragamuffin was one thing. But the infernal woman was the bigger danger. He'd sensed it in the carriage—an awareness that she was female and he was male and it could be a heady combination. Bringing home a woman from outside a brothel could not end well.

He'd kept reminding himself not to take notice, yet he'd been aware of each time the carriage jostled her. As if his reflections had summoned her, she moved into the room, her eyes taking in the surroundings in a glance. She acknowledged his presence with a subservient nod.

She didn't seem as defeated as she had the night before. Her eyes were downcast, but somewhere inside her was spirit that had been lacking earlier. Perhaps it was in the straightening of her neck or the fluid movement she made as she entered the room.

She was a widow. It would have been hard to leave a woman like her behind.

'Ina told me the boy is gone.' He put the rest of the bun down. 'Do you plan to stay?'

'Of course,' she said. 'I could not leave my new post.'

A firm statement. But her throat bobbled as she swallowed afterwards.

He pushed the plate aside, twirling the knife between two fingers. He let the utensil clatter on to the dish and clasped his hands together. 'If you count Stubby, this is the third time I have had to replace a manservant. Beldon hired Crisp, a sweetheart of his. The one before disappeared in the night and I discovered he'd been drinking his way through my liquor.' Addison had been tempted to summon the constable and pay him to bring the butler to justice, but it would have meant the risk of drawing unpleasant notice to himself. He needed none of that.

Crisp had kept a tidy world and the next butler had done well enough. But he'd been cautious on how he wrote his letters of reference, mentioning dates of service, bookkeeping and cleanliness skills.

Over the past year, more and more things were altered in ways he didn't like. He also wondered if he'd heard the full story when Mrs Crisp apologised, eyes downcast, on behalf of the servant whom she said had broken the Meissen figurine. Crisp claimed the girl had left in tears, but not to worry, she'd been replaced. With her own niece.

She reassured Addison that she'd cleaned up every last piece of broken porcelain and she'd put an urn on the shelf. He'd doubted anyone could break the urn with a hammer.

It hadn't felt right to him.

'Besides you, there is Cook, a scullery girl, Ina, who did as her aunt directed, and, when he is replaced, a manservant. The coachman does not live in, but is amazingly adept at understanding my schedule. Do you think you can handle a household of this size… particularly without Crisp to instruct you?'

'Of course.'

He could have told her the roof was caving in, the walls were aflame and a cannon needed to be moved into the sitting room and she would have answered the same.

'I have work to do today and I've no time to spare with the minutiae of the daily duties.' He unclasped his hands and moved back in his chair.

'Beldon worked as my valet as much as my butler. I'll have my man of affairs searching out a new manservant for me immediately. See that I have hot shaving water in the morning.'

Again, the same response from her.

'Can you read?' He watched for honesty.

'Yes. Easily.'

'Good,' he muttered, the muscles in his legs stretching as he stood. He straightened his cuffs. 'I'm not sure Ina has mastered that skill and you will need to do the account books until a new housekeeper is hired. I gathered Crisp's and Beldon's ledgers last night.' He indi-

cated the volumes on the far end of the table. He'd not
wanted them exiting with Crisp and Beldon.

'Why did you leave your last post?' he asked.

'Mrs Roberts died. Her family no longer needed me
to care for her.'

'What other posts have you had?' he asked.

'I lived at my mother's home until I wed, then after
my husband died, I discovered Mrs Roberts was ail-
ing and needed help with her care. I was thankful for
the work. I couldn't return to my mother's because she
had passed on and there was hardly enough money to
settle the debts. Mrs Roberts was kindly—a women I'd
known for years—but her family was unable to care for
her as they wished. The son had a large family of his
own that he could barely support.'

'You took care of the entire dwelling? No one to oversee, or to give direction?'

'Only Mrs Roberts. It was a small home,' she admitted.

'Can you provide the location of your former employer?'

'Yes. Her son and daughter-in-law. They live in the
house next to Mrs Roberts's home.'

'This afternoon, when you hear the carriage, give
the coachman the location of your previous employer
and tell him to check your reference tomorrow and report back to me.'

'Certainly.'

'Unless you hear otherwise from me, you are to manage in Mrs Crisp's position. Starting at this moment.'

Her brows rose. 'Are you certain?'

'Yes. With both the butler and Mrs Crisp gone—and
her niece could plan to follow—you are the one avail-

able. The books will assist you in ordering of supplies…
whatever is needed. I want no interruption caused by the
change in staff and that seems obtainable with you here.'

Addison stepped around the table, placing himself
directly in front of her. He wanted to give her an option and she must understand that his domestic life was
important to him.

'While I may speak with Cook as a friend, and she
is, it does not mean that I expect less than perfection
from her, or any other employee.'

'Of course.' She spoke as if there could be no question.

'If you fail, the consequences can be swift. Do you
understand that?' His peacefulness would suffer if he
overwhelmed her, but she needed to know what she
was taking on.

The lashes swept up and he saw the concern behind
her eyes. He wanted her to understand his expectations
and needs, but he didn't want to trap her because she
had nothing else. He had to give her another option.

'But if you'd prefer, I'm sure Crisp's niece will be
pleased to take over these duties. It is not my prefer-
ence, however.' He softened his voice. 'The housekeeper
will have more responsibilities, particularly as I have
no manservant for the time being.'

Her expression showed she was contemplating what
he meant and he wanted her to determine if she should
accept the lesser post.

Moments passed. He saw dignity in her shoulders
and the way she carried her head, but the placid expression didn't conceal her concern.

'If it takes that long for you to make up your mind—'

Her chin rose. 'A housekeeper is a fine occupation. I will take it.' Her throat quivered a bit as she spoke.

'No margin for error.'

'I will not need one,' she said firmly.

He put his bent fingers over his lips, a thumb at his cheek, hiding his humour. The scared little miss had stared him down.

Sophia studied his library closely, her dusting cloth in her hand, trying to see through the furnishings to the man who lived within them. The one who'd given her another chance in life.

The desk appeared more table except for the deep circular shapes carved around the top sides. The brace underneath was made of curved metal to give stability and still allow him room for his legs. He had one near-empty ink pot, with a full one beside it.

The tabletop was covered with a sheaf of documents near the ink. Three papers were precisely placed. One had numbers and lines on it. The other had tiny writing from top to bottom and the last, a few lines in a language she assumed was Latin.

He trusted her to clean the library and she supposed it to be his most personal room. True, he had no samplers on the wall. No portraits. In fact, she'd not seen a drawing or a painting on the walls, except a few plain engravings. Nothing of a nature to tell what he held dear except the one urn on the mantel in a place of honour.

She wandered to his desk and the small table beside it, which had been left clear except for one page. Then she read down the other written paper—a list of his duties. Some, so complex she didn't understand what they were, had a line drawn through them.

He had a mountain of work facing him. A mountain.

Then she saw an empty ink pot beside the second, half-filled one. She gripped the container. For the time being, she'd substitute the one in her room and later she'd find paper and make her own notes to follow.

She glanced at his cluttered desktop and saw another page filled with figures. The amount of them made her gasp.

Now she studied the area differently, seeing Addison's personal nature. It glared at her from the walls which had sconces attached, but nothing else affixed to them. Light to work by. The shelves holding old ledgers. The two straight-backed chairs, one in pristine condition, the other a little worn, facing his desk.

The wood surface completely covered so that he had a table placed at the side.

No wonder he did well in his life.

She recalled his bedroom. The wardrobe with differently hued waistcoats and cravats, yet little variety other than that. Everything austere in her view, except the one comfortable chair which appeared ignored.

Hats and gloves.

A bed that appeared made to fit his specifications. A shaving table in the small dressing room. Stands for three pair of boots which added the scent of boot blacking and leather over the softer shaving soap. A bootjack. Nearby a chair to sit in when he donned the footwear.

If he were royalty, she doubted he would have directed the rooms differently. Perhaps a few more waistcoats and cravats, but she didn't think he would have truly cared.

She'd seen notable ladies with their beaux or husbands. The men had had little things to twirl or hold.

Umbrellas, or fobs, or canes, or snuffboxes. Addison appeared to have none of those, but instead he had his eyes to direct attention and his shoulders and his stature.

No wonder Addison did so well. It was as if the world had been designed for him and he could grasp how to work and create the best life around him.

Chapter Five

Sophia heard the carriage return and knew the coachman had investigated her previous employment. A few minutes later, she heard him whistling as he moved up the stairway.

If he had spoken with Mrs Roberts's daughter-in-law and son, he would find no aspersions about her. The son had never paid her, allowing her room and board in exchange for caring for his mother. He was a stern man who'd rather scowl than speak, but he only knew of her life with her own parents, not her married years.

Her grandmother had been friends with the elder Mrs Roberts and as the woman aged, her senses waned. Sophia had almost begged for the post to be created after she'd discovered her mother-in-law's machinations. She'd even taken in sewing to aid with the household expenses.

Then the woman had died and Sophia had had no money left. The woman's son had insisted his mother's house be sold and, for a time, the wife had allowed Sophia to help with their children.

Then, the family's finances had taken an even worse

turn. The daughter-in-law had cried when she told Sophia goodbye, but both knew nothing could be done.

Sophia's next step had been to search for Merry at Mrs Wilson's because her cousin had been trying to help find Sophia reputable work. Then she'd met the little boy and Addison.

She'd never seen a man who appeared so in control of his surroundings and himself. She couldn't imagine Addison ever being anything but disciplined.

After she'd cared for an older woman who thought it an adventure to escape her home, and then four children who felt the same way, she expected the housekeeper duties to be a pleasant change.

Sophia heard Ina bump something against a wall. Ina had stopped short of refusing to do anything the day before, until Sophia had reminded her that Addison had let her aunt go.

The extra clatter of the woman's mop handle against the stairways, and the clunk of the bucket had been part of her not so silent resistance and she'd even spilled the used mop water down the stairway, barely missing Sophia.

Sophia had sent her back with towelling and told her to save time for the extra laundry needed to clean the mop cloths.

That night, their supper had been a mood-laden affair, yet with food fit for royalty. They ate around Cook's table, all silent except for the contact of utensils against plates and a few comments from the scullery girl about her beau, until Cook quietened her with a glare.

Sophia had savoured a crisp outer layer of the roast that she'd not known could exist. The vegetables melted in her mouth and she wasn't certain they'd not been dotted with something special to add flavour, plus, she'd gasped when she saw the wine bottle. Cook's smug nod, and the scullery girl's easy acceptance of it, reassured her it was approved by Addison.

The first day had been a trial, but the last meal made everything worthwhile.

She heard the carriage driver leave and then the bell jangled.

Sophia rushed up the stairs.

Addison waited, jaw shadowed, but reminding her of the marble statue she'd seen of a Roman commander. She wondered if she touched him whether she might find a chip of stone. Inside, perhaps, but his exterior had been fashioned by a different sculptor. One who worked in light, reflections and vibrancy.

'I wanted to let you know that Caldwell checked to make certain your little brother made it home safely. Caldwell was to remind you not to forget your promise to visit.' A soft smile flitted behind Addison's eyes.

Sophia didn't know what to think. No man in her previous life would have been concerned about a youngster they'd met so briefly.

'I also wanted to inform you that the lady Caldwell contacted couldn't stop praising your work. But I wondered, is the lifting here too much for you?'

Not idle conversation and not a question to be taken lightly.

'No.' Her resolve faltered. The lifting had been minimal. Less than she was used to.

'Things clattered and clanked more than they ever have before in the servants' stairway. What was the problem?'

Her stomach sank. The sounds Ina had made had carried into the master's quarters, the not so silent actions of her pretending a struggle as she managed the simplest task.

Eyes studied her.

'I will be more careful,' Sophia said.

'I could have promoted Crisp's niece. I didn't, though I suspect she toiled as hard as her aunt did. Is Crisp's niece adjusting to you?'

'Well enough.'

'Your answer is not a yes and it is not a no. It is a response that suggests otherwise.'

She swallowed. She'd never had someone notice her speech so carefully. In the past, she would have guessed most of her replies had been ignored.

'I wouldn't have liked it if a new person were brought in either,' she admitted, 'and my aunt was let go.'

Addison again looked like a marble statue, only his eyes were colder. 'Doesn't matter. I gave her a chance by not sending her away with Crisp. If she doesn't do what she is capable of, and you don't let her go, then the onus is on you.'

She wasn't entirely sure what he meant by the onus being on her, but she got the idea.

She saw the butler's tasks, Ina's tasks, Mrs Crisp's duties all being relegated to one person and she wasn't sure her shoulders were large enough to take on all those responsibilities, particularly as she wasn't used to them. No matter how hard she tried, it would take adjustment. She'd not even been sure what was beyond the doorways that the servants' stairs led to, afraid she'd be entering the wrong room at the worst time.

She'd just learned which bell was for her, but she supposed if she was the solitary one to answer the rings it would be obvious whom they summoned.

'I would like to give her more of a chance and I will speak firmly to her.' She tightened her clasp. She would be direct with Ina.

'Do you have any queries for me?' he asked.

She batted away her fears. It would not do to show any weakness. He might have sent the driver to check on Stubby, but he'd also sent away Crisp and the butler, and seemed inclined to rid the household of Ina. Her standing was too shaky to risk any more upheaval.

'I've no questions.'

'No one brought my shaving water this morning,' he said.

She put a hand to her neck and imagined herself following in Crisp's footsteps. 'I did not think of it.'

'No matter.' He shrugged, then studied her a moment longer. 'Truly. Relax. It doesn't matter. I didn't ring for it because Beldon wasn't here.'

'I'll bring it myself until you get a new manservant,' she said. Then she bit her lip, afraid he would somehow take her response as a criticism because he'd let his servants go.

'Sophia...' He indicated a chair. 'Sit.'

She had no choice.

He moved, then propped himself on the desk edge, crossed his arms, lean legs relaxed. 'I had a first day on a job as well.'

'Yes.'

'It's not easy.'

'No.'

'You're learning what is expected.'

'Yes.'

He spoke, each word precise. 'The sky has purple dots and rainbow clouds in it.'

She spoke softly. 'No?'

He uncrossed his arms and stood. 'That is a statement my employer once said to me. I would suggest you always agree with my wishes in the end, but it is acceptable to tell me tactfully when you consider another option.'

'I don't think I will—' she gulped in a breath '—will consider another option.'

'Perhaps you shouldn't in the first fortnight,' he said. 'But in time. Just don't be so frightened.'

'It's—fearful being without work.'

'I suppose,' he said and studied the urn on the mantel. 'But you were at Mrs Wilson's. She offered you work?'

'I don't think I could have taken it on,' she admitted, eyes downcast. 'My cousin and I talked of it once…and I said I would starve first and she told me we weren't far from it then. And my father died and my mother had nothing, and she was so ill. But my cousin and I both had beaus by then and we both hoped for the best.'

'Beaus?'

'I married mine. She was not so fortunate.' Then she gulped, shocked at her words. 'Yes. I was the fortunate one.'

His lips firmed and he seemed to lose interest in the conversation.

'See that my shaving water is brought to me in the morning and be sure this room is cleaned tomorrow while I am away. I'm working to get more assistance. My man of affairs has sent a message that he will have two candidates for the manservant position, arriving the day after tomorrow. Show them to the library.'

He kept his gaze on the urn, went to it and reached into his waistcoat pocket. He dropped something into the container, several jangles sounding. 'If you ever wish to leave—on your last day, take the ghastly pottery and its contents with you.' Then he frowned. 'Assuming no one from the staff has helped themselves to it before you. It is up to you to watch over the vase and contents.'

He rubbed his stubble again and watched her. 'Life is full of cold pieces of metal and sometimes they are handy. We are the lucky ones. We survived.'

Addison couldn't sleep. He'd dozed, but a noise had awoken him and he supposed it was the clanging of his conscience.

He'd not minded Crisp and the butler leaving. They could have accepted the situation and stayed. But Sophia was in over her head. He saw it. As did she. And yet he could sense an inner spirit from her that seemed emboldened by it.

Kicking the covers away, he moved out of bed. Pacing. He'd dropped gold coins in the urn, likely tossing them to the wind.

But, blast it, he was tired of having a thief in his midst and not knowing who it was. Better for her to take the money and run to Mrs Wilson's and he could put aside his wish to speak with his father a little longer.

At least Ina could manage the washing and he would have good meals from Cook.

Promoting Ina had been almost an impossibility, because he didn't trust her. He'd not wanted her in the upstairs any more than necessary when he was there and he'd let her know early on. No matter what happened,

Ina could never have been in charge for long. She had too much welcome in her eyes when she walked into a room with him. Stood too close. Lingered.

Sophia's compassion for Ina surprised him. Crisp had kept her niece on her toes. But she must work with Sophia, and not against her, and he didn't think Ina had that much kindness or wisdom in her.

The woebegone appearance of Sophia had hit him hard when he'd taken her from the street, but the fear he saw when he'd suggested she let Ina go had jarred him the same way a horse had when it put him flat on the ground.

If she was going to run off in the night, best to do it now while he still had Crisp's niece to take care of the household's basic needs. He certainly didn't care for Ina, but still, Cook said she knew her duties.

The man of affairs did exactly as instructed with the financial matters and understood them. The steward wouldn't trust a single dot on a ledger page without verifying it, but put a friendly individual in front of him and the person could convince him of their sainthood and undying devotion with half a smile. Having him search for staff might not be the wise course as the errors would be for Addison to correct. But right them he would.

Donning his trousers, he planned to fetch a drink from the decanter in the library and take the glass to the gardens. The night air would clear his brain. If the moon was too bright to see the stars, all the better for watching the peaceful shadows of the night.

He slipped the shirt over his head, grabbed his frock coat for warmth and tugged it over his shoulders, not buttoning it.

He could not let his life fray. He was so close to having the course he wanted and feeling more respected for changing his ways. His mirthless laugh surprised him. He'd possibly received more notice because he'd been such a rakehell and now he did all but write the sermons for Sunday services.

Pausing, he contemplated his household.

This home had no memories of his mother and father raging at each other when his father visited. Or after his mother had passed, the disappointed and distant visage of the butler as he opened the door for Addison to attend some festivity, the neighbour averting his head if he happened to see the woman Addison escorted.

He'd not cared, or really noticed his neighbours, until he'd arrived at his childhood home after the difficult walk from gaol. Then he'd been aware of how people perceived him and it had mattered. The spectre of his actions had jeered at him, slashing him like arrows with poisoned tips.

His illegitimacy had been his parents' decision. His rebellion against his father had been his own choice. And the punishment would have been for him alone.

On every step home the day his life had been given back to him, he'd been able to see himself from a distance, see the world around him with a clarity that had never been visible and he'd hated the moment when the butler had opened the door for him. Addison had kept his haughtiest scowl on his exterior while his insides had burned as if a fireplace ignited in him. The butler had peered beyond Addison, ever so proper.

Even if he'd wanted to sack the butler, Addison couldn't have. His father paid the man's wages.

He'd sworn an oath to himself that he would find a

way to pay the salary of each and every person under his roof and own every thread he wore, and he would never be wrapped in the stench of gaol again.

After that, he'd weighed every action before he took it.

At first, he'd felt he was balancing on a slender reed-sized bridge across a crevasse, but then the bridge became easier to cross as he made better choices.

Since he'd moved to the structure he owned, he'd silently shaken his head while living the staid life he preferred. He considered the banking staff—and the rest of society—a congregation whose good opinion he must retain to the highest degree.

Moving to the library entrance, he congratulated himself on his efforts. He'd done it. He'd been in a joust with his old self, but in truth, it hadn't been difficult. He detested the youth he'd been after his mother died.

A soft clunk, ever so muffled, sounded before he stepped into the library.

No one should be there at night. It was where he did his work from home and to be attended to when he went to the bank.

Damn. Not again.

Without making a noise, he crept to the door and held it firm to control the creak of the wood. The scent of beeswax lingered, but he ignored it as the light shuttered, the servants' entrance closed, leaving the room in darkness. A board creaked from the servants' stair.

If it was Sophia and she was leaving in the night, she might not be limiting herself to a few coins in an urn, but stealing half the fixtures he owned, having found an accomplice to cart them off for her. And he would have to hire someone to find the items quickly or count them a loss. It wouldn't help his standing for mention of that to get about.

His trustworthiness and the respect others gave his judgement were vital. They trusted him with their livelihoods.

He'd managed when the first butler had left with a few candlesticks and things he'd not expected Addison to miss. Addison hadn't had time to pursue it, nor the inclination to risk anyone finding out he'd been duped. Better to take the cost and learn from it. But he would not do so now.

The coachman had told him of the constable living nearby and the man had agreed to assist Addison if needed, but he didn't want to admit his hiring errors or have his judgement questioned.

He left, charging down the main stairs, making little noise and rushing through the corridors to the servants' stair entrance. The door was open and the sound of soft footsteps reached his ears. He stilled, staying in the shadows, waiting to see what she was carting down the steps.

A tiny bump and water sloshed. Sophia stepped out, juggling a candle, with a mop angled under her arm and against her hip. She put the bucket outside the servants' door and propped the handle she held against the wall. She used the cloth over her shoulder to daub at the wetness on her brow. Then she shut the door, picked up the tools and moved away.

It was as if he could see through all the darkness in the world and beyond. He'd made the best hiring decision of his life, it appeared, outside that brothel.

He trudged up the stairs as silently as he'd descended and moved into the library. Dampness underfoot reminded him of the mop when he stepped inside, and the scent of the polish on the furniture made him feel as if he'd stepped back into the rooms of his youth, and the maid of all work had handed him a cloth and told him if he was going to chatter so much, he might as well clean while he talked.

Even though he could see nothing clearly, he needed no light. The library had been arranged for his comfort and his work. He reached the decanter, but didn't pour anything for himself.

He tapped the bottom of the empty glass against the fireplace mantel, letting the clink remind him he was not alone. He felt he couldn't tell anyone about Sophia's dedication. Not even her. Which made him feel isolated. Which he shouldn't. He had Cook and the coachman to speak with at home. He had the banker and the officers of the bank and the steward around him during the day.

His world was crowded with people. Sometimes, too many of them.

For some reason the image of Sophia standing outside the brothel, the fringe of her shawl waving, her eyes filling with hope, kept revisiting him. And he kept comparing it with the shadowy picture of her struggling with the mop, candle and bucket.

And he still found her alluring.

The glass clinked a little harder before he decided to resume his trip to the garden. He'd have to solve this or he'd be awake every night listening for noises from the servants' stairs.

Cook had once told him he needed a society wife. A woman born into wealth who could oversee the housekeeper and would enhance his own status. She would be the last step in showing everyone that his past was a youthful folly. He was settled, mature and not someone on the edge of society, but worthy of their esteem, trust and acceptance.

Something his mother had never achieved because of her rebelliousness. She'd lived among the rich, but not been accepted, nor wanted to be. It was as if she'd ignored the influential, saying her freedom was more important than their restraints, thank you very much. She would have their luxuries, but not them.

He saw no reason not to have both.

He was certain he could manage the right invitations if he put his mind to it. His children could have the same advantages as their cousins.

Marriage to the right person would firm the path over the chasm he'd once made. He'd noticed earlier that not all the invitations he'd received had been due to business connections. Some had been because, as the banker said, a mother with an unmarried daughter might like her daughter to be partnered. The banker had jested that Addison was an adequate dancer, but you'd think he was unrivalled by the way the mothers with daughters fluttered around him.

He tried to recall the ladies presented, but he imagined them as chattering magpies too innocent for interest, having blank blinks behind their lovely smiles and perfect dance steps.

Cook had assured him that one day he'd notice the daughters and see one as a life mate. He tried to imagine that. And couldn't. Sophia's image fluttered in front of him.

Addison yawned when he awoke the next morning, then frowned as the realities appeared in his memory.

He yanked the pull beside his bed. He had no manservant. No experienced housekeeper. And Ina's attentions were too intense.

He found his trousers draped over the chair back, retrieved the dressing gown on the bottom shelf of the wardrobe, wrenched the garment from under the stack and shook it as free of creases as was possible. He put them on, feeling smothered by the clothing when he added his dressing gown. He would definitely have to hire the next man who arrived, because getting dressed as soon as he rose was not his preferred method of waking up in the morning.

Perhaps he had not thoroughly weighed the prospect of having Sophia in his quarters.

Almost before he finished tying the sash closed, he heard someone in the servants' hallway by his dressing room.

He opened the door for Sophia and she came inside, two cloths shielding her hands from the warm container, her hair dampened from steam, her cheeks red, struggling to catch her breath.

Whatever the opposite of insubordination was, he had certainly found it in her.

He asked her to set the pitcher on the dressing table, afraid if he moved to take it from her, she'd somehow burn herself.

An apology bubbled inside him, but he waited.

She stepped back, the two cloths crumpled in her hands, unsure.

He poured half the water into the bowl, ignoring the steam as it escaped.

'How long was the water boiling?' he asked.

'Not long.'

The perfect answer from a well-trained servant, but not what he asked. 'An hour?'

'Thereabouts.'

He hid a smile. 'If I ring too early, without letting you know in advance, I will accept the lukewarm water as my reward.'

'The scullery maid starts it boiling.' She kept her backbone straight.

He'd never shaved in front of a woman. Ever. Even if he were married, he would not be shaving in front of his wife.

He appraised the situation, feeling reluctant to cross a boundary he'd set in his own mind. He held a palm over the bowl, the heat rising, and the steam moistening his hand.

The water would cool soon and he could send her away now. But it was better to get a snare untangled early. Always.

It was simply that if he did straighten this, he might be creating a different kind of predicament that would take even more cautious steps to control.

He searched inside himself and assessed his strength, bearing in mind the times he'd had to make tough decisions and how he'd never regretted the struggle to pilot his life in the direction he should take it.

'I want to do well.' She moved a step forward, interrupting his contemplation. 'The food is tremendous here.'

He suppressed his smile. His home had the best food he'd ever tasted and it had seemed a waste for him to be the only one to enjoy it. He'd made certain Cook prepared enough for everyone and he'd expected it to buy him some loyalty from the staff. Perhaps it had at first, but Crisp and Beldon had become so entrenched and seemed to take it as a right to rule his household for him and let their position chip away at his authority.

'I know. But I cannot have you— Your brother, Stubby, would say you need a chance to find your sea legs.'

'I'm sturdy.'

Crisp had been sturdy. Ina was sturdy. Cook was sturdy. She was slender. A woman who might struggle after a night of mopping while everyone else slept and not even be aware that the toil reflected on her appearance.

He dropped his hand from the steam. That water would take the whiskers off and keep them off.

'Would you fetch some unheated water I can use to dilute this and perhaps the basin can be partially filled during the day? When you bring the cool water, knock and leave it outside the door if you're concerned with the sight of my chest and I will talk with you afterward.'

A shadow passed behind her eyes and made the darkened smudges beneath them even more prevalent. 'I did not think of the water being too hot… I had a place near the fire that I always set the kettle for my husband and it kept it the right temperature. I guessed this the same.'

'The valet always had a portion of water in my basin and then, in the morning, he added heated.'

She nodded. 'I will bring cool water. I didn't realise the bowl was to be half filled the day before.'

'I understand. As I've said, it's acceptable to knock and leave the water outside until a manservant is hired and he can take on these duties.' That would be best for both of them. She shouldn't be exposed to his nakedness and he would be able to maintain the line between housekeeper and master. He couldn't shave with his collar in place.

'I've seen a man's chest before,' she said seriously and turned a little too quickly, grasping the door handle a second time when her hand slipped off it.

She left and he lifted the comb to his hair, and knew he'd made his path to do the right thing more difficult for himself.

He should have simply given her a list of specific instructions. Written areas for improvement and told her where she could find the paper after he left for the day. But lists could be misinterpreted.

He'd not earned his place at the bank by leaving things to chance, or by not investigating to learn about the situations he encountered.

That one life-changing walk home, those years ago, though truly it was only a few miles, had impressed on him the realities of his world and how fragile he could make it.

Perhaps he'd been wrong, but the sport the other prisoners had of jeering at the condemned, who were soon to be removed from the world, made him think not of people, but of buzzards feeding on their comrades' carcasses. He'd never before wondered what happened to a fallen vulture, but the jeers had answered his unasked question.

Recently, he'd spoken quietly to a few friends, on condition of anonymity, and asked them to reflect on a portion of Sunday Services at the gaol. He'd asked if the coffin could be removed. The wooden shout to the prisoners of the wages of their sins. An ominous whisper that death could be their next journey and they must consider the hereafter. He'd recently heard that the box had been taken away. A fortnight before.

A small thing. Truly nothing to an outsider. But that coffin had appeared in his dreams and after he'd heard it had been removed, his sleep had been quiet.

He didn't doubt that his actions, no matter how small, could make all the difference in a person's life. All the difference. And the one life that the most minute actions made the most impression on was his own.

He had to take care with Sophia.

Ina loitered by the broom cupboard when Sophia rushed down the stairs and was still there when she returned with the cool pitcher in her hands. On her way up, Sophia put her foot on the bottom stair, stopped and directed, 'Mix furniture polish if you've nothing else to do.'

Then she went to Addison's room, not depositing the pitcher outside the entrance for him to collect and pour. She didn't want him to be adding the possibility of another error in her duties. Her whole body ceased movement when she stepped inside the door.

She'd not lied, obviously, when she told him she'd seen a man's chest. Only she'd never seen a man such as Addison without his shirt. Shoulders gleamed in the dim morning light, taking up all she could see, and fading everything else for a brief flicker in time that she would recall for ever.

She was happy the mirror didn't point in her direction. Now she understood why male artists painted so many pictures of unclothed women. The male body, in the right proportions, could be intriguing, too. She regretted that there were not more female artists with appropriate models. Those renderings would be intriguing.

She didn't know why she'd not been aware of such a thing before, except, apparently, her husband's chest hadn't been so well formed.

Now, she noticed Addison had a cloth knotted haphazardly at his neck. She'd not even seen that before, as her awareness had entirely been consumed by his muscles and their movements.

Fixing her eyes upon the pitcher, she kept her expression averted and walked sedately to the dressing table. She poured the water into the bowl.

'Do you mind to stay a bit?' he asked.

That sort of question generally didn't end well.

She stepped away and he put his fingertips into the water. Then he dipped the towel into the basin and lifted the cloth.

'I appreciate your efforts…'

But… He was going to say *but*. He had recognised she was struggling. He would let her go. Cook didn't like her. Ina didn't.

'But you are one person.'

He patted the towel against his cheek and rotated towards her. 'Do you understand what I'm saying?'

He *was* letting her go.

She hid her sigh. She'd half concluded that was why he'd wanted her to stay after she'd brought the water. Thankfully she had the little boy to search out and the man Broomer. She should have left with the lad.

Addison appeared to be trying to stare through the mirror and into her soul. 'You're doing the job of Beldon this morning. You cannot do the job of a butler, of Mrs Crisp with her bookkeeping, and Ina as well. You know I am in the process of hiring a manservant. And if you need another maid, I give you leave to hire one.'

'I am to hire my replacement?'

'No,' he slammed out the declaration. 'You are to hire your helper, if needed.'

Helper? She put her hand to her chest. She should have assistance? Examining the room, and then the hand she'd briefly raised, she was certain she was hearing properly. Fairly certain she was standing upright. And wondering how she managed to slip into someone else's life.

'Certainly,' she said, relieved at the prospect and controlling an urge to break into a smile.

His brows knitted and his eyes locked on her.

She gathered herself and measured the situation. She was pleased he wasn't sending her away.

'You're smiling,' Addison said and he resumed attending to his stubble.

Immediately, she regained her housekeeper demeanour, not wanting to let him know how much she'd been expecting to be searching for another position. 'I'm pleased that you are agreeable to additional staff.'

'Take care with the hiring,' he said. He flicked the blade over his skin with a soothing rasp. 'And try to have better luck than I had.' He wiped the blade. 'If it were not for Cook and the coachman, I would doubt my abilities to select a staff.' The blade tipped down and then something warm sparkled from his eyes. 'And you.'

Oh, this was much better than being married.

She didn't have to worry about cooking in addition to cleaning. Meals seemed to appear as if by magic.

Bills were paid and disappeared without her having to struggle.

Life in service was more appealing than a life of wedded nightmares.

He interrupted her wool-gathering, his conversation going in an unexpected direction. He'd put down the razor and patted his jaw with the towel that had been around his neck.

'I want the upstairs cleaned today and I would like Ina to do it. Not you. All rooms but the library because I will be there working. If the cleaning is not done to my specifications, I will tell you and tonight you are to reprimand her in front of me.'

Her shoulders fell slightly. 'That will not be easy. To reprimand her in front of you.'

'It will be ever so simple.' He moved closer, still holding the towel and speaking as if sharing a secret. Her heart beat faster and a warming sensation invaded her. She waited, not for his words, but for the way he spoke them. 'Because if you impress upon her that it will be reported to me and when she gauges how I will react, she will not want that and will do the job as she knows how to do it. That will save both your time and mine.'

He stepped away, dropping the towel beside the basin. 'Let Ina take care of emptying the water when she cleans the bedroom. She is to do right or she is to leave.'

She nodded.

'Make it an early night for yourself,' he added. 'That is not a request.' He paused, emphasising his statement. 'And please ask Cook if she has time to prepare some berry tarts for tonight. Work deserves a reward.'

Oh, she knew Cook would have time to create something special for Addison and she couldn't blame her. She'd never had berry tarts and no doubt there would be plenty for everyone.

At that moment, if she'd had a cape she would have spread it over the floor in the mornings just to keep his feet warm.

She pulled the door closed behind her and, at the sound of it shutting, an ember of comprehension sparked in her, causing a ripple of warmth. He'd requested the berry tarts—as a treat—for her.

A housekeeper on Addison's staff had all the best parts of being a wife, and yet without a husband.

She went to the servants' stairs and heard footsteps. Ina had likely been listening outside the door.

Moving quickly down the steps, Sophia caught up with Ina and relayed the message of what she was to clean during the day.

The anger rose in waves from the sullen maid, but her head bobbed in a swift upturn. Sophia didn't spend time fretting about it. She had too many other concerns to attend to.

Like eating berry tarts.

Then she grasped the flowery posies she was painting around Addison in her mind. That was beyond foolishness.

She had spun magic dust around her first marriage before her vows and that had not been wise, but a folly of large proportions. Marriage had been the biggest mistake she'd ever made, but she'd needed somewhere to live, believed in love and hoped for the best.

She felt herself spinning the same illusions with

Addison. He was a man who needed servants and she needed employment.

She took in a deep breath, aware of the aroma of Cook's baking. Aware of the sunshine she couldn't see from the hallway and, most of all, aware of Addison.

When she reached the kitchen, she relayed Addison's request for tarts. Cook spared a glare at her, not pausing in the zesting of lemon peel.

Cook must have read something in her demeanour. 'Addison is not as innocent as you are.'

Innocent. She felt anything but and was secretly pleased that she could be perceived so. 'I've been widowed.'

'You are still a babe in the woods compared to him. Need I spell it out for you?'

'No.'

'I will anyway.' The blade darted around, corralling the zest. 'Addison's mother was graced with all the outward perfection nature could bestow on a woman. It was claimed she was one of those women who had people agog at first sight. She first wed an older earl who'd already sired children. After her husband died, his sons inherited all. She was hanging on by her beauty and her wits.'

Cook used her fingers to load the blade with the lemon. 'It's said she understood metals and could melt gold right out of men's pockets. The Duke of Oldston noticed her, supported her and she had a child. Addison has his father's stature. But he inherited his mother's eyes and smile, and knowledge of the upper reaches of society. The Duke knows Addison is his son. Everyone does.'

She paused, sliding the lemon zest from the metal and letting it land in her bowl. She directed a question at Sophia. 'Doesn't it make you feel better just to be in the same room as him?'

'He's my employer. It would not benefit me to dislike him.'

Cook snorted. 'Imagine his mother, a woman who affects men as Addison does women. Would you like to know what is said about Addison?'

Sophia knew from the tone of Cook's voice that she wouldn't, but neither would she be able to stop Cook from telling her.

'His drive is to do as well as his half-brothers. Or better than they do. And that includes the one who will take their father's title some day. That is a powerful goal.'

'That has nothing to do with me. I wish him well.'

'It could have a lot to do with you.'

'You sound like a mother warning me away from her son.'

Cook's expression brightened and she laughed. 'My wages and my place are dear to me. So perhaps I do feel as if I'm the mother of the people who eat in my kitchen.' Then she placed both palms flat and pushed herself up. 'When he marries, I will keep my post. He says he'd starve without me.'

She straightened her apron. 'I'm a Wellington of the kitchen. It's a wonder the Prince hasn't tried to snap me up. Addison said that's why he doesn't like my skills being known. Is afraid someone else will try to hire me.'

'I agree. That would be his loss.'

'Addison has weaknesses, or strengths, depending how you interpret it. He appreciates the loyalty he gains from us.'

'I saw him let the butler and Mrs Crisp go.'

'They weren't loyal to him, but to each other. I didn't let Mrs Crisp's haughty ways bother me because I could hear his patience wearing thin with her. He didn't trust her or the butler.'

Cook lifted a cloth from the table and brushed it absently over the clean wood. She eyed Sophia. 'If the servants around him don't give him the notice he believes is his due… It's a fine line for you to keep. A servant who must treat the master near an equal and yet not step from her place. And you don't cook.'

She scrubbed at an invisible speck on the table.

'He doesn't feel he has true family now with his mother gone— His father rebuking him. Servants— those are the people he is closest to. Addison has been known to talk for hours with the carriage driver. I didn't catch on at first and, because he was the master, I kept from sending him out of my domain. I was surprised that he would give me the time of day. Yet he kept appearing here time after time.'

She waved a cloth, beaming at the memory of Addison treating her as a friend.

'The pinnacle is the society folk whom Addison wants to live among eventually and he plans to do it. But now, he feels comfortable among us. I've heard of people having such ways before, though. Once he marries and has a proper family, he'll fall into the natural order of things. His wife will pull him along with her and he'll find the life he wants. It's in his grasp.' She held out her fingers to indicate a pinch. 'And he's this close.'

She wrapped the towel into a twist, then snapped it at a chair rail and sent a fly to the floor. 'Trespassers to my kitchen are not welcome. But no matter how many times you tell a fly that, it never listens.'

'What you said about the servants—' Sophia rushed on. 'You make it sound as if he cares more about them than family. And you do manage to keep in his good graces, but you are an exemplary cook.'

Cook frowned, taking the compliment as both her due and the distraction it was.

'Addison's soul needs nourishing. On occasion, he toils late and gets hungry in the middle of the night, and he rings three quick jingles, but I know what's next. I get up and prepare him a bite. Nothing fancy, perhaps bread and jam, or whatever is at hand. And he comes to the kitchen and we talk. I love him as much as I could a son of my own and he knows it. He can be ruthless when he feels someone is against him and he has no remorse for moving aside those who don't value him. Anyone who cares for him would want him to have his wishes and his dream is to stand side by side with his blood relations, and he's got powerful tall blood relations.'

Sophia didn't answer.

'Don't you be ruinin' what you got here. Most 'specially don't be ruining what I have. Don't you be upsettin' Addison's life.'

Cook took her towel and washed the table top with a vengeance. 'One smile from him and I feel years younger. The reason Crisp's niece didn't leave with her aunt is because she's besotted with him. Woman's got a scar that runs down her back. Almost didn't survive her mother's love. Crisp took her in.'

She snapped the towelling towards Sophia. 'Tread light. Addison has been jaded by his past. Taught to be cautious. He guards his heart closer than any miser guards gold. He has no reason to share it with anyone. Women give him what he wants easy enough. Now be off with you and I'll have the scullery maid take the berry tarts to Addison if he's here when they are fresh from the oven. We'll have ours at supper. You need to keep your distance from him.' She grimaced. 'But I know you won't.'

Sophia started, bolting upright in her chair, her sewing falling to the floor, awakened by the rap on her door. 'Enter,' she called out, momentarily forgetting her location and reliving her terror at the possibility of being discovered.

The scullery maid peered in.

'I took Mr Addison his tart and he said if you weren't abed, he wished to talk with you. He's in the library,' she said, leaving.

Sophia jumped to her feet, her feelings all askew.

Then she rushed to Addison's quarters, feeling a flush of pleasure when she saw him at his desk, a half-eaten tart in his hand. He took another bite.

'Don't forget that I will be having interviews in the library for the manservant in the morning and then, after the last one leaves, we will discuss their demeanour.'

She nodded, prepared to depart.

'Wait,' he instructed, finishing the treat. 'How did your discussion with Ina go?' The words stopped her.

'It went well… I suppose.'

'Sophia. You've got to be firm and more staff is needed here. You may feel you're in over your head, but that is usual with any new position. In a short time, you'll understand the staff and anticipate what needs to be done before it occurs.'

She lowered her eyes, then checked his expression, finding warmth. 'I'm learning. Just not as quickly as I'd like.'

'Even if you were absorbing slowly…which I don't see…it's all forward progress.'

'I never thought I acquired knowledge as easily as my cousin Merry.'

'Don't compare yourself to others,' he said. 'Tomorrow, when the last interview leaves, meet me in the library. When you get there, look around you at the plants. Caldwell planted many flowers to bloom at different times. Numerous shades. Heights. It makes the beauty of the summer last longer.'

'If you… I'm sure you're correct.'

He paused. 'Sophia. Stop fretting. I'll let you know when mistakes are made and you can amend them.'

She didn't anticipate joy in being told about her errors.

His lips tightened, but she could see the smile behind them. 'You are not being corrected, but assisted.' He seemed to be waiting for her reaction, but she wasn't sure what it should be.

'I'll leave now, if that is acceptable,' she said.

She could tell he was considering his next words and he seemed to lose a battle with himself, and gave an apologetic smile.

'It appears you were awoken. I had no idea, or I wouldn't have summoned you.'

She brushed a hand through her hair, straightening it. 'I fell asleep sitting up.' She heard the embarrassment in her voice and explained, 'I've not done that before. I could not imagine a housekeeper's room to have such a soft chair.'

'Crisp caught a cough soon after she arrived and Cook told me that the housekeeper was having trouble sleeping when she retired for the night. The chair had been one of a set in my bedroom. I just had it moved and never had it returned.'

'Oh.' She felt she'd done something wrong. 'I will get assistance and I will put it in its rightful place.'

'It is in its place,' he insisted, waving away her statement. 'I can't sit in two chairs at once. If I'd needed it, I would have had Caldwell take care of that years ago.'

'You are my superior.' She considered her words carefully. 'And it is my first fortnight. So, I will not dare disagree.'

'Good on you.' Then he raised his brows. 'The tarts were delicious. Weren't they?'

She sighed. 'I did not know such a treat existed.'

He nodded. 'I hoped you would enjoy them. Pleasant dreams, Sophia.'

Outside the door, she stopped moving, her insides fluttering. As she suspected, the tarts really had been for her. Cook had probably grasped it.

She'd been rewarded for working so hard.

Staring down at her reddened fingers, with a blister on her thumb, it had been worth it. She would become the best housekeeper ever.

Chapter Six

The prospective butlers had arrived and she'd been cautious as she spoke with them, trying to size them up and committing the details to her memory, then showing them to Addison's library.

As soon as the second one left, she moved outdoors, finding the space in the rear of the house empty.

The walled garden was small, possibly less than half the size of the one below the rooms she'd shared with her husband, but that spot had been merely untended grasses shaded by overgrown shrubbery. This one spoke of serenity.

One large tree dominated a corner, shading it. Underneath, two benches faced each other, an alcove which encouraged visitors. A matching table sat between them. Stones were inset into the ground, with the soil surrounding them only visible enough to let a few tiny sprigs of grass grow, except at the perimeter where plants of various sizes and shapes flourished. Then she noticed portions of the walls were offset, possibly to welcome breezes.

Addison strode from the house. 'My favourite spot

to be when the weather is good, but it seems I never have enough time to enjoy it,' he said. 'Mostly only Sunday afternoons.'

'It's lovely. A room—with foliage to enfold you and sky for the ceiling.'

'Caldwell tends it for me. It was nothing more than grass when I moved here, with a pen for chickens in the corner. One overgrown hedge surrounding. I didn't have plans to change it. But when I started on the interior of the house, Caldwell said it would be a shame to ignore this area. I told him to do whatever he wished with it.'

'He did well.' A breeze brushed her face as she contemplated her surroundings.

'He always does. He's exemplary. Much more than a coachman,' he said. 'He's advised me several times. Somehow, I can't see either of the men I spoke with today joining the staff seamlessly. One had worked in a much more affluent house and I couldn't see him adjusting to here and I didn't take to the other at all.'

She almost stumbled in her surprise. Her trip up the stairs to his room had taken longer than it took for Addison to discuss the decision with her.

He must have read her astonishment because he laughed. 'I didn't expect to make up my mind so fast. But the last two manservants have made me wary.' He strode to the alcove and she followed.

'Perhaps I could find a temporary assistant for a few evenings,' he said as he dusted a few twigs from the bench. 'I am hoping to have a guest. I want someone here to at least answer the door and show him to the sitting room. It's extremely important. Though I don't know how I could find a decent butler for a short job, if I can't find one for a longer one. The coachman would agree to do it, but he would be uncomfortable if I tasked him with it.'

He studied her. 'Sophia, make another short night of it. I don't want you doing any chores late into the night. I can tell you're not getting enough rest.'

'I'm sleeping well.'

'I can imagine. Because you're so tired after doing all the cleaning.'

He watched her, his expression not condemning, but telling her she'd been caught out. 'And you must take some time away from work soon. You must.'

She couldn't answer.

'I'm not angry with you. Merely concerned that things go in the correct direction.'

He undid the buttons on his coat. 'And ask Cook if she can spare the scullery servant to help you, but assure her she knows it's her decision. Perhaps it will be easier to replace her than a maid and the scullery girl might prefer different duties. You are doing too much.'

She'd never expected the master of a house to think of the lowliest servant. She'd not even envisioned asking if the young woman would be interested in different duties.

He held out a palm to indicate she sit on the other bench and she did, unable to resist the respite. She'd no idea one could create such an inviting garden.

'This is so lovely,' she admitted.

'Well, if you see me out here, don't be surprised by my reading material. Beldon used to collect the scandal rags for me, though he would insert an equal number of more reputable newspapers. But I relax here on Sunday evenings when the weather is good and peruse them. I know not to believe most of what's written in the lesser sheets, but it can be entertaining.'

He looked heavenwards. 'I tell myself it's business to know what's going on in the world, but it does get to be a habit.'

She turned her head and pressed her lips together, wondering if he remembered the story in the papers about Ophelia.

'Don't judge me harshly for my weakness.' He laughed his words away, and she grasped he misinterpreted her response. 'I've left my serious vices behind and decided it's a much better failing to read about others in the rags than to see my own name mentioned there.'

She tapped her fingertips on her skirt. 'I cannot imagine you ever doing anything to be mentioned in such horrid papers. Please, can we talk of something else?'

'Don't be upset for me. In the past, I've done enough to deserve my name there. I'm far from perfect. Guessing by the stories, few are. If my family is mentioned, I like to know of it. That's how I found out my father planned to marry again. And it's nice to know these things.'

She interlaced her fingers, unsure of what to say.

He loosened his cravat. 'It was better than reading the wager in the betting books about whether I would die before my twenty-fifth birthday.'

She put a hand to her mouth. 'Unthinkable.'

He shrugged. 'I took the wager. And lost. I don't have to win every time. Just enough.'

She wasn't certain he didn't wink at her.

'And the day of my birthday, I worked from home

and went to sleep early.' He stood, took off his coat, draped it over his left arm and said, 'Now, I must get back to the important papers awaiting me in the library. They're not nearly as interesting as the latest on dits, but relaxing in their own way.'

She stood and dusted the wrinkles from her skirt, walking beside him as they returned to the house. 'I would have thought you would have bet the other way on the wager.'

He moved purposefully so she couldn't read his expression.

'I generally consider as many facts as I have available before making a decision. I came closer to winning that one than I would have liked.'

He paused and took her arm to guide her inside. She thought the touch was to comfort himself.

'I'm pleased you lost,' she said, capturing his clasp briefly, and giving it a light squeeze. 'I need the employment.'

'I'm pleased to be here to provide it,' he admitted. 'Very pleased.'

Chapter Seven

The next morning, Sophia noticed Addison asked her a few brief questions about her duties when she entered, making sure all was well. He seemed to be waking up as he shaved, companionable, but not talkative.

The sound of scraping of the whiskers was the only noise breaking the silence and the shaving soap scent infused the air.

She hoped all her future mornings could be so peaceful.

She'd left him and been downstairs for about a quarter of an hour when the sound of the next bell caused her pause.

Quick snaps that boded ill and her heart reverberated with the jangle. The intensity of the ringing had caused her stomach to plummet and her slippers flew as she darted up the stairs.

Something in the rapidity warned her.

A quick, timid rap on his door. From the other side, he snapped, 'Enter.'

She stepped inside, then hesitated, unmoving.

His waistcoat, unbuttoned, with the rich fabric reflecting the window light and making it appear as if it had been spun with golden threads. His trousers black as night, encasing his legs to perfection. The sleeves of his shirt billowing as his arm moved. The cravat, tied to an exact, but trim knot at his neck.

His face. Shaven.

His eyes. Dark.

He was dressed and held out his arm.

True, she saw the anger. But in another part of her mind she saw the dark hair falling over his eye, the lean length of him and the male wall of his chest. Even as her mouth dried in response to his scowl, she could not shut away her awareness of him.

She clasped her hands.

'What happened to my shirt?' he asked, his voice well past the calm before the storm. Invisible lightning sparking in the air, singeing everything in its path. 'You could have told me or removed the garment. What happened?'

'I don't know.'

He waited.

She walked forward. She could not imagine what had happened to the clothing.

She tried to pull herself together. The fabric was dear and the shirt had taken a lot of material.

The scent of the fabric that touched his body, a foreign spice scent, surrounded her. He towered above her, larger by the proximity.

He was angry, but the control he exhibited let her know she was in no danger. A fact that surprised her.

'Are you attending?' he asked.

'Yes,' she answered of habit, not sure what he had said before that.

'This,' he said.

He held out a section of the sleeve closer to her. It appeared to have ash and wax on it. As if someone had taken a snuffed candle and smeared it over the fabric.

Her throat constricted.

His eyes pierced her. A person she'd never seen before stood in front of her. 'Who has been wearing my clothing?'

'I didn't— No one has.'

'Then how did this happen?'

She knew. Ina.

He waited. Then his voice became quiet. 'This wasn't an accident. Was it? You knew nothing about it.'

'I didn't.'

'You are in charge of the maid.'

One forceful blink from his eyes and she couldn't speak. The entire room, if it had been able to creak, was silenced while Addison gathered his breath.

He spoke in a soft voice, with an underlying thread of steel. 'I understand that you are new to this and that Ina is not accepting you. I told you. You may replace as needed.' His brow furrowed and his voice softened. 'I do not need to concern myself about my clothing in the morning. Ina has been ghastly with her duties since you arrived. She is testing you to see how far she can go. And you must put a stop to it.'

His eyes challenged her. He took in a breath and she imagined she could hear the air rush by her ears.

She didn't know what to say.

He unbuttoned his waistcoat. The fabric twisted and

rotated as he slipped the fastenings through the button-holes. 'And see that this shirt is gone as well.'

'I can try to mend it. To get out the wax. Or get similar fabric and replace the sleeve.'

He spoke, a slow swirl of command. 'I never wish to wear the shirt again.'

'I will take care of it.'

The waistcoat fell open. 'Be aware, Ina has had years of service here, yet she destroyed my property and didn't care how her actions affected you. Let that make your decision easier.'

Biting the inside of her lip, she pulled another shirt from the wardrobe. 'I will try harder.'

'You do not need to try harder. You are trying enough. You need to try differently.'

He glanced to the window, seeming to forget she was there. 'If a man has a shovel and is digging a hole in the wrong place, trying harder just makes a deeper hole.' He didn't seem so condemning, but more thoughtful.

'I will do better.'

'Of course you will,' he said and let the silence invade the room.

The air whooshed around her, bringing an awareness of his maleness, their closeness and her knowledge of the gulf between their stations.

She feared anything she said would land her in more trouble.

'It is your choice, but if I were you, I would let her go.'

'I've never done such a thing before.'

He could send a butler and housekeeper packing without a blink and she grasped that she had no other options.

'I would suggest you deliberate on Ina's actions. I do not think she wishes to work here any longer. She is taking your preferences from you.'

He seemed to be gauging her reaction to his words. 'Years ago, I made decisions which narrowed the paths I could travel. Let's blame it on youth, but that's unfair to children. When I was forced to see what I was doing, I could have been angry with ten or more other people, but I chose the right person to be furious with. Myself.'

'The only path I know I've selected...was marriage.' Perhaps she'd deluded herself. 'I don't know that I had a sensible alternative.'

'If that was the only route you considered sensible, then you deserve a halo.'

Eyes pierced her again, but not with anger.

'Wait here.' With that, he went into his dressing room and shut the door.

She wilted, holding the tall footrail of his bed for support. She ran her fingers over the smooth wood. She imagined a whirlwind as similar to Addison. He could gather all the forces into the room inside himself and be stronger for it, leaving everyone else depleted.

Within what seemed like seconds, he had returned, dressed perfectly, with his coat on. He gave her the shirt.

'Go to the tailor's today. He should have a new waistcoat for me. Order a shirt.' He paused for a heartbeat. 'Select and lay out my clothes in the dressing room afterwards so I will have them ready tomorrow.

'And, Sophia...' he lifted his hand at his side and something in his eyes flashed defeated '...these have never hurt a woman and they never will. Don't flinch when I speak with you. I didn't intend to sound so harsh.'

'I beg your pardon. I didn't know I did.'

'I will remind you if you do it again. But do not expect me to keep my voice light. It lets people know I am serious.' Then he straightened his cuff. 'And I am serious even when my voice is soft.'

With that, he left.

But he'd told her he would never strike her and she believed him. He'd not hit Stubby. He'd been upset about the shirt, but he'd not lost any control of his statements, nor had he stormed about, sulked or jeered at her. His voice had risen in volume, angry—and she understood because fabric could be so dear and Addison was so precise about his clothing—but still, he'd not lashed out at her as he might have.

Addison handled anger in ways that she wasn't accustomed to.

She examined the garment and brushed it against her cheek, the fabric softer than any she'd ever felt. Yes. The sleeve had been ruined, but it was a fine shirt. Still useful. In the past, she would have been expected to repair it and she would have done so, or reused the cloth for something else.

She gasped, comprehending he'd just sent her on an errand she had no idea how to accomplish.

She followed him from the room and moved quickly down the stairs.

'Where is your tailor located?'

She stared down at him, but he wasn't diminished at all. She might as well have still been looking up. In fact, he appeared larger.

'I'll send my driver back for you. He will know where you need to go. Until we get staffed, you may use the carriage when it's free—you can move about more quickly. Let Caldwell know your plans.'

He gave a nod to her. 'When you bring my shaving water in the morning, if you have any other concerns, we can discuss them then. I will wish to know how you handled this.'

As she trod the stairs, Ina—chin up, arms crossed—stood just out of Addison's sight, challenging. She'd heard the conversation at the doorway. Saw the shirt. Had a smug smile on her lips. 'Oh, my. Did Mr Addison's clothing meet with an accident?'

Sophia looked at the stain, folded the fabric before tucking it under her arm and raised her own chin. 'You are let go. Be packed by the time the driver arrives for me and we will drop you at a nearby location after we retrieve your last pay from the man of affairs. Or you can leave now, with no funds, and walk where ever you wish to go.'

The woman acted as if Sophia hadn't spoken and strutted from sight.

Sophia went to her own room, falling against the door. She would have never been able to do such a thing had Addison not given her leave to do so.

But that didn't help her at all with the chores.

Chapter Eight

That afternoon, Sophia heard the wheels of Addison's carriage and knew she would have to give him the bad news.

Running to the kitchen, she made sure Cook didn't need assistance and waited for the soup to be warmed and dished up.

She gathered the tray Cook prepared and darted up the stairs, the aroma of Cook's favourite beef soup that they'd all tasted earlier making her mouth water again. Perching the tray on her hip, she knocked on the door.

'Enter,' he called out and she marvelled at the timbre of his voice. Even without seeing him, Sophia could hear the strength in the assuredness of his tone.

She moved inside. Briefly, Addison's presence took everything else from her mind. He imposed on the space around him and yet, with nothing more than a flickering change of expression, he welcomed her into the room. Warmth enveloped her and pulled her closer to him, and their eyes met—his puzzled. He expected the scullery girl as Cook often sent her with a meal since the manservant had left.

'The scullery girl had to leave suddenly,' Sophia told him, putting the tray on the table by the door. 'Her beloved proposed and the master where he lives has a position for her. She was tearful, but felt she had no choice but to leave immediately. Cook is upset and was washing up and stumbled over a bucket the girl had left behind. She is walking gingerly. Her knee is out of sorts. I will help her.'

'Are you sure Cook isn't hurt badly?' His gaze narrowed, and he tensed, moving close.

Sophia touched his arm, reassuring him, shocked that the master cared so much for the servants, but then Addison seemed different than any other man she'd ever met.

'She said it doesn't hurt at all now as long as she doesn't jostle it and it's so much better than earlier.' Sophia took in a breath. 'But that isn't all of it. I let Ina go.'

'You did what had to be done.'

She shrugged. 'I worried that Ina might not have a place to go. *That*—' her shoulders dropped '—that worries me.'

'She tried to sabotage you.' He shook his head. 'The butler's brother works at a country estate,' he said. 'Likely he already had a position there and one for Crisp as well. Cook knows of the place. If the niece doesn't secure a post, she'll have her aunt to fall back on. They are close.'

'I am relieved.'

'Do you know anyone who might work as a maid?' He waited for her answer.

'Perhaps. I have been thinking about it.' She and her cousin had sworn to be there for each other and now she had a chance to help Merry.

'But she must be of outstanding moral values. Ina wasn't. She had to be told to keep her distance from the coachman several times. He's married and didn't appreciate her lingering when he worked in the garden. He said that telling her nicely to be on her way didn't last for more than a day.'

She took a step away and her lips firmed before answering, 'I'm not certain. I might know someone. I wrote her a message earlier and asked the scullery maid to deliver it as she was leaving.'

She'd not wanted anyone to tell Addison that she'd sent the message to the brothel and, since the scullery maid wasn't returning, it would be unlikely for him to discover this and she'd been happy to deliver the message as her last chore.

'Good. It's too much for you to take on.'

With a sideways glance, she indicated his table. 'I make lists now, like you do.'

'Thank you for all your efforts.'

When she studied his azure gaze her efforts were rewarded, but when he averted his attention to his desk to take his pen—and her mind could work again—she grasped the situation. If her cousin was employed, that might mean she had another person to watch as carefully as she'd had to do with Ina.

'I may be overextending myself,' she admitted.

Addison smiled and dipped his pen in the ink. 'I'm writing a note to my steward now. Since you have a potential maid, I'll tell him to work on obtaining a scullery girl first. Cook must be helped, especially if she's limping. You are a remarkable woman, but you're still merely one person and can do no more duties than two as a rule. Three for only a brief time.'

Remarkable woman, he'd said. Happiness flooded her. The highest compliment anyone had ever given her, ringing all the more true because it came from Addison.

She wanted to tell him she appreciated the statement, but she could tell he already knew.

He finished penning the note, stood and placed it with the top sticking out in a blue ledger. 'Tomorrow morning I'll have the coachman deliver it.'

He was even taking a chore that he might have given her if she'd not been so busy.

He walked to her and put a hand on her shoulder. Time stilled and his regard infused her with his strength. 'Don't worry about this. You will have help soon. We just must take care, or we'll find ourselves back in the same situation of needing employees. I don't want another Ina. I didn't know if she was taking things, or if it was Crisp, or Beldon. And I suspected all three of dishonesty at various times, but I could not be certain who it was.'

'I don't know about her honesty—or how she worked when her aunt was here—but she wasn't impressive with me. She spilled water down the stairs. Which made no sense as she had to clean it up and get new water. She only made more work for herself.'

He stepped away. 'For most, I guess the secret to wisdom is learning not to be your own worst enemy.'

'Sometimes it is difficult to judge what is the best path to take, or your mind could even hide it from you.'

'You're right. I suppose we must have compassion for those who are bungling their way through life. Compassion,' he reiterated. 'Not unawareness.'

She didn't want to make the very mistake they were

talking about and she could feel herself becoming closer to it.

Her mind told her she must go. It would be inexcusable if he comprehended how her feelings were changing. She was the housekeeper. It would even be intolerable for her if she became attached to him.

Her feelings for Addison had transcended what she'd first felt for her husband many times over. She couldn't let Addison comprehend how her affection had grown so quickly. He would likely try to find her another location to work. Or, at best, distance her.

She didn't want to live in the shadow of his affection, waiting from behind a window for a glimpse of him in a carriage as he rolled out of her life in the daytime. Hoping for the scent of his shaving soap, touching paper he'd held, or staring at the boots in his room.

Being helplessly besotted would be a curse she'd put on herself. Little different than being wed to a man who was as demanding as a child and expected her to do all for him that he could have her do.

Her husband, excellent at carpentry, and skilled at running from beam to beam, had tried to become an actor, but his performance had always been wooden.

Finally, the theatre owner had taken a chance and cast him in the role he pursued and immediately her husband had believed himself the best thespian to walk the boards or jump above them.

He had weakened her with his needs for praise and reassurance. Addison strengthened her.

But she imagined the fulcrum swinging the other way and her affection for Addison taking more from her spirit than anything else ever had. Dwindling her into a speck of who she was and the fragment only living when he noticed her, and the rest of her hurting when he didn't.

She could imagine giving her love to him and it would be hard to survive with her heart beating for him, and his heart oblivious to her, or attached to one of the women Cook claimed best for him.

And it was true. She was a servant in his household, not someone who would be able to walk about on his arm and provide a home for his children to move among the best families.

He'd mentioned people who didn't look out for their own best interests. While she had in the past, she wondered if it was because she'd had no opportunity to do otherwise. Falling in love with a man above her station would not be wise.

She imagined herself being introduced to a new lady of the house and knowing she would report to her.

'Goodness. I mustn't keep you any longer. It's later than I recognised.'

She darted from the room. A crushing weight seemed to take over her thoughts and she ran up the stairs to her room, but truly, she was trying to run from the truth she wanted to erase.

The next morning, Addison's hand stopped before ringing the bell for Sophia.

He wondered if he was becoming his own worst enemy again. If he'd been so reluctant to hire one of the men who'd shown up for the interviews because he wanted to see Sophia first thing in the morning.

True, he was friends with Cook, and the coachman, and he'd thought becoming acquainted with Sophia would be no different, yet he knew it was. Something stirred differently inside him when she arrived in the room.

He went to the mirror and stared at himself. He wasn't a youth. The visage he saw had changed. It should have gained wisdom with the years. It had. But he feared he was returning to his old ways. Maybe just one step here and another small step outside a boundary there and he'd be tumbling about without a purpose again.

He'd had a momentary lapse by being attracted to Sophia. He could control it. Blazes, he'd ended many similar feelings for women in his past.

After Sophia had left the night before, he'd moved to the kitchen to check on Cook and she had been waiting, as if she'd known to expect him.

Then he showed her the note sent by his father.

And he'd talked quietly with Cook and she'd reminded him how hard he'd worked, how much he'd moved forward, and that the banker's daughter was likely still besotted with him. Even if she wasn't, other influential people had unmarried daughters and would appreciate having a son-in-law like him.

She'd reminded him his first duty was to his future self—and his wife. That he could never disservice a woman by looking back and thinking if he'd wed someone else, his life might have been better. That his wife had hindered him.

No wife would want a husband thinking such.

Addison relaxed, seeing his strength in the mirror again, and moved away. Confident he'd corralled his thoughts and would have no trouble with a friendship with Sophia.

He rang the bell.

A few minutes later, Sophia rushed in, her hair held in place by a few pins. A flyaway wisp caught his attention and she brushed it back in place, an unthinking motion, but his fingertips responded with an awareness as if he'd been the one touching her tresses.

He stared at his hand, as if it had betrayed him. The early morning sweetness of her still invaded him, tinting the world a little brighter, but he could not begrudge her that. It was his own failings which he had to contain.

He put his attention to his shaving, but he paused briefly. 'My father might visit soon. Nothing is more important to me right now. I'll tell you as soon as I know when he is to arrive and, on that day, I want everything he would see from the front door to the library to be perfect. Can you manage that without another servant?'

She nodded.

'If you have worries, let me know.'

He caught her view in the mirror. 'My father and I have not truly spoken in years and he could determine much of my future. That's why his visit, and goodwill, are vital.'

'It sounds like you have obtained his goodwill if he might visit.'

'I don't want him to work against me.' He flicked the blade against the whiskers. 'Though I suppose he never has.'

'I'm sorry you do not get on well.'

He stopped shaving, deliberating. 'That's a hard judgement to make. You might say we've got on better in the past few years than we ever did. I suppose I miss him. Possibly because no one in the world can anger me like he can.'

He held the razor, unmoving, at his cheek, aware of how closely she followed his movements.

'Thinking of watching your husband shave?' he asked softly.

'No. I try not to.'

He studied her briefly before continuing his actions. He took another swipe along his chin, studying his jaw in the mirror, but not truly seeing it. 'Do you miss him?'

'No. We rarely had a conversation.'

He remembered the spirited arguments of his parents. 'Is that a bad thing?'

'Before we married, I expected we would remain friends afterward. We didn't. I was his audience and the performance was always a repeat.' She bit her lip, recalling. 'I've tried not to reflect on him much. He became sullen if he wasn't praised, yet you couldn't give him enough notice.' She waved a hand, as if brushing away her statement. 'But...' She clucked her tongue softly. 'My husband was years older than me. It just didn't seem so...'

He dipped the blade in the basin and rapped it on the side, tapping the water free, addressing his own view of matrimony. 'My mother and father usually didn't live under the same roof.'

He stilled. 'I hadn't understood it before. But perhaps their shouts and drama constituted a performance to them, too.'

'Were they friends?'

'Possibly. I suppose when they were getting along best, I was left to my own devices. I didn't mind at all. I preferred it.'

He put down the razor and swept up the towel, brushed it over his face, and gave a swift lift of his brow when he lowered the cloth. He rubbed his cheek, checking the shave.

He studied her. 'The order I get from my life means a great deal to me.'

'You like the peacefulness of it?'

'Yes. Suppose I do.'

'I will do my best to keep the quietness around you.'

'Then you'll be the perfect housekeeper.'

He forced his attention to his shaving, trying not to let his mind linger on her.

'To be fair, Crisp kept a soundless house.' It had put him on edge, much like the oppressive demeanour of the butler of his youth. 'So maybe a small amount of relaxed noise is welcome in a home.'

She appeared to deliberate on what he said, lips pursed, and he felt the need to explain.

'Like chatting with you in the morning.'

Her cheeks brightened above her blossoming smile. The image of innocent happiness hit him so strongly, he moved so that he couldn't see anything but his own visage in the mirror.

He heard the door shut and rotated, transfixed by the empty space she'd left behind. Blast it. He'd lied to himself. He was still a youth inside.

Chapter Nine

Sophia heard a rap at the outer servants' door and assumed it odd a delivery was arriving so late in the evening.

Opening the door, she discovered her cousin, Merry, eyes red rimmed, clutching a wadded handkerchief and cloaked in a cloud of the vilest perfume which covered her far better than her bodice. Behind her stood a man in a ragged coat with a portmanteau and a crate.

The man doffed his hat, dropped the case and crate, and gave an apologetic nod as he scurried away.

Merry sniffled and, voice trembling, said, 'I got your message and knew I had to come now. I couldn't wait another second. I refused to entertain even one more person and Mrs Wilson tossed me out.' She clutched Sophia. 'Please. When I saw your letter, I knew it was the answer. Please let me work for you.' She gulped in a breath. Her remarks ended on a plaintive note.

'But this time you must—'

'I won't take anything and I won't misbehave. Just let me sleep in your room. I'll make a pallet on the floor.'

'You must promise…' She couldn't ignore her cousin. They'd nearly starved together.

Merry released her clutch on Sophia and made a prayer-like gesture. 'Please.'

'We'll both go hungry together before I let you go back to the brothel.' She regarded Merry. So much work needed to be done. 'But Addison wants someone with good morals.'

Merry's head rose and she brightened. 'I can have good morals. I've been a virgin lots of times.'

Sophia studied her cousin. 'But what if someone recognises you? You've always attracted notice. Always.'

'True,' her cousin agreed. 'But I've been noticed enough now. I don't want to be an actress any more. Or a courtesan.'

'You need to tell the truth, but not all of it. Don't mention the theatre.'

'I never worked there anyways. At least on stage.' She paused. 'I don't want to go to another brothel. None is as good as Mrs Wilson's and it terrifies me. She promised I would find a suitor and be able to leave, but I can't wait for that.' She gave one large sniff. 'And I won't be like I was when you introduced me to the actors. I promise not to cause any rows.'

'This may be your last chance to start over,' Sophia said. 'It's a chance for both of us.'

'It will be almost like we were children again and your mother took me in, with the good times we had when your father was away drinking.'

'No. You have to work. Real chores. I will have no choice but to send you away if you don't do as you're supposed to. I'll give you what funds I have and we'll try to find you another position, but I will not let you stay if you jest with all the men and don't help with duties.'

'I will. You will never know I'm here, except for all the work I'll be doing.'

'Just don't mention the theatre to Cook, or anyone.'

Merry agreed. 'I won't. That is behind us. Your mother-in-law was evil. Trying to have you hanged. Going to the newspapers time after time. I was thankful your dolt of a husband never called you by the right name.'

She grimaced. 'It was endearing when he courted me.' Sophia had often read plays with him and he'd decided the name fitted her best. After they'd married, it wasn't worth the fight to correct him. He'd refused to call her Sophia and his mother didn't know her by any other name.

His mother had hired a constable to have *Ophelia* arrested and tried for murder. When her friend Humphrey had warned Sophia what her mother-in-law was doing, she'd been able to move swiftly, hiding, being the housekeeper for the elderly woman, Mrs Roberts.

She'd been careful to keep herself from view. Humphrey had taken care of the errands she needed at first, until drink had taken first importance in his life. Merry had helped Sophia keep out of sight, though truly Sophia appeared nothing like the engravings in the newspaper.

She had the good character Addison required. At least, when people got her name right. She grimaced when she remembered the headlines:

Hamlet Killed When Ophelia Pushed Him from Window!

* * *

Cook had already instructed her to take a plate to the library when he'd not arrived after supper and she'd known it would not be long before he returned. The squeak of a brake alerted her to Addison's carriage and she put aside her stitching.

He'd been working late, not carousing. He wasn't like her husband or her father.

She remembered the notes she'd seen. Goodness, she'd never known of anyone before who had an occupation where he'd needed to keep notes of what he was to do. She would have doubted his powers of recollection if her own mind hadn't become jumbled at the length of the list and the amount of figures.

Jumping up, she secured her lamp and ran to the doorway, unlocked the latch and opened it. He stood with a huge satchel under his arm, a sheaf of papers in one hand, and he was retrieving the books he'd set at his feet to free his hands to be able to manage the entrance.

'I'll help,' she said, taking books. Their fingers connected, and her senses soaked in the masculine scent of him, stirring a longing that burst into her like a spark on tinder. She backed aside while he entered, shocked at her body's awareness of Addison.

She concentrated on securing the door, trying to smother the waking embers she'd discovered inside her.

'Thank you.' He moved closer, his presence cradling the space around her. 'You didn't have to wait up. I would have got in.'

The soft sound of his voice mixed with the deepness that rumbled through her was caressing in a way she didn't remember ever being embraced with before.

Addison seemed to pull her closer, sharing the secret of their moments when they'd talked earlier.

'I wasn't asleep,' she almost whispered, arranging the books so she could hold them and pick up the lamp. 'And I'd fear for my life if Cook heard you rapping on the door and her rest was disturbed.'

The papers nudged her up the stairs. He waved her ahead of him. 'How is she?'

She moved enough to increase the distance between them and instantly felt colder. 'Much better.' She paused. 'I hired a new maid today…if that meets with your approval.'

'I'm pleased you have assistance and I see no problem with that.' He used the papers in his hand to tap her elbow in a pat. 'Well done.'

They moved to his library. 'And the coachman knows someone who has a daughter who can help Cook for the time being. So, things are improving.'

A weight had been lifted from her shoulders, but she wasn't sure if it was because new help was arriving, or because Addison was nearby.

'The desk.' He indicated where she should put the books and he followed behind her, adding his own load to them.

'This appears to be a lot of work.'

He shuffled through the papers, separating them into three stacks. 'I was hungry. The carriage driver had been waiting far too long and I wasn't finished. Besides, I was starting to make mistakes. I needed to let my mind take a moment to rest and reassemble. I'm pleased your day was more productive than mine.'

He unbuttoned his jacket, studied the desk, then put the jacket on the back of the chair. He interlaced his fingers as he put his hands behind his neck and stretched, giving a tiny groan of tiredness.

Then he stopped, moved and took the wine glass Cook had insisted she put out for him, taking a sip before putting it back in place.

He shook his head, reached for the bread and the knife for butter.

'I still need a manservant. It's not fair to you to be waiting on the door and helping me in the mornings. Not fair at all. Plus, I got a message earlier. The Duke will be here tomorrow. I wanted the butler to be at the door when he arrived. To give the right impression of my life. A minor thing at first glance, but important to me. The Duke has said before that a man without a butler hasn't reached the pinnacle of success.'

He snorted, more at himself than anything else. 'I know that's ridiculous. And an odd thing to find important, but…'

She so wanted to please Addison. 'If you need a temporary butler, I may have a friend who can—possibly—help. One night. Until you find someone else.' The words rushed out, and then her brain caught up with them. 'Er… I'm not entirely sure he is available, though.'

She'd pondered on Humphrey, the actor who'd lived in the rooms below them. He'd been a performer most of his life, but she didn't think he could act well enough now to convince anyone he was upstanding and the drink had inserted itself between him and his profession…most of his friends…and a roof over his head.

He was the only man she'd ever seen who could recite Shakespeare while so foxed he couldn't remember whom he quoted.

The tavern had been his address since his house had

burned down. Usually, he'd stayed inside the structure. But when she'd last found him, he'd been sleeping under the boards at the back, almost in a little nest he'd made, but coherent and sober.

'He's by no means perfect.' But he had a rather elegant way of speaking that he'd learned for the stage.

'The Duke has the highest standards.'

'Then Humphrey isn't the man for you. But he can be grand on occasion.' Not that he'd had many of those occasions of late, though he'd assured her that he was taking a respite from drink as it always improved the taste of it when he swallowed his next drop, which he claimed the curious saving grace of sobriety.

Addison ruminated for a moment. 'All I need for tomorrow is someone who can appear formal.'

'He possibly could. But you should meet him first and I'm not sure he's available.'

'Is he of good moral standing?'

She pursed her lips. 'I would say he is of medium moral standing. His standing is always a bit wobbly, in more ways than one.'

Addison's eyes narrowed in question. 'You think— this man could convince someone he is a manservant?'

'Possibly. I've seen him gather himself at the last minute and do well. But perhaps… I'm not sure.'

Addison drew in a breath. 'Could you get your friend here before tomorrow night for me to speak with him?'

'Possibly.'

'It's only for one night.'

'Mr Talbot can be on his best behaviour…if it's a night. He can manage a few hours. But only until you find someone else…' She didn't think Humphrey could be at his best for long.

'Yes. My true butler must be above reproach with excellent references.'

Humphrey could never provide excellent references. He'd told her his stories and, true, he'd confessed fault on some occasions. He understood that drink had taken a toll on his employment and he'd admitted that he'd been enthusiastic with helping tavern owners in exchange for a sampling of their wares.

But he'd claimed drink the single love that had remained with him to his old age and he didn't see himself abandoning it. True, he was trying a break from it, but he judged it a limited performance and not one to go on overlong as when he had enough sobriety to find work to purchase more of the elixir, he would then again happily trot off into a numbing haze of comfort.

Addison studied her. 'I'll speak with him and make my decision.'

She understood she was lingering, getting a comfort from his presence that she'd not received from anyone before. 'Is there anything else?'

He shook his head. 'No. Expect me to ring late for my shaving water in the morning.' His eyes drooped. He yawned, and she refused to chatter on.

Addison spoke before she left the room. 'You're doing well, Sophia. A treasure. I'm pleased your little brother brought you to my attention.' He took the door from her, holding it open a second longer. 'Though I doubt you could have escaped anyone's notice.'

She left the room, emotions flooding her. He only noticed her because she worked for him. He just was aware of the people around him. It wasn't because she was singular to him.

She stood in the darkness, again unsure of the path in front of her and not only because of the darkness.

A sound of skittering.

She didn't move. Gathering herself.

It was only that this life was so different than her own.

Nothing like the moments of her husband arriving home after lingering at a tavern, saying he was with other actors and they were working on an idea to make them all rich.

She gripped the banister, engulfed by the deep uncertainties she'd often felt.

In the past, she'd liked the darkness, seeing imagined happy scenes in the dark shapes, but now her imagination turned everything ominous.

Her father had died when she was eighteen, but he'd often left them alone night after night and they were the happier for it. In his drunken state, he'd often considered the men in the taverns a good match for her. Her cousin, Merry, had given her advice and suggested she tell her father she was waiting for a widower with a good fortune and wouldn't that be nice if she married into money and the man took in her family as well. They'd spun silken tales for him, pretending agreement with his grandiose plans, bolstering his imaginings.

Merry had convinced her that it was always better to agree with someone you disagreed with who had power over you and tell them the beauty of their plans as you convinced them they were having an even better idea.

Sophia had tried so hard to follow that advice after she'd wed.

After her mother passed, she'd been alone and vulnerable, and marriage hadn't improved things much. She'd seen her father die of drunkenness and expected her mate would meet the same fate, but he hadn't...exactly. Not as she'd foreseen.

Suddenly, the last remnants of affection for her marriage arose. The aftermath of that night. The sadness and struggles she'd had after he'd died engulfed her. A lump lodged in her throat and she paused, controlling her tears.

The past surrounded her as alive as if it had happened seconds before. Her mother passing. Her father terrifying them. Her husband playing his foolish jests and jumping at her from the darkness.

At that moment, a shape hurled itself at her feet, sending a shard of pain through her leg, causing her to stumble, and the globe of the lamp dislodged, falling with a clunk on to the stairs, not breaking, but tumbling down.

The shape thumped down the stairs, tangling with the globe, sending it clattering down the stairs, and the creature scurried away.

Sophia couldn't move, her fingers gripping the banister. Frozen. She knew what was happening. Knew it had not been a monster of any sort, but still, she was unable to speak. To stop shaking. To do anything.

In those moments, her mind had reacted beyond its ability and the sensation of fear gripped her, entrapping stronger than any bonds. Her hands locked in place.

She was prey. Captured. Controlled by fear that paralysed.

Addison charged from the library.

'What is it?' he called, surveying the area around her

in an instant, stopping, puzzled, shirt hanging loose. 'What happened? I heard something.'

Shaking, she couldn't speak. She stood gripping the lamp and the banister, shivering, the globe finally resting at the base of the steps.

'What's the matter?' He reached for her, taking her arm, pulling her closer, yet still she couldn't let go of the banister, shaking, her mind locked in terror.

'What did you see?' He retrieved the quivering lamp, sitting it close to the wall behind him, then he put an arm around her and removed her fingers from the stair rail.

Addison drew her close, shielding her and guiding her up the stairs.

She could feel Addison. Knew he was there. Had an awareness of her surroundings, but her body had trapped her. She couldn't move.

Sophia stood, unable to do anything but shake. Addison kept her at his side.

'What was it?' he asked, precise softness adding force to his tone.

She couldn't answer. She couldn't. Her mouth trembled, but nothing came out.

'Was it a person?' Addison asked, holding Sophia, turning her to him.

Sophia stood silent, unable to stop shivering. Her heart pounded.

He tugged at her, but she was unable to follow.

He put both arms around her and held her.

She gasped for a breath and started to weep softly into his shoulder.

He held her. Comforting. Standing with her, letting her cry.

She seemed powerless to move. Incapable of stopping the tears.

Addison stood, clasping her, caressing her back in soothing motions, letting her cry on his shoulder.

She couldn't stop crying.

She could hear Addison murmuring to her. Softness. Gentleness. And for some reason, the soothing whispers tore at her and made her weep anew.

Finally, she gained control of herself. She moved her hands. She gripped his waistcoat. 'I'm sorry.' Barely loud enough to be heard. 'So sorry.'

He didn't answer, but knelt, seizing the lamp on the floor, and took her into his sitting area, holding her snug against him, his muscles moving beside her, a fortress of molten, fluid strength.

In the room, he sat the light on the first flat surface and stood with her.

'I'm sorry,' she repeated.

'Was it someone?'

She shuddered, trying to control the tears. 'No. A cat, I think. It pounced on me and I wasn't expecting…'

He led her into his dressing room next and took the flannel from the table, dipping it in the water, wringing it with one hand and holding it to her, but he still clasped her side.

She wiped her face, not shivering as much, but still not herself.

'There's no cat in my home.'

'I'm sorry. It lunged out of nowhere and grabbed my leg. Claws jabbing me. My mind stilled.'

'You've nothing to apologise for.'

He led her back to the sitting room, sat on one of the floral sofas, pulled her against his side and held her.

She rested her head on his shoulder, the flannel tightly clasped.

'I was thinking and it was dark, and the cat—I didn't see it. I didn't expect—'

'It could have tripped you. You could have fallen down the stairs.' He kept her in his arms, holding her close.

'I'm fine, though.'

He moved away enough to speak. 'You are not fine. Do you know how a cat got inside?'

'Perhaps Merry, the new maid… She had a crate. I didn't think. I didn't think of not telling her… But I didn't know she had a cat.'

'I will send her packing.'

'Please don't let her go.'

'*Her blasted beast could have killed you.* It could have caused you to tumble down the stairs. You had a lit lamp. So many things could have gone so much more wrong.'

'I need her here. I do.'

His voice was almost a growl. 'You could have fallen. Been killed.'

'But I wasn't hurt. Merry would never let something like this happen on purpose. Never. She's not that way.'

He groaned. 'If that's what you wish. She can stay. But the cat goes.'

'Thank you.' She reached out, clasping him tightly, and he hugged her, the thin cloth of his shirt not much of a barrier to the warm skin beneath it. The muscled forearm. 'Thank you for holding me. I've never—nev done that before.'

'These last few days have been trying for you I'm sure that had something to do with it.'

They were trying in more ways than he understood and she'd not even grasped it. She was attracted to Addison in a way she'd never experienced. Feelings had grown and she'd not fathomed them more than a pleasant reaction to an appealing man, but now they peaked within her.

And he wasn't someone she could easily walk away from. Moments between them could lead to little else.

She would be adrift, both in heart and employment. It wasn't only the awareness of falling from the stairs that had frightened her. She was falling from her life. Again.

True, she'd had no alternatives before. She'd done everything correctly.

The knowledge slapped her. She'd done everything correctly and ended up with a bag in her hand and standing in front of Mrs Wilson's.

'Falling down the stairs would have been horrible.' She shuddered. 'My husband died from a fall. I didn't know if I would catch my balance. I could have set the rooms afire. It was terrifying. But the most frightening thing of all was not being able to move afterwards. I just couldn't.'

'You've had long days, long nights, I suspect, and you've had upheaval. It's not easy.'

But he'd made everything easier for her.

'Thank you, again. No one's ever held me like this.'

'But you've been married. Widowed.'

'Yes. But my husband would not have held me.'

He didn't respond.

'He wasn't demonstrative. Like that.' She ducked her head.

'I'm not either. With most people.' He reached out

and left a trail of heat behind the brush of his finger against her cheek.

She raised her eyes. The fear left, replaced by an awareness of the man. Her whole body felt more alive than it ever had. Again, she couldn't move, but this time it was from the warmth in Addison's eyes.

'Sophia, if your husband didn't hold you, then I pity him.'

She didn't answer, but he seemed to form his own conclusion.

He stood, moving her to her feet, one hand remaining at her waist, making sure she was steady before he released her.

He waited. 'Better?' he asked.

'Yes.' But she didn't want to leave. She didn't.

And he didn't move either.

'Let me see you get to your room safely.' He brushed his hand along her elbow.

'It's no more than a few stairsteps away.'

'I know. But you've had a fright. Your knees may give way. Or the damned beast might jump at you again.'

She shuddered.

'Are you sure you're fine? You can stay if you'd like. You can stay in the sitting room as long as you want. All night if you'd prefer.'

'I want to be held again.'

He moved, enough that she could fall into his arms, and she did.

She looked up and he bent his head.

The kiss was sweet, gentle, caressing, and brandy scented.

The second one—a taste of lips, longing, and need.

His arms clasped her tighter and the third kiss was an exploration of her lower lip, moistening breath against it. An awareness of him erasing everything else in her world.

'Soph—'

She moved against him, hearing the regret.

Their kisses lingered and she was aware of her own need, his desire and an emptiness she'd never experienced before.

He ran his hands down her back, past her waist and to her curves, pulling her closer, causing her body to tremble with need, securing her against his hardness.

His cheek brushed against hers before his lips took hers again. A touch of tongue, intensified by the soft sideways movement of his body as he angled closer, taking her mouth with hungry passion.

She mirrored his kiss, matching him with the pressure of her body, flattening her breasts against him, kindling an explosion of sensations in them she was hardly aware of because her whole body responded.

He paused. Moved back. 'This is…a situation…that will have a bad end. You'll be hurt. We have to stop.'

She stared at him, dazed, not knowing what he was talking about, or why he felt he must speak. But then he stopped and she needed him to continue, to use his voice to pull her back from the edge of the precipice. She was dangling in mid-air, waiting for his touch to draw her into the comfort of his body.

'I've had romances before. It never ends well.'

After she'd fallen into the precipice of Addison, he'd taken a firm step away from the edge and away from her.

'You're right,' she said, trying to hide the need that

pulsed through her. Trying to brush her hair into place as if it were just another day. 'I've been married before. It didn't end well either.'

'Let me see you down the stairs.'

He took her arm and secured his lamp.

She went with him downstairs and the temperature dropped with each boot fall on the stair, and the night darkened inside her, replacing all the feelings she'd embraced with a dismal bleakness that frosted the air she swallowed.

She stopped him at the last step and their attentions locked on each other. She spoke softly because she didn't want anyone else to hear. 'When our—time together ends, I could find other employment.'

'That is a horrible idea.'

'Why?'

'I need you here.'

She observed him. 'I don't understand—'

Addison's grunt expressed irritation at the situation. 'I'm concerned. That you, because you've been sheltered in marriage, might make a mistake that would ruin your life.'

'I understand. I am good at making mistakes that could ruin my life. I somehow feel I came close to it tonight. But I don't care.'

She left, before she could say anything else. He'd kissed her. He'd desired her, yet he'd felt himself so far above her.

'Wait.' He clasped her arm.

She rotated out of his grasp, facing him, back straight, chin level. He had so much more than she did, but she stood in front of him as an equal. 'Yes?'

He took her fisted hand and she pulled slightly, but

he followed, his touch gentle. She relaxed. He lifted her hand and kissed four knuckles, then his fingers slid and ended with their hands clasped together, which he lowered.

'It was I who made the mistake, tonight. You did nothing wrong. Everything right. Can you forget this happened?'

'I will reserve a decision on that.'

'Fair enough.'

'The first time in my life I've been held with compassion and you wish me to forget it. I must have mistaken the moment.'

'No. You didn't. You deserve more than a man who cares for you. A woman should have a man who places her above all others. Above himself.'

'I've never heard such a thing.' She put her hand to her chin. 'I've always estimated caring was enough.'

'It isn't. It's never enough.'

'Tell me.' Her fingers brushed his shirt. 'Have you ever seen a person like this? I mean…where might I find such a specimen? Is there a menagerie where this sole person is kept? I don't think I've ever seen someone like this.'

'Caring is a part of the connection between a man and a woman. If we make love, it will change things between us, at least for a time. The kisses have. I don't know what it will bring.'

'You have said the kisses have altered things between us. That means I am not merely a housekeeper in your eyes. That I am also someone who may give you my opinions. Or am I misunderstanding?'

'I would like to be your friend.' He soothed over the

rejection. 'Friends have disagreements sometimes. It doesn't always end their connection.'

'It doesn't.'

He caught her jaw. 'You are beyond measure beautiful. You've captured my attention and awakened desires. I don't want this to tumble around our ears. If we became closer and something went wrong between us, we would both suffer. Friends are hard to find. Good friends are rare.'

'True. No friend has ever made me feel like you do.' She put her fingers over his and took his hand from her jaw, but clasped it to keep her balance. She tiptoed, steadied herself, and put a kiss on his cheek. 'Goodnight.'

He gave her the light and she stepped inside. As the door closed, she heard his voice.

'Night, Sophia.'

The sound of her name on his lips caused a renewed longing. Bursts of feeling that almost took her to her knees.

She put her hand to her forehead, disbelieving the words she'd heard coming from her lips. Never before had she been so demonstrative with a man. Even her own husband. Yet she'd been unable to consider the ramifications of what a closeness with Addison could lead to.

Her first romance had led to a marriage which nearly destroyed her. This one could take her heart from her.

She stood in the darkness of her room, arms clasped around herself, her mind lingering on Addison.

The kiss had been a tragedy waiting to happen. A pleasant, wondrous mistake. But neither of them had meant for it to happen. Perhaps they could both erase it from their minds and continue on.

Addison was her employer, but she wanted him close because of their conversations. Because of how he made her feel appreciated.

The cat wouldn't have scared her so much if she'd not been thinking of her husband. On no occasion should she think of him. She couldn't bring him back and, if she did, she doubted he'd stay long. He'd never been able to see beyond the next adventure or lark.

In order to survive early on, she'd welcomed her marriage. Welcomed it. True, neither she nor her husband had been thinking of love at first, but more a case of working together. She assumed he wanted someone in his bed and someone to cook for him. True, his job at the theatre wasn't the most steady, but he assured her life was brimming with opportunity and he wanted them together.

But she'd not met his mother. It hadn't been an oversight on his part. She was certain of that or he would have mentioned, in passing, that he didn't live alone, but had been a kind understanding son who lived with his mother, above stairs in a dwelling owned by the actor Humphrey Talbot, and she mostly supported her only child…and his mother was a woman who might, on occasion, drink a bit and he might be compelled to spend an evening at the tavern imbibing with her as it soothed her evil heart to be with him and other people whom she could tell at length how wonderful her son was, assuming anything could appease her.

And her mother-in-law had been as surprised as Sophia was when her husband had introduced them after the marriage.

It was the single time Sophia had ever seen the woman enraged at her most precious son. Seeing her much older thirty-five-year-old husband's ear twisted nearly off had not been how Sophia had expected to start her married life.

True, he had been older than her in years, but by the end of the first year of her marriage, she accepted that she was more advanced than him in every other way.

Then she understood why he'd proposed. His mother had been complaining about her health. About new pains and being unable to do all the cleaning. He determined it would help if he had someone to stay behind and take care of the chores while he was at the theatre and his mother were at the tavern. He wanted to be certain everything was taken care of.

She'd not done a perfect job at that and she never wanted Addison to know. She had failed at her most important duty. Keeping her husband from destroying himself.

Chapter Ten

Addison stepped into the library and lifted his fork from the floor. His mind remained on the scene at the bottom of the stairs.

He'd heard the clattering and known something was amiss.

He'd bolted out, unaware of dropping the utensil, or of the need for a lamp, and found Sophia clutching the banister, unable to move, terror consuming her, but nothing there to scare her.

Then he'd wanted to hold her and reassure her. And he had. He'd not expected it to end in comforting himself. Holding her had made him comprehend how alone he was. How solitary he'd made his life.

After university, even after he'd modified his life, he'd not been celibate, always having a woman who would welcome him in the late hours, to whom he promised nothing. Then one day he understood how well and often he was delivering on that promise and he'd striven to spend more of his evenings alone. Work had seemed the answer. And the harder he'd toiled, the more he'd found needed to be done.

He'd felt the aloneness then, but over time, he'd accepted it as the price for more success.

He'd been wary of courting. Of stepping into a union similar to his parents, but with no means of escape. He'd known it would have been unfair to the woman and himself.

After growing up, listening to his mother's complaints about husbands and men, he could find strangers to disparage him easily enough. He didn't need a wife.

His mother had said that having half a man was better than having a whole one, and sometimes even half a man was the wrong half, whichever half it was.

Her first husband had died, leaving her penniless. Bitterness about that had overshadowed any good memories she might have had of him. She'd decided then that she didn't want a man to control the funds in her life, ever again. If that meant no marriage, then she was fine with that.

She'd even refused a duke, she'd boasted. Her declaration on her unwed state.

Addison had understood. His mother and father's romance had been a constant bicker because their joy was in verbal gouges and thrusts. His father would live with them a few days at a time, leave for about the same length and then his carriage, ducal crest for all to see, would arrive at the front door. The butler, Wooten, would open the door with a flourish, helping His Grace with all the respect due to the Duke. Wooten did all but add trumpeters to complete the welcome.

Whether Addison's mother greeted the Duke with a smile or with a shout depended on the day.

Addison realised he'd been like his mother. Rebellious.

And he'd rebelled with a vengeance.

He'd followed along with that kind of life, until he'd had three very long days to think about it.

Then he'd decided to keep upheaval to a minimum and over time it had surprised him how much he liked a life without strife. He'd even let Mrs Crisp and the butler stay longer than he should have because letting them go would disrupt things. He'd hoped for a trouble-free home. But it wasn't working out. It wasn't the smooth well-ordered life he'd planned.

Sophia had clung to him, shivering. He could have fought an army, but he hadn't been sure how to handle tears. And when he'd sat with her she'd relaxed and he'd felt stronger than ten men.

In such a short time, he'd become accustomed to her presence. He liked having her nearby. Their mornings had evolved into a little ritual of sorts, rather like he'd had with the butler, except absolutely nothing like that.

The first manservant had been agreeable and too loquacious. The second, Beldon, had stayed to hold Addison's shirt and rather annoyed him with his stone demeanour and wall of perfect silence. He'd never felt at peace in the room while either was assisting him.

Sophia would investigate something as she stood, not always in the same place, and relaxed or fidgeted or studied something, even if it was appearing to examine the back of her hands while her mind was far away. Sometimes the mirror reflected her expressions.

She didn't seem able to be completely still. Sometimes she would ask him questions about whether he'd noticed any dust, or did he mind if she replaced a table covering or she'd beg his pardon for leaving an upper storey window unlatched that he'd not even noticed open.

Sophia had a serenity about her. A peacefulness. Having her near relaxed him. Reminded him that the world had simpler times. She was an intricate treasure of serenity. So innocent. Their kiss had been like a thousand first kisses all rolled into one.

He should never have tasted her lips. He'd never be able to convince himself that the kiss didn't truly happen. That it was a mirage.

Nothing so beautiful could be false.

He'd been aware of the hooks on the back of her dress. The femininity of hooks fascinated him. Perfect little latches. He touched his thumb to his fingers, imagining the crisp twist of them under his fingertips.

And then he'd mentally cursed at himself.

His housekeeper was busy and did not need him thinking about her. Or kissing her. The moment of holding her had been necessary. She'd needed reassurance, but a kiss wasn't supportive. At least the ones they'd shared.

He didn't need to be spending his hours with her in such awareness, aroused by the way her actions captivated him and her smiles flourished inside him.

His well-ordered household had been swept away with her tears. And a kiss to cherish. A kiss to ruin his well-ordered plans.

He didn't want her to leave.

If the romance didn't go well, how could he bring a wife into a life with his former lover in it?

But then he tossed out his reservations. The work had been going well. He could set her up in a residence of her own and take care of her. She would be protected. He saw himself following in his father's footsteps and remembered the harshness his parents shared with each other. A life like that would not be good for anyone.

She couldn't be his mistress and he didn't want to wed. A wife would not understand the hours he needed to devote to his success. Would not understand how little time he had for her. Then there could be children and he recalled how distant his own father had often been. How he'd felt when one parent pulled him one way and the other, instructed him differently and he'd seen no option but to rebuff both directions. If he'd chosen one parent's wishes over the other, the results would have been even more explosive.

People had noticed his composure when taking on the most intricate and tense projects. None had been as involved and thorny as his childhood.

He appreciated both his parents. They had prepared him, accidentally, more than they could have ever grasped, for the investments.

But they'd not prepared him for marriage. Only to avoid it.

Sophia opened Merry's door without knocking.

Merry sniffled, a huge black cat in her arms.

'I can't go back to Mrs Wilson's.' Merry's voice rose. 'I can't.'

Sophia sighed. 'You can stay. But the cat has to go. It caused me a fright…on the stairs.'

Merry moved the cat around and Sophia saw mournful eyes on both of them.

'It's Rufflestiltskin. Ruffles needs love, too. Ruffles has been there for me. Day in and day out. Mrs Wilson hates Ruffles and she would never let me bring Rufflestiltskin back. You know what it is like to struggle.'

'I'm sorry. For both of you. But it must go. In the morning. Or you are going with it. And you should never have jeopardised my employment like that.'

Merry sniffed. 'I told it to go out the window when it needed to roam. I opened the door and it got out before I could catch it and I didn't know which way it ran. I was trying to find it when I head the clatter. Rufflestiltskin came running back and tried to hide in the crate.'

Sophia's lips thinned. 'The beast pounced on me out of nowhere. I could have tumbled down the stairs.'

Merry lowered her head.

The cat gave a soft meow. Almost a beg.

She shook her head, but her heart softened. She couldn't bear to see an animal suffer and this one needed a place to live as much as she had.

'We can't keep the cat. Addison will be furious.'

'I will explain to Ruffles it is all your idea.'

'You should have told me.'

'I meant to. But Ruffles was nervous about moving. She casts up her accounts when she's nervous and I didn't think that would get the two of you off to a good start. It certainly didn't with Mrs Wilson.'

'Merry…'

'I know,' Merry admitted. 'But I love Ruffles.'

Sophia wondered if she'd made a mistake. 'I'm going to find Humphrey tomorrow…to see if he'll be a butler here for one day. Keep Ruffles in the crate and perhaps we can talk Humphrey into taking him when he leaves. Maybe Ruffles will keep Humphrey from freezing to death when it gets cold.'

'I like Humphrey, but it's safer to keep the cat here than it is to let Humphrey in the house. Rufflestiltskin has never got foxed and taken a nap in the middle of a performance.'

'I know. But Humphrey can usually keep a part for one day. I'll get him here, in costume, and get him out. The former butler left quickly and apparently the master has his coat and trousers because he left them behind. They'll fit Humphrey well enough for one day.'

When she left the room, a warning bell sounded in her head. She knew she should listen to it.

But if Humphrey was able to act the part of a butler for one evening, Addison would let the coachman take Humphrey and Rufflestiltskin back to the tavern. The cat probably wasn't used to living in such meagre surroundings, but it would have to make do, just as she was with Humphrey.

He loved a performance, at least on opening night. Unfortunately, he couldn't always abstain from drink until the finale.

The bell rang and Sophia ran for the heated water, pouring it into the pitcher and going quickly to Addison's room.

Her heart thumped in her chest and it wasn't all from the movement up the stairs. Part of it was her reaction to seeing Addison again.

She paused at the door, then gave a brief knock and walked into his private rooms. He stood by the basin, shirtless, brushing his hair. She moved forward and he stepped aside as she poured the water into the bowl for him.

Her concentration was on the night before. The moments of him holding her. The kiss. And what he'd say to her. Yet it seemed a different world in the morning light and they didn't seem the same people.

They weren't looking at each other or speaking, but it somehow seemed their bodies were remembering, connecting and reliving the kiss.

He mixed the shaving soap and lathered up.

She knew, if he had a valet, the man would likely have done that for him. But she'd never felt right about moving forward and asking if she could help. He would have said no.

He lowered the brush into the soap, unmoving. Appearing to gather himself. So unlike him. 'Are you recovered from last night?'

'Yes. Again. I beg your pardon for being so nervous.'

'Again. Nothing to apologise for.'

He gave her a glance. Just a glance, held for a moment, and again their bodies spoke.

She comprehended that she stood closer than she usually did and he shaved more carefully, slower, and with the grace a perfect sculpture might use if it came alive.

He finished shaving and she watched the muscles move beneath the surface of his skin. He was well formed, words which didn't do him justice. Much in the same way a person might have suggested Michelangelo was of moderate talent or da Vinci was good enough for an artist.

And he did need a haircut, she supposed. She probably should have offered to cut it for him. She'd shorn a man's hair many times, but the main requirement had been to remove most of it. Perfection hadn't been expected and she would hate to be the one who butchered those locks.

They curled around his ears and, while she hadn't touched them, she could feel them. They were luxurious. Soft against the man who had more strength in his muscles than he had a right to have.

She'd been told by Cook he sometimes toiled at the docks when shipments arrived, moving crates aside, checking manifests and showing other employees what was expected. The efforts showed on his body in a way other men would be envious of.

She'd already examined each picture on the wall… both of them. What she didn't know was why he had an engraving of a knight battling a dragon and the other of the dragon, one foot on the knight's chest and with the sword raised high.

She deliberated on the images. 'Why do you have those pictures on the wall? Is it some days you slay the dragon and some days he gets you? Life.'

He lowered the blade for a moment, smiled, gave a brief perusal of the engravings, as if he'd never seen them, and then continued shaving, speaking around the swipes of the blade.

'They came with the house, I believe.'

'Oh.' Well, she'd asked. She took in a deep breath. 'I told Merry the cat has to go. We've not found a place for it yet.'

'Ask the coachman. He will be certain to give it a home. He doesn't believe a person can have too many horses, or pets—unless they are eating something he's planted. And a cat is fairly certain to leave greenery alone.'

'Merry will be so pleased.'

'Perhaps I overreacted. I saw how terrified you were, though, and never wanted that to happen again.'

He'd finished shaving and was wiping his hands, and as the moment expanded, again the air changed, but this time it was with a feeling of separation.

Eyes full of compassion, he said, 'I don't need anything else this morning.'

Disappointment filled her and perhaps a bit of relief that the kiss no longer seemed to linger in the air between them. The next time they met it would be the same as if it had never happened. Which somehow made her sad.

She prepared to leave, but then something caused her to hesitate and she caught his gaze on her. Warm and riveting, in a way she'd never seen anyone else observe her.

For a moment, neither moved, held together by the longing in his eyes and the same emotion inside her.

'I wish I'd stayed last night,' she said. 'With you.'

'Sophia.' A caress. Soft, low and not just the use of her name. 'I apologise.'

'You did nothing wrong. Unless you feel it was incorrect to comfort me.'

'I suppose it was. In the way that I did it. I should have called Cook or the new maid.'

'I'm grateful you didn't.' The moments between them had given her solace the rest of the night. Only the intensity of the feelings of comfort Addison gave her could erase the terror of being unable to move, run or even scream.

'I shouldn't have held you.'

She didn't believe that. She really didn't. She suspected if she didn't get him out of her yearnings, she would need to find a position somewhere else so she didn't long for him. 'I understand you feel that way. And

I hope you aren't affronted by my belief that it's nice to have a man in my life who reacts to me as a person in my own right. And perhaps that will be enough for me. It is a new experience and I like it.'

She shook her head in amazement. Addison was one man who had the right to treat her in a subservient manner, yet, in their short time together, he'd treated her better than her husband ever did in the way he respected her.

'Every man in your life should treat you well.'

'I agree, but it isn't logical to expect that.'

'Not all marriages are happy. They seem a way to trap two people who might like each other more if they could both leave. Although that didn't create happiness for my parents.'

'I've yet to see a marriage or a romance that is truly happy. I don't think I've ever seen a romance, in fact,' she said.

'They can be fun. Spirited in a good way. It's the ending that is so difficult.'

'If you wish to offer it, I would like a romance with you. I've never had one before. And I would like one.'

He didn't flicker an eyelash. 'A romance of the intimate kind?' He walked closer, the towel still in his hands.

'Preferable. But if not, I would like that also.'

Cupping her cheek, he put the barest kiss on her lips. Hardly a touch at all, but infusing her body with the feel of him. It was as if they had embraced again, yet she didn't move.

'Based on how I've seen things progress from kiss to caress, before long, we would be sharing a bed.'

His mouth touched hers again, more of a miss than a

kiss, but his warm breath against her cheek heated her skin as intensely as if he'd spoken words of love within it. For seconds, his forehead rested against hers and she could have lived in the feelings growing inside her for the rest of her life.

He was correct. The ending would be painful. Unthinkable if they stayed in the same household and he began raising a family. Her heart would not continue to beat.

She had to find a new life…a place to retreat to should Addison make love to her and the end reach the natural conclusion of a master and a servant. The one Cook had warned her about. And she didn't want to stand in the way of Addison reaching all the success he deserved.

Nor did she want to hurt herself more than she had to. And making love to Addison might be necessary. Her body cried out for his and she tried to remind it that she couldn't destroy her life. Her future. For lovemaking.

But then she wondered if the memories might be worth it. She had lost one man she never truly loved and didn't want to lose a man she truly loved without ever touching him.

He stepped back and she slipped out the door—not dismissed, but hoping to collect herself and needing to make sure what she'd asked for was indeed what she wanted.

An ache within her answered her questions with an unexpected clarity. Leaving the room and knowing it would be hours filled with long minutes, before she saw him again, caused her to feel bereft.

She imagined ten years in the future, without Addison, and knew she wanted the memories of a romance with him. She would hold them close the rest of her life.

With that lodged in her mind, Sophia couldn't rest. No matter how much Addison didn't seem inclined to let her go, if they had the romance she hoped for, the ending might be more painful than she anticipated. She would have to leave.

She'd made a promise to the little boy to visit him. If she waited, Stubby might forget all about her and, if a possibility of a different job remained, she wanted to find out.

Her curiosity compelled her to plan a visit. Best not to wait until she had no other options. Planning for future catastrophes would make her feel better.

Addison had offered her the carriage to find her butler friend, but she'd refused, knowing he needed it for the morning, and suggested she'd take a hackney if it met with his approval and he wouldn't mind the expense.

She didn't want the coachman seeing Humphrey's surroundings, fearing he would report them to his master.

After she and Merry cleaned the necessary rooms, she grabbed her reticule and set out to find Humphrey.

He wasn't at the tavern as she'd hoped, but the owner said he'd likely be back before morning and he would give Humphrey her message.

Instead of returning to Addison's, she took the hackney to discover if she could find the sailor's abode, allotting herself enough time to make it back to Addison's home before dusk.

When she found the oars, she asked the driver to wait. She ran to the door and knocked.

A man, truly bigger than any she'd ever seen in her life, both in width and height, opened the door. In a few seconds, he'd sized her up and a chortle escaped his lips. 'You be Stubby's new sister?'

'I was dropping by to let him know I'm doing well. Is he in?'

Stubby's head popped into view. 'Hello, Sister. You here to help us with the place?'

'I can't stay,' she said. 'The hackney's waiting. I just wanted to let you know I'm fine.' And to see if he'd told the truth.

'Well, we can take you home,' Stubby said.

He waved the hackney on, but the driver didn't move, watching Sophia.

'Sure can,' Broomer said. 'I'll pay him and send him on his way if you'd like.'

'We can show you the docks. I know 'em fore and aft.'

'I don't think I can,' she said. 'I need to return to Addison's soon.'

His woebegone droop changed her mind and she gave a nod to let the hackney driver know it was fine, and Broomer paid him.

'What you think of movin' here?' Stubby asked as the driver left. 'We got extra room and you won't have to do much 'cept the usual things.'

Sophia discovered she didn't want to leave Addison's house, or him. 'It's the best place I've ever lived and I—' She couldn't tell Stubby she had family there now.

Broomer returned. 'I'll let Peg know to watch things

while we're gone, and to get the carriage ready.' Then he trudged away.

'Peg used to sail 'til the waters started attackin' 'im. I found him on the docks and brought him for Broomer to take care of 'im.' He paused and she could see the thoughts churning in his mind. 'Mr Addison hired a butler yet?'

'No.'

'You think Addison might want Peg to take my place? Be a butler?'

'I don't think Addison would like that. Sometimes I'm not sure he'll let me stay.'

'If you ever are in need of a job,' Broomer said, returning, 'come to us. I've been keeping things shipshape here for years and I'm in charge of all the hiring, and we have a fine crew to work with.'

'I will remember that,' she said, 'and think about it.'

'Sometimes you'll have to pull Peg out from under a bed 'cause the spirits been chasin' him,' Stubby said.

'If he was my size, that'd be a problem, but he's hardly bigger than little Stub. I lift the bed up and snatch him out,' Broomer explained.

'I bet that's a sight to see,' Sophia said.

'You could see it all the time if you lived here,' Stubby said. 'You sure you don't want to stay?'

'I've already been given the housekeeper job. It's an honour.'

'You're about as high as Broomer now. Maybe Addison isn't so bad.'

'He's kind.'

'You're not courtin' him, are you?'

'No.' A jab went into Sophia's heart.

'Don't see why not. You're fine enough.' Then he

puffed out his cheeks and took her past another harpoon and into a seafaring sitting room filled with artifacts she'd never seen before, and started explaining where the objects had been found.

Then a spindly man hardly bigger than Stubby came into the room and told them the carriage was ready and Broomer led her to the carriage.

They went for a quick ride around the docks while Stubby chattered about each place they saw.

She had no idea of the time when Broomer walked her to Addison's servants' entrance and left her with an elegant bow.

It was like being in a fairy tale, but not exactly.

Broomer was nice, much the same way Stubby was.

And he would be a better man to work for because nothing about him made her senses stir and reminded her of the pleasures she could have with Addison.

Chapter Eleven

It wasn't unheard of for a coach to pull up on the street and stop. On occasion, it happened. Perhaps the bank's owner would send someone with paperwork or a message. Perhaps a friend would stop by.

But most of his neighbours lived more modestly than he did and rare occasions called for them to rent a hackney. So he'd noticed when the coach arrived well after darkness and he'd not been able to refrain from standing at his window.

He'd seen the coachman getting the lantern and taking it to the vehicle door. This was not a hired cab. Then an overgrown man stepped out and helped Sophia ever so gently from the carriage.

He couldn't hear her laughter, but he could imagine it as the oaf led her to the servants' entrance. Led her to the servants' entrance, as if he was a prince bringing home the princess disguised as a housekeeper.

He wasn't angry. He wasn't angry at all.

Addison got no more work done that night. He'd paced, unable to concentrate on anything except the recollection of the man standing in the darkness with Sophia. He couldn't hear them speaking or see their expressions, but it galled him that the man had not provided a chaperon.

Addison decided he must be coming down with some plague and he knew what kind of illness it was. He had to clear his head of her. A romance would bring nothing but discomfort around him and he needed everything to run smoothly. He did not need his life or work interrupted when it was going so well.

The next morning, he decided he did not need warm shaving water. Cold shaving never killed anyone. And if it had, better to die of cold shaving water than an overheated heart. Then he examined the basin. The water could suffice, but a morning without Sophia wouldn't.

He rang the bell.

She arrived, almost swirling into the room. 'Good news,' she said. 'Cook is so much better this morning.'

He nodded, relieved.

Then Addison asked a question, which he'd tried to ask quietly, but he heard an edge in his voice he'd not expected. 'Who brought you back last night?'

'Oh, that would be Broomer.' Nostalgic reflection flavoured her speech.

'The little scamp's friend?'

'Yes. He truly does know an earl and a sea captain.'

'I know the Earl of Warrington. I've assisted him with business decisions. And I'd heard of the ship that the lad claimed to sail on. I'm not surprised.'

'I was. Broomer confided in me that he'd been little older than Stubby when he struck out on his own. If it weren't for the goodness of strangers, he would never

have survived. He feels it an honour that he can sometimes do for others the kindness that was once given
him.'

'Mmm,' Addison answered. 'Were you trying to find
out if that Broomer would like to be the butler here?'
He finished patting his face dry.

'Oh, there is no chance of that.'

Addison's brows popped up.

'Not because he would not like it here.' Her expla-
nation rushed out. 'But because, there, he is so much
more than a servant. Two brothers share the dwelling,
but neither ever visits long and it is more like he is the
owner, and he said he can hire those he feels in need.
The owners never question his actions, but thank him
for taking such good care of the household and they
hear of the others he's been able to help because of the
amount of trust they place in his decisions.'

'He walked you to the door.'

Her mouth opened. She stared at him.

'I heard the carriage,' he said. 'It was outside. On the
street across from my window.'

Then she laughed, shook her head and looked heavenwards. 'Goodness. More fool me. For a moment, I
imagined you sounded jealous he might hire me away.'

He took a moment, collected himself and watched
her. 'Isn't he trying?'

She ducked her head and her cheeks brightened. 'He
did offer me a job, but it's more of a seaman's world and
full of males, and I—'

'He offered you a job. He just met you,' Addison
ground out the words.

'What is so preposterous about that?' she asked. 'You
did the same.'

'But you were at that brothel and— The boy was going to take you—'

'But you knew, knew the man he spoke of. Knew he was truly offering me a place to live.'

'I know *Warrington*, but you and I had an imaginative lad in front of us, searching for a mother, and he claimed you as a sister. It was impossible to tell whether he spoke the complete truth at first glance. Who could tell if the job offer was only in his imagination? I discerned this would be better for you. And I don't like that the Broomer fellow is trying to steal you away.' His gaze passed over hers. 'I hope you stay.'

'You held me.' Her cheeks bloomed again as she glanced away, then into his eyes. 'And I understand that sometimes a simple gesture could be misconstrued. And I don't want to tumble into something that I can't tumble out of if needed.'

Her sincerity silenced him.

'I don't mean that—I just mean that it would be unpleasant for me to develop an affection for you and it not be returned. And none of us is truly in charge of our hearts.'

'We are.'

She didn't verbally disagree with him, but her averted eyes did. Then she faced him again, sincerity infused in her tone. 'My cousin Merry has assured me—um, reminded me—that a heart can be broken once or twice and a person can survive. But it's best to let it get bruised and go on about your day. I have not had a perfect time in the past and I want nothing more than an uneventful life and a quiet world around me.'

Words he could have said.

The earnestness in her impressed him. True, she admitted she'd not had a perfect life, but then, neither had he and everyone knew of his transgressions. His half-brother, the heir, had walked by him once and asked him how he'd liked being in gaol. He'd retorted that the Sunday Services there had been much the same as anywhere else, but the new friends he'd made had been rather bland by comparison to his usual set.

His brother had snarled and Addison had responded with a smile, and moved his arm in a broad half-circle, punctuated at the end with a rude gesture.

'Sometimes I've relapsed into my old ways,' he admitted. 'But I have changed and rarely give my brothers rude waves now. So, I must respect that you've grown as well.' Though he didn't know if he'd moved ahead enough not to let the Duke's eldest son goad him into doing something he might regret.

Edward had made him angry, but he hoped he'd got past that. His eldest brother reminded him of a dog with a sharp nose and a blood lust for sniffing out prey no larger than half his size, and his other brother, Benedict, panted along after him, staying in his shadow.

'For me, the path to moving ahead has not been to be concerned about who might remember an instance in my past, but to assume everyone knows everything. And if they can't see that I've put away the excesses of my past, I can't dwell on it. I must live every day as respectably as I can, in honour of the people who had put their trust in me. The ones willing to listen and welcome me when I returned, when they could have dismissed me fairly and condemned me.'

She nodded. 'I've tried to do as I should, yet sometimes that gets misinterpreted.'

'At least you tried. For a time, I didn't give a moment's notice to what I should do, but rather what I wanted to do or what sounded like the most enjoyment at that second. For those transgressions, I have to live a bland life so that no one questions my actions. But it's not difficult. It's rewarding in its own way.'

A sparkle shone from her. He could see too much admiration in her gaze.

He stepped closer and gently took her arm, below her elbow, and when he spoke his voice sounded much kinder and gentler than he'd ever heard it. 'Miss Marland. Sophia. I was graced. The best of life. And I squandered it.'

The light in her eyes didn't dim. 'But it has made you more compassionate to others. Understanding of their mistakes.'

'I wouldn't agree. Concern didn't pull me from the edge. It sent me deeper into an abyss. When you showed Ina kindness, you see how she rewarded you.'

'I suppose you are right.'

He didn't want her to be sad. While still holding her elbow, his other hand clasped her fingers, pulling them near his heart.

They shared something and he supposed it was the moment of both of them knowing they had their past behind them. That they'd both started over.

He dropped her hand and stepped closer to his wash stand. 'No one truly knows what the future holds, but I hope you'll be happy here.'

'Thank you,' and on those words, she slipped from the room.

He moved to get his shirt, letting the crisp clean scent of it waft above him as he donned it over his head. Grateful Sophia hadn't been the one who'd had to launder his clothing on the day he'd changed his life. She wouldn't have gazed at him with such admiration in her eyes.

He remembered standing outside the prison with the Duke's man of affairs, after three days of living worse than any rodent in his father's stables would have. That time, he'd not even committed a minor offence. His new acquaintance had pretended friendship, stolen funds while Addison was nearby and left him to face the blame for a crime he'd not known about. Addison had discovered what had happened when the magistrate and constable arrived to take him and it was too late then.

The Duke's man of affairs had finally appeared, roughly seventy-two hours later, and delivered the message. He could still hear the oil in the man's voice.

'His Grace has seen that you will not be transported. His Grace refuses to be contacted again and, should the necessity arise in the future, he is undecided about attending your hanging.'

Then he had never been handed a document so pristine and with such a flourish. He'd read it immediately. A bill for his education, plus the amount for reimbursing the victim of the fraud.

He hoped to cancel that debt.

Sophia hadn't seen Addison since morning, but she guessed if she took all the instances when she'd not reflected on him since then, she wouldn't have had enough time to take a sip of water. He stayed in the recesses of her mind, like something left on the back of a stove, simmering, and always there while she went about her day, and she couldn't brush it away.

Merry had travelled to search Humphrey out and

return with him if possible. She'd told her cousin to explain to Humphrey that the performance would last one evening, but must be perfect.

Merry had returned with him and secreted him in the butler's quarters and was ensuring no one saw him before he'd cleaned up.

Sophia didn't know whether to be pleased or upset with herself that she'd sent for him. But he was the single person she'd ever seen that could sleep in a stack of hay in a stable, then stumble out and charm anyone he met. Well, almost anyone.

But now that she'd hidden him and given him strict instructions to bathe and dress in the clothing she'd procured for him, she was asking him for the performance of his life. Without a drop of drink. That would be the concern. She didn't think Humphrey could act without liquids propping him upright.

But then Merry collected her and she went to view the actor. She had to admit, with his silver hair and austere being, he appeared the part.

The trousers had been quickly taken in to fit Humphrey and the hem of the legs had been unfolded, adding necessary length. Even without a hem, they weren't long enough, and neither of them had stockings for him. A bit of ankle peeped out if he walked quickly.

'Do you not have any boot blacking for my leg? Fetch it,' he instructed Merry. 'This isn't the first time I've not had a costume that fits well, but one of many. My sincerity of performance will keep attention from short trousers.'

As her cousin rushed away, he held out a palm, spread his fingers, and let his hand drift towards the ceiling.

'I will do you proud,' he orated. 'I will act the part of a butler. Once I am in costume and on the stage, I become the character. I have not had a drop of the treasure of life for several days and I am still able to stand. Miraculous.'

Then he crossed his arms, returning to the Humphrey she knew. 'But I do not see this performance going on overlong. I am not a soul designed for the trivialities of work.'

'You're not working.' She mirrored his actions. 'You are merely acting the part of labour.'

'Ah,' he said. 'I can do that.' He shut his eyes, a glimmer of a smile wafting across his lips. 'I have performed the actions of toil on stage before, briefly. This will be an extended performance.'

She heard the carriage. Addison. But he was arriving too soon. Then Merry returned and they both worked to paint stockings on Humphrey's ankles.

Humphrey gave himself a nod of approval when he peered in the mirror and adjusted the simple black cravat with a demure loop.

Then she went quickly up the stairs to alert Addison that the new candidate was ready for interview.

Addison sat alone in the library, studying what appeared to be a mountain of papers, lost in the world of his work.

'The manservant is downstairs,' she said, after rapping on the doorway to catch his attention. He lifted his eyes and her heart fluttered more rapidly. The sight of him drummed awareness through her with a pounding intensity, but she pushed it aside. 'The man for the temporary butler position. Humphrey Talbot.'

'Good.' His smiled rewarded her. 'My father is still scheduled to arrive tonight.'

She bit the inside of her lip, trying not to react. She didn't know if Humphrey was up for this performance, fearing she had made a tremendous mistake.

'I don't know...'

'Bring him up.' He stood and she knew as she hurried off that he would straighten his cuffs, check that his cravat was in place and wait for Humphrey, impatient, but not expressing it aloud.

She rushed to the butler's quarters to check on Humphrey. He barely acknowledged her.

'I like this room. It's got a window. With glass.' He shook his head. 'Gathered the only way I'd get a roof over my head again was in a coffin. And those are sadly lacking in windows. Or openings for air. It was rather confining the last time I was in one. Felt more permanent than I would have wished.'

'This is to be temporary,' she said.

He remained in his role and raised a brow at her. 'All things in my life have been temporary, except my appreciation for fine liquids. And the theatre, which has sadly let me down.'

She understood and gave him one last instruction. 'When you walk in,' she said, 'and you stop to meet him, after you bow, discreetly straighten your cuffs.'

'Bow. Stand straight. Straighten my cuffs. You forget, I am a thespian. This is an easy part for me. I have played Macbeth on the same night I played the most intense witch—after surpassing a real one for the role.'

'Be on exemplary behaviour.' She clasped her hands in a prayer-like pose. 'Please don't let him down. He has been so kind to me.'

'I will act the part of good behaviour.' And with that, he swung his arm wide and stumbled, catching his balance against the wall.

Then he held his head high. 'You think I will not get this part.' He grabbed the lapel of his coat with one hand, steadier for the grasp. 'It is that I have been a little dry on drink for some time and apparently it all settled on one side and I was used to that. It is hard to balance without nourishment.'

'You are doing wonderfully, but please don't let him know you are from the stage, as he will send you away. He wants the most respectable of homes and his staff to be exemplary. But I would so appreciate it if you could do this.'

'Exemplary?' he scoffed. 'With Merry here?'

'She is going to be.'

Her voice commanded respect, but he gave a nod worthy of both Mrs Crisp and Addison's old butler.

'I am not doing this for you, Miss Sophia. Acting is my lifeblood.' After the superior glower she received, she had to remind herself he was playing a part.

She led him upstairs and decided that if Humphrey didn't get the job, it might be for the best. Merry was doing a quick scrubbing of his clothing, to get the hay out. Humphrey would have a warm meal, a soft bed, and would have cleaner clothing for the next day when he left.

At the top of the stairs, Humphrey paused. He took in a deep breath. His chest expanded and he walked past her and into the library. He put one arm behind his back and one at his stomach and bowed.

'Humphrey Bonette, at your service, sir.'

'I gathered your name was Humphrey Talbot.' Addison examined Humphrey.

Sophia bit the inside of her lip, feeling impending disaster.

'Yes.' He straightened and arranged his cuffs ever so slightly. 'Humphrey Talbot Bonette. Talbot was my mother's name. My father Bonette. During the skirmish with the French, it was best that I forget that for a while. Bonette? Talbot? *"What is in a name? That which we call a rose by any other name would smell as sweet."'*

Addison was silent.

'I am here to apply for the temporary butler post and I hope I can be of service to you.'

'What are your qualifications?'

'I have few adequate qualifications for this post, though I dare say that most men would be insufficient for it. I was a tutor once for a young man in Manchester and, of course, you cannot tutor a child for the whole of your life. The little ones grow. A butler's life might be a chance to keep a dry roof over my head. Rain doesn't do much for the complexion at my age.'

'Married?'

Humphrey took a breath. 'Alas, it is possibly for the best that I have only had marriages of the heart. None with a cleric involved.'

'You're familiar.'

'Ah...' He smiled. 'I have been told that many times. It is a rare gift I have. To take on the guise of others.'

He clasped his hands behind his back. 'Might I pour you a drink, sir? I feel that the true test of whether a man should do a job is not the particular endeavours he has attempted in the past and ones which brought him to the point of needing employment, but his skills for the required work.'

Addison blinked. 'I am not sure if I am willing to overlook any endeavours you may be alluding to in the past.'

'As most certainly you should not.' Humphrey went to the decanter on a table at the other side of the room.

He carefully opened the decanter, lifted it and filled the glass beside it to what seemed to be an exacting amount as he poured it so slowly. Then he lifted the glass, walked to Addison and held his palm flat, presenting the drink as if it were on a tray. He didn't stumble, although his breaths quickened.

Then he stepped away, stopping at the side of the door.

Addison took a sip.

'Are there any other questions you would like to ask, sir?' Humphrey stood straight and, with the slightest twitch, adjusted one cuff before again clasping both hands behind his back. He waited.

'Experience as a butler?'

'I have also been employed by Mr Andrew Townsend and I worked for Mr Townsend, in various capacities, for nigh on a decade. When a butler was required, I stepped into the role.'

Sophia swallowed. She recognised the name of the theatre owner Humphrey had worked for.

'Why did you leave?'

'Mr Townsend and I parted ways due to my fondness for spirits.' He let out a long, wavering breath as he studied the rug. 'I fear I let him down due to indulging myself with my entire salary. On many occasions.

At the end—every occasion. But I have not had a taste in what transpires as a lifetime now.'

Addison blinked in recognition of the information. 'Did you drink from his supply?'

Humphrey took an inward breath and his head darted up. 'Heavens, no. He did not know good liquor from tree sap.'

Addison nodded. 'You are to drink neither my good liquor or tree sap while you are in this post.'

Humphrey raised his palm near his chest and, in a fluid motion, swept his hand out. 'I would not dream of it.'

'Later tonight, I will have a guest. The Duke of Oldston. Be sure you are at the door to open it for him when he arrives. He will likely not stay long. Show him to this room and make certain to be at the bell should I need anything else. I will ring the bell once quickly when he is leaving. Get the door for him then as well. Do not make him wait half a heartbeat.'

'Of course. If there is nothing else, then I will await my duties near the entrance so I will see him arrive. Please summon me at any moment.'

Then he took one sharp step back and was out the door before she knew it.

Addison stared at the door, briefly, then directed his attention to her.

Sophia was relieved Addison had not recognised his own shirt on Humphrey and she'd watched for Humphrey's ankles. The blacking had done a good job of disguising them.

Since Humphrey had admitted it and since Addison studied her so intensely, she volunteered, 'He promised he would remain upright tonight. You do not have to concern yourself.' She would do his worrying for him, in fact. 'I am certain he will do the job correctly.' He would not have a drop of spirits until the Duke left. Merry was to guard the liquor.

'Thank you for the efforts,' Addison spoke.

They both heard it at the same time. A carriage. The Duke had arrived.

'I'll make sure the new butler's waiting.' Sophia flew down the servants' stairs and peered around to the entrance to check on Humphrey.

Humphrey stood at his post, but flicked her away with a wave of his hand, and she disappeared into her room, hoping for a miracle.

Chapter Twelve

The Duke walked into the library and Addison gave him a bow. A respectful one.

'Why have you summoned me?' his father said, both hands clasped on the gold-handled cane. His clothing was immaculate, except for a rumpled paper, rolled into a tube, protruding from his waistcoat pocket, which was visible when he moved. 'I do not like to be summoned.'

'I invited you.'

The Duke shook his head. 'It was not an invitation.'

Addison opened a portfolio on his desk. He took out some creased paper. The bill. And then he added the note from his bank. He held it out to his father. 'Reimbursement.'

His father glanced at it but didn't take it. 'You should have sent it to my man of affairs.'

'I wanted to give it to you myself. But if you wish, I will send it his way if he is the same one you had when the invoice was presented.' Addison tossed it to the table.

A short nod answered. A scowl. 'I'm still undecided about attending your hanging.'

'I decided I would not be there.'

His father snorted. 'You've always been contrary that way.'

'Like my father.'

The Duke didn't move. 'I would not call your father contrary. At least to his face.'

'I've always been difficult that way as well.'

'True.' He studied the room. 'I did not like to bring the ducal carriage here, but I wondered...'

He glanced around the room, shaking his head. 'In the future, you can obtain an appointment with me and see me in my office if you want to talk. I do not plan to be summoned again.'

Addison hadn't been to the ducal estate since before his mother died. 'Would that not be awkward for you, my being among your family?'

'Not for me. And if it is for them, it is their problem.'

'You would agree to an appointment?'

'It would depend, I suppose, on how the day was going.' He glared at Addison. 'Do not expect any more favours. I fathered you. I fed you. I clothed you. I got you out of that gaol.' He took several steps and glanced at the paper. His lips moved into a hard smile. 'But you took care of your education. And the amount for the theft.'

'My education. Where I stand. The horses I own.' Addison heard the challenge in his voice and the pride.

His father waved the argument away. 'But you use my tailor,' Oldston said, eyes gleaming as if he'd proven a point.

That his father knew such a detail surprised Addison. He didn't respond. It hadn't occurred to him that it was possible to use anyone else.

'Your mother insisted I go to him,' the Duke said. 'No disrespect to the present Duchess, but I still miss your mother. She was the most challenging woman I've ever seen.'

'She once said you were generous to her.' In fact, she said he'd treated her far better than she would have done had their positions been reversed.

The Duke grunted. 'I had to be. She insisted as soon as you were on the way. If you received any of the softer qualities in life, you didn't receive them from either your mother or your father.'

'Are you certain? I always deemed you too soft-hearted.'

The Duke chortled.

'And the butler? Where did you get him?'

'I recently employed him. I've not had a chance to send him for a well-made coat and trousers.'

His father raised one brow at Addison. 'He's different. I've never been called Your Grape so elegantly.' A guffaw burst from his father. 'Surprised you didn't do that when you were a lad.'

'I didn't think of it.'

His father nodded. 'When I got your missive, I expected you to ask for some sort of help.'

'You've done enough.'

'Yes. I have. You are the most stubborn of my sons. Even as a little mite, you'd bow and you had a way of bending either too fast or too deep or too shallow. Not respectfully, somehow.' He stopped, reminiscing. 'My other sons did not have to bow to me when we were alone and neither did you. And yet you did.'

'You were the Duke. My mother insisted.'

'That was like Vera. She never forgave me. And I would have made her a duchess.'

'Can you blame her?'

'Yes. Of course.' His father glared at him as if he were mad to suggest such a thing. Addison didn't respond.

'You were baseborn. You didn't have to be. That was wrong of her. I sent you to university as I did my elder sons. I would not have a child of mine be uneducated. Then she died while you were there and you returned worse for the university. Drinking. Women. Gambling. I perceived I'd made a mistake giving you an education. My first one. But you ended up securing a position with your Oxford friend's father.' He laughed, a true laugh, but not wholesome.

'What's so humorous?' Addison didn't smile when he directed the question to his father.

'You exceeded both my two other sons in gambling, harlots and then in finance.' His father shrugged. 'Bloodlines. You can't help it. Your mother could have thrived eating nails and dirt and been more beautiful for it.'

'She wasn't always the easiest person to live with.'

Now the Duke's laughter was full throated. 'I know that well.' Then his voice softened. 'But she was harder to live without.'

He moved to the shelves and thumped the urn with the back knuckle of his middle finger, then frowned. 'Ugly pottery.'

'I agree.'

The Duke walked to the doorway without a backward glance, but then he hesitated, adjusting his cane, and briefly tucked it under his arm. He retrieved the folded paper from his pocket. 'Almost forgot this.'

He held the missive towards Addison and Addison didn't feel he should take it.

The Duke took a step and tossed it next to the urn. 'My wife sent it. She's got a soft heart. Curious about you. Or she wants to get a laugh in at my other sons. I dare you to attend.'

Then he stepped to the corridor.

Addison gave a quick tug of the pull so Talbot-Bonette would be at the door to let his father out.

Then he picked up the paper beside the urn. His father had dared him to attend whatever event was mentioned. A sincere request in his father's terminology.

'Is there any baking going on?' Addison walked through the kitchen doorway. 'I think I smell a pie cooking.'

'Will be soon. Peach in the oven. And I've just finished slicing the apples,' Cook answered. 'In case one pie isn't enough.'

Addison leaned against the door jam. 'Is Sophia in her room?'

Cook grimaced at him. 'Likely.'

He glanced towards the servants' quarters.

'Tread lightly with her. You had nothing to lose when you were younger. And I don't see a happy end in it for her.'

'What are you talking about?' Addison straightened.

'You know what I'm talking about. You've been working all hours for a long time. Stopping to eat and sleep. Now you have a pretty woman right here under your nose.'

'It's not your concern.' Addison put emphasis in each syllable.

'Fine. I see how it is.' Cook sniffed.

Addison walked over and put an arm loosely around Cook's shoulders. 'No one can cook as well as you and it would be a sin not to share it with others.' He put a kiss on the wrinkled cheek and she beamed brighter than any of her cherry pies.

'Get away, you scoundrel,' she said, laughing. 'You'll cause me to cut myself.'

He stepped backwards to the entrance, bending to peer sideways and call down the hallway. 'Sophia. You are needed in the kitchen.'

'Phht,' Cook said and mumbled under her breath, 'I'm the only one needed in this kitchen.'

Addison smiled at Cook, but he listened for Sophia, relieved when he heard her footsteps.

In moments, Sophia appeared. Her eyes darted to him. She seemed startled, as if she'd been caught doing something wrong. She acted almost afraid to step inside. 'Did the butler do as you required?' she asked Addison.

'Yes, he did. We spoke for a moment afterwards. He apologised for his nervousness. But I let him know that the Duke had no problems with his actions and that Oldston is intimidating and can be a difficult man to win over. The butler achieved it—and did it much faster than I did.'

Truth be told, they'd both done it on the same day.

Addison had an urge to lift Sophia up and swing her around the kitchen. She had no need to look worried. The visit had exceeded Addison's expectations.

'Where did he go?' Sophia took in a breath and appeared to be glancing about for Talbot.

'Don't be concerned about him.' The man had shown such regret and feared he'd not been suitable for Addison's guest. The remorse had touched Addison and he envisioned Humphrey traipsing the same steps Addison had walked after being released from the gaol. They'd talked a few moments longer and Addison had sent Humphrey to the butler's quarters to get a good night's sleep.

Now he indicated the oven. 'Join us. We are celebrating the imminent arrival of a pie. A taste unequalled in other kitchens and better than any others created in the entire world.'

'True.' Cook put the pastry in the dish, trimmed it with a few flicks of the knife and poured in the apple filling. She then added the top, making quick work of thumbing the fluted edge of the dough into shape, finishing with slits in the top to let the steam escape. 'The usual fare, suitable for angels, prepared by a mere mortal and sometimes sampled by people with devilish smiles.' Cook dusted off her palms. 'I had planned to eat it all myself, but you discovered the ruse. Now I suppose I must share with everyone.'

'You definitely have to share with me.' He glanced to Sophia, giving her a smile. 'Everyone else can fend for themselves.'

'So did the Duke stop here and ask for directions?' Cook asked. 'Sad his driver getting lost.'

Sophia stilled, waiting for the response.

'He said he'd never be back.' Addison delivered the statement easily.

'Oh.' Happiness faded from Sophia. 'He's not returning.' She gripped the apron edge. The visit had been so important to Addison.

He reached to his waistcoat pocket, holding up the rolled paper. 'This is what it is.' He put it in Sophia's hand, and for a moment, their fingers touched.

'It's a note the Duchess sent. Inviting me to have supper with them on the occasion of their fifth wedding anniversary.'

'To their estate?'

'Yes. I've not been to my father's estate more than a handful of times. All when I was a child and without my mother. She refused to set a foot inside.'

'Will you attend?'

He nodded. 'I already have the support of the bankers. Whether I have Oldston behind me or not, everyone will believe that I do. It's as good as an invitation to the finest events in London.'

'I think we should have a celebration.' Cook bunched one end of the towel and held it to the corner of her eye.

'You are looking for an excuse to create more treats,' Addison said.

She gave him the kind of blink that a mother gave a favourite son right before she gave him a meaningless scold. 'That's what good cooks do,' she answered. 'Especially this one.'

She tossed the towel to Sophia. 'Would you take the peach pie out of the oven and put the apple in? I'm going to get a bottle of wine that we've saved for a special occasion.' She moved out, still dabbing her eyes, and Sophia expected she was using the time alone to compose herself.

'Were you truly pleased with Oldston's visit?' Sophia asked when Cook had left, in part to reassure herself that Humphrey had acted the part well.

'Yes. In fact, today was the first time we've spoken

in a long, long while. I've felt that a few doors have been closed to me for fear of invoking his wrath. He has the power to make it difficult, if not impossible, for me to succeed further. I've crossed paths with him when I've been out, but it has always been as if there is an invisible wall between us, and we've shared less than the minimum communication to be civil.'

'Did it bother you?' Her eyes widened.

'I can't blame him. I acted the fool.'

He rested his knuckles under his chin. 'The last time he acknowledged me was at my mother's funeral. My mother's funeral.' He shrugged away the memory. 'He arrived, said to me, *"Condolences"*, then immediately left after the service.'

'Were you angry?'

'No,' he mused. 'Grieving. She was not the kind of mother one expects to mourn, but I suppose I did. They said she took a cough and, suddenly, she was gone. The Duke sent his coachman with an extra horse to fetch me, but I didn't arrive in time. I wasn't even told why I must return to London.'

'Perhaps he wanted to spare you worry.' She remembered the distress she'd felt when her own mother had succumbed to her frail health, but they'd really always known she was sickly.

'When the door was opened as I stepped into the house, the mirrors had been covered in black and the butler had a matching armband on. I tried not to believe the truth in front of me, but I had no choice. I was directed to—I said goodbye to her in the main sitting room.'

He shook his head in memory. 'No one expected her to die. She never showed weakness. Never. But it was as if my father and I blamed each other for her death, yet neither one of us was with her because she'd sent both of us away. I don't think it was entirely anger on her part, but merely what she felt was best. Best that I get an education and best that she not depend on the Duke too much.'

Addison's reminiscences brought silence from him.

She glanced at the oven, wanting to let his memories settle around him without interruption. She took the towel and used it to open the oven door and remove the peach pie. She placed it on the table. She put the remaining apple pie in the oven.

He took the towel from her, which surprised her, then he flicked a crumb of the crust from the hot pan and tossed the cloth near it.

'My mother and the Duke often fought about marriage,' he said. 'Their favourite topic to fight about and they had many. I didn't know during my childhood if either truly loved the other,' he continued. 'But no one would argue with her so much and keep coming back if he didn't truly care for her. If you can hear adoration, grief and loss, I believe I heard it in my father at her funeral.'

Addison watched as she folded the towel he'd crumpled. 'He said *"Condolences"*. That was all. The only word he spoke to me that day. Yet it took more effort for him than any other utterance I'd ever heard him say. I thought he was going to fall at my feet and his brother stood at his side as if to catch him.'

He tilted his head back. 'In that instant, I knew he had cared deeply for her. But I was angry. Furious. I don't know why. Perhaps it was grief for what might have been for them.'

She wanted to touch his hand and the glance he gave her told her he understood.

'Then, after I left university,' Addison admitted, 'I lived the life of a duke's son without the funds. I had been selling the things he'd given my mother. Then, one day, I needed him and he sent his man of affairs to help me when I thought I was alone in the world.'

Cook opened the door, sniffed long enough to draw air completely into her lungs, and gazed at the waiting pie on the table. 'Beautiful,' she said. 'Perhaps it is a sin to eat it.'

Addison moved, utensils clattering as he searched for them, finding forks and a clean knife. 'Only if it's cold.'

'Well, you're right,' she said and pulled out plates. She put them on the table and took the knife from him. 'Let me. I don't want it butchered.'

The solitary sound was the quick ring of the blade against the side of the dish as she moved the knife.

'Did you cut two pieces bigger than the others?' he asked.

'Of course. I wanted to be correct. I'm cutting it and you're the master. You and me will each get the biggest ones,' Cook answered. 'Takes more food to keep us moving. We must be fair to ourselves.'

Then she put a large slab of pie on Addison's plate and gave it to him.

He took a bite, a drop of the crust lingering on his lip before he licked it off. 'Definitely formed by a goddess.'

'Ho. Ho. Ho,' Cook said. She handed a piece to Sophia.

She took a bite and sighed. 'Never have I had better pie.'

Cook stretched, but it was more of a victory movement. 'Wait until you taste the apple. It has figs, raisins and pears, and a sprinkle of saffron.'

They finished eating, then Cook got another piece of pie for herself.

Merry appeared in the doorway. 'Did I hear my name called?' she asked Cook.

'No,' Cook answered, 'but you can have a slice anyway, if you take one to that manservant.'

'Mmm,' Merry said, moving in to sniff the aroma.

'Well, I will be off to bed,' Sophia said, leaving the table.

She heard footsteps behind her and knew they belonged to Addison, and the *hurrumph* was from Cook. Merry's chatter filled the air, but it didn't matter. All she could sense was Addison's presence behind her.

'I don't want to work tonight, Sophia,' he said, softly before she reached her door. 'Would you like to celebrate with me?'

'How?' she asked.

'For me, it would be by being with you.'

'Will you promise to kiss me again?' she asked.

His lips moved closer. 'If you insist.'

'Of course.'

Chapter Thirteen

She went with him to his sitting room and saw the sofa where he'd held her when she was terrified by Ruffles. The recollection caused her to want his reassurance again.

She threw herself into his arms, burrowing under his coat and pressing herself against him, cloaking herself in his intoxicating scent and feel. She'd never known a man could emit power from his presence. His body was so much stronger than hers, a fortification of strength.

'Your assistance with my father's visit is greatly appreciated,' he said.

Suddenly, a wave of sadness, and almost irritation at herself, overwhelmed her. She'd toiled to help Addison with his father's visit and she would do it again, but she feared she'd hastened his departure from her life.

The thought caused her to clutch more tightly at his waist. 'I wish…'

'What?'

'I just wish to be held,' she said.

'How long?'

'Perhaps…until I fall asleep.'

He put an arm around her waist and put a kiss against her hair before they moved inside his bedchamber.

He angled her chin up, his breath warming her lips, and a whisper of peach flavoured his kiss.

A thunderstorm broke out around her, but she was sheltered, safe and secure and with all the searing intensity of lightning and the sensations of soft summer raindrops whispering against her skin.

He pulled away, studying her. 'I'm afraid if I touch you, you'll be gone in the morning.'

'Not if you do it right.'

His mouth fell open and then a smile spread. 'I will do my best to make certain you'll still be here tomorrow.'

Her smile was enveloped by heated flourishes from his lips, softening hers.

His fingertips across her back brushed over the placket of her dress and his hand spread so that he clasped her, drawing her closer, and she strived to feel all the height and width of him that she could.

Finally, she breathed, aware of her senses flourishing and the famished feeling that he was sating.

She pushed herself back, fingers on his waistcoat pocket so she could not lose the connection to him.

'Sweeting, is anything wrong?'

'It's so shocking to feel desire again. To want to make love. And be held close. A miracle I didn't know I could feel. Kisses stronger than I am.'

He swept her up in his arms, carrying her to the side of his bed, until he could stand her on her feet and place the ledgers he'd left open on the counterpane on the bedstand.

Even as he released her, his presence kept her close

to him. She couldn't let him go, moving knuckles over him, needing the touch, unable to stop herself from stretching her fingers out so she could embrace him better.

Then he held her shoulders, caressing her lips with his. His fingers rested on the hooks at the back of her dress. 'May I?' he whispered against her mouth.

'Yes.' She moved her head slightly so she could speak, but burrowed against his neck, letting the slight stubble on his jaw brush against her, savouring the blunt ends and the roughness. She reached up, her fingers intermingling with the strands of his locks. 'But you may not ask me any more such questions. I am able to speak and I'll tell you if I want this to end.'

'If you're certain.'

'Very. And I know I don't want you to stop.'

He altered his stance, moving to undo each small hook, his fingers precise, and she kept a clasp on his waist.

Then he undressed and afterwards reached to help her from her dress and corset before pulling back the covers.

The sensual awareness multiplied and he lowered them on to the bed and began an exploration of her body, the curves reacting to his touch, giving her a voluptuous feeling she'd never experienced as her skin seemed to rise against the pressure of his hand. The boundaries disappeared between them into a swirl of sensations they both appeared to feel at the same time.

When they were side by side, he whispered her name mixed with endearments, her breasts excited by his touch, and when his palm brushed over her, she could tell he was aware of the hardened nipples through the fabric of her chemise, because he slowed, making the moment a joy to savour.

She lost awareness of anything but him and the feelings he created. Even the fabric of her shift moving against her heightened her senses more.

Then he ran his hands down her body, his fingertips bringing her even more alive as he cloaked her in his touch. Her thin shift moved aside as she pressed closer to him. He understood her needs and held her most intimate place, caressing.

Then, before she expected it, she felt her release and he held her so tightly they could have been intertwined.

'Stop,' she said, letting herself return to the moment, and he did, instead using his cheek against hers to keep their connection and his hand at her waist, holding her close.

She tugged her shift higher and he helped her remove it, then she pulled herself astride him, her moistness evident, and they slipped together, her joining with him as if she'd done the same each night a thousand times before.

She watched him, male beauty before her, his lashes closed and suddenly she was infinitely aroused again, more so than before.

They coupled, fevered moments, and she knew he was about to release, and she couldn't contain herself, letting the waves carry her a second time.

Before he finished, he'd pulled aside, holding her tightly, a gasp escaping.

She lay beside him as their breathing relaxed, resting so that she could see his profile in the darkness.

'I'll send for French letters tomorrow,' he said.

'If you send someone for them... Are you comfortable with everyone knowing?' She rolled to her side, bathing in the sound of his voice, the magnificence of his body—even the manly scent was an embodiment of his strength.

'I don't mind. And my schedule is so busy, I don't have time to go myself. Plus, I don't want you to feel forced into marriage as you might if a child was on the way. Because, trust me, I would try to persuade you into marriage. The child would be mine as well and I would want him near me.' Then a soft laugh escaped his lips. 'Or her. I definitely would want to be wed first if I were having a daughter.'

'When I was a wife, at first I wanted a child, hoping my husband would see it and become a better man. And more mature. But after a few years, I could be thankful for not having one.'

'He might have seen the baby and reconsidered his ways. I did without a child.'

'Yes, but you wanted to. He didn't. He would have been jealous of the attention it received. He never once mentioned wanting a baby and I never did either.'

She'd mourned after her husband's death. Truly mourned the life lost on a few occasions when she could summon a happy memory. But she'd also felt equal parts relief.

'My husband was young for his years. I didn't expect that when we married because I was inexperienced, too. I didn't grasp that he had grown as much as he ever would and I would keep maturing until I felt so much older than him. I'm sad that he died. But there was no lost romance. I was an always available audience and I soon lost interest in the same jests, day after day.'

He'd made a game of jumping out at her and making her flinch. But it was better than having a sullen child. And his mother had encouraged his nonsense. Sophia expected they were near the same age on the inside.

'Do you think he would have ever matured?'

'No. He was more than a decade older than I. It was who he was. The man-child his mother created. The sponge looking for attention.'

Sadness enveloped her as she considered options and her past. Surprisingly, she'd missed her husband in small fragments of memory. But it had been the occasional companionship, she supposed. Then she decided she was deceiving herself because those were the feelings a widow was supposed to feel. She was sorry for her husband's death, but she never missed the marriage.

Alone, with all its uncertainties, now had fared better for her.

Marriage. Entrapment for women. A snare for men. Hardly worth the time it took to say the meaningless vows. And then there was supposed to be moments of sweetness afterwards. Not bitterness. Not finding out that your husband had forgotten to tell you he lived with his mother.

She admitted to herself she'd agreed to wed within weeks after they'd met, but then her options were dwindling and she'd seen the path Merry was taking.

Her husband's frustration with his lack of success at the theatre had worn on him, but he had progressed to securing the role he'd always dreamed of—Hamlet. That had worked out as she should have foreseen.

She'd always envisaged she would have taken it well if he'd told her his truths beforehand. But she never would have got along with his mother. The woman blamed her for the few weaknesses she saw in her son.

He'd hero-worshipped Humphrey and Humphrey had introduced him to several others who could help him at the theatre, but memorising the words he was to speak bored him and he never wanted to give the same performance twice, he said, except his beloved Shakespeare's roles. Yet he would play the same tricks on her time after time.

In truth, he'd scared her by diving out the window on occasion, tumbling down the offset roof to roll on to the ground. Then he'd pretend to be hurt and jump to his feet and pounce at her when she reached him.

She'd expected the charade the last time, but it had been in darkness and a cat had yowled. After nudging him on the cold ground with her foot twice, and pinching his nose, she'd screamed.

Addison sensed she was reliving her marriage and hugged her close. 'Sweeting,' he said. 'Are you with me now, or in the past? I want you here with me.'

She put a palm flat on his chest, over his heart, and he clasped it, savouring the small hand in his. 'I'm here.'

His lips found hers, completing him, and he lay back, his mind opened in a way it hadn't been before.

'Hell. I've just grasped that in the past, my mind was halfway out the door after lovemaking. But I don't feel that way tonight. I never believed anything could affect me, in an instant, as much as the three days did.'

'Three days?'

'In gaol.'

'You've been in gaol?' She spoke as if she'd misheard him.

'Not recently. Some day I will tell you about it, but

there's really nothing to mention except it stank more than any offal you can imagine. My father saw that I was released. He saved me and then work did. I needed to be busy.'

One of the other bankers wanted him to fail. It oozed from him. His eldest brother wanted him to fall flat on his face. 'I embraced an awareness that some waited for my downfall and used it, and work, to keep me going forward when I wanted to relapse into old habits.'

He mused for a moment. 'Gaol was just the exclamation point at the end of a life of revelry. I had nothing else and I had to replace my old forays with something to keep me occupied, and the bank was happy to keep me toiling. My old friends were rabble.'

'I cannot imagine you as anything but serious, dedicated and responsible.'

'True. I've always been that. I was serious, dedicated and responsible to being the biggest rakehell in London. Failure wasn't a consideration. The noose was.'

'You?' She pulled away and studied him. 'A rake?'

'Yes. A reformed one who has been tempted beyond satisfaction by the beautiful Sophia.'

Then she snuggled back against him. 'It sounds like a jest to call you a rake.'

'It's not. But I changed.' He ran a hand over the counterpane. 'My father owned everything I had. I hated living on the Duke's property and, in a short time, I discovered that it would be a relatively simple matter to set up my own household. At first, I endeavoured to support myself and I expected nothing but employment and an opportunity to step from my past.'

He'd been almost ashamed of living in such a grand

place as he had because the town house had been handed to his mother, the Duke's mistress.

'Here, the surroundings are my own. Cook is here. The stable master, Caldwell, is an uncle I've never had. I have true uncles, but I've seen them no more than a few times. Proximity makes for family.'

He stretched and folded an arm behind his head. 'I never had much awareness of it earlier. My own roof. My own walls. My own maturity.' He examined the ceiling. 'One day, I realised the numbers I laboured over were funds. And I watched as people made them bigger and it seemed easy enough. A challenge that I dealt with in numerical form.' He rubbed the back of his neck. 'I celebrated privately when the investments did well and people noticed. You want to keep the winning streak on your side. It's gambling, but you can shift the odds if you think them through.'

'You're so alive when you speak of funds. It would have terrified me to gamble in such a way. I've seen some of the numbers on your papers.'

'They called me the fortune teller. Behind closed doors, the owner of the bank still calls me Fortune. He said I'm the first person he's known, besides him, who could wager and predict without a flicker and didn't let my desire to win override sense.'

'You don't have to struggle with the numbers?'

'I was born with wealth around me and it was only figures. But I enjoyed the challenge. The game. I never thought much of it until now. But it makes me feel alive to see the money and what I have accomplished. Early on, I didn't grasp I was dealing with people's livelihoods. Structures and houses and businesses with potential for bankruptcy and creditors. Homelessness for others.' His words slowed. 'By the time I understood, deep inside, what I was doing, I'd passed the uncertainty and knew if there was a gift to it, I had it.'

But nothing made him feel the same as Sophia did. As if he finally had the home around him. The past behind him. A companion in his arms.

Yet he dreamed of more.

'Still, I can't move forward. Even with my superior helping me all he can. I've been to the best estates and the best events, championed by the bank, and yet I am an employee caring for their money.'

He took her other hand and they were locked in a twinkling of time before he released her and the air chilled without her touch, but he had to explain.

He watched her, and hoped she comprehended. 'My older brother will some day be in the House of Lords. Huzzah for him. The bank will be passed on to the owner's heirs. But I am finding funds. I will not receive a gift of money or title from others. I'm making my own.'

Shutting his eyes, he relaxed. 'I received a great inheritance from my parents, but I'm sure the Duke is conscious of it. Not property or lands, but the blood in my veins. A hidden heritage I can squander, or work with and make grow. I am proof that you can have everything… everything…and still be a wastrel. It takes more effort to keep the gifts than it does to lose them and blame others.'

He lay back with eyes closed and couldn't stop his smile. 'I have people against me and that helps. I want to do well to show them I can. To tip my hat at them. To give them a bow. My eldest brother is a marquess and some day he will be Oldston, the Duke. That's as it should be. But I want to…'

He waited a bit too long. 'My father said I always had rebellion in me when I was a child. Perhaps I'm letting that arrogance work for me now and not against me. I could be defiant enough to be proving I am worthy of a place in Oldston's family. Perhaps not just to my father, or to society, but to myself.'

When he slid closer to her, he heard the pride in his voice. 'To work hard doesn't make a man wealthy. To have intelligence doesn't bring riches. But to toil hard, use your head, keep an eye to the future and to have luck, those bring the best results —and the satisfaction of seeing the fruits of your labour. It's probably wrong to want to do well to show others you can, but it's like adding the spice in a chocolate drink. The extra bite of flavour.'

He took her hand a second time, watched her expression and he saw the sunshine in the darkness. 'I am the most fortunate man I know. The luckiest. The head of the bank shares the secrets of wealth that he has learned from his father with me. My father cast me out when I needed it. And I am with you at this moment.'

Chapter Fourteen

When Sophia left, Addison lay in bed, not staring up at the ceiling, but inside himself, waiting until morning. Waiting until she returned. He'd never considered the motivations of his life until Sophia lay beside him.

He took each section of his existence and considered it as a group of teamed pieces on a chess board. One side, together, planning forward actions. A unit to achieve a goal, yet in this case, he didn't want to lose even a pawn. The goal wasn't to remove the players from the other side of the board, but to retain and strengthen what remained around him.

And the queen could move in so many different directions and change the play.

His world was whirling ahead at a pace he couldn't control. He'd started the fire, but the flames grew of their own accord, blazing ahead.

He'd been so cautious about romantic entanglements—never letting himself get close enough to the woman that she might consider herself a part of his life. Yet Sophia was a part of his life even before they'd kissed.

He wondered what had caused him to remove the

barriers he'd set inside himself. And he knew without question. The repayment of his education. It had freed him. To move forward without restraints. To have a life of his own.

From the time since he'd walked those streets after three days living as near to hell as he ever wanted to be, every ambition in his life had centred around showing his father that he could pay him back for his education.

It had been his quest, overriding all other considerations in his life. Shaping them.

He'd truly been innocent of the crime, but it hadn't mattered at all because it had appeared he wasn't. Without his father's position, and intervention, he would have perished.

At the time of the incarceration, Addison had been living in the town house where his mother had lived. Owned by the Duke. He'd expected a knock at the door after he'd been in gaol, an eviction of some sort. He'd awoken the next day aware of how fragile his financial situation was.

He'd sat at his table, eating an egg prepared by the maid. He had a butler and two female servants, all paid for by his father…a man undecided about attending Addison's hanging.

By nightfall, he'd contacted five men, knowing they'd agreed to speak with him on the strength of his father's position. He had no illusions. And when he arrived for the appointments, he told them of his arrest, admitted the Duke had repaid the victim and that he would not again find himself in such a situation.

He hadn't touched on his innocence. It hadn't mattered. He'd done enough to cast aspersions on his character and the men hadn't shown they cared about his past, but his future direction.

Within a fortnight, he had employment. He suspected the timespan between talking with the banker, Burroughs, and the position materialising had to do with his father being contacted. He'd never asked, but he was certain Oldston could have blocked the chance of employment with little more than a grimace when Addison's name was spoken. And he'd only been entrusted with small sums at first, but he'd done well with them.

Now, he didn't live in an elite location as his mother had lived, and his father, but it suited his needs. He'd had to economise. He'd paid for the expense of a carriage so he could get back and forth to the bank quickly, but the vehicle also gave him the air of success he needed. Fodder and care for the horses cost him more than the food for the people he fed, but that was to be expected.

When he relocated, he'd sent a note to the man of affairs for the Duke of Oldston saying that the house would be vacant by the end of the month. He'd signed that with a flourish so big it could have choked someone.

At first, he'd noticed the drabness of the new residence, even if it hadn't mattered much because it was his own. A place to sleep and work without memories attached. But later he'd given Belden a sum and they'd examined each room while he noted repairs to be completed.

He rose, sensing the arrival of daylight, dressing in trousers and a shirt, spurred by his need to see her, knowing stealthy footsteps wouldn't carry on the servants' stairs.

He padded down, gave a soft rap at her door and moved inside.

'Soph?' he whispered, pulling the door shut behind him and placing his lamp on the small table.

Covers rustled. She pushed herself up on her elbows, awakening, and he stilled, awed, discovering her exquisiteness again.

Reaching out, he sat beside her, holding her, intertwining his fingers in her hair, needing the strands around him so that they were even more connected, and relishing the joining of only the tiniest touches of their bodies.

But he forced himself to give her no more than a kiss at the temple, letting one lone finger trace the outline of her jaw, once, and then again. Savouring their intimacy of being together when the world was waking, the day was starting, and it giving the impression that everything stirring was separate from their togetherness, yet embracing them from a distance.

But so much had happened to both of them recently and he feared they were sharing reassurance with their bodies. She was solace and he wanted to be the same for her. Yet he wasn't certain either of them could trust their feelings.

He stood, moving to her dressing table, finding a brush and nudging himself into the bed behind her so she could sit with her knees propped up and he could run the brush through her hair while they talked.

'My father has influenced each day of my life since I left university. Each footstep. Decisions I've made, though I take responsibility for the errors. And I doubt he even knows it. I released myself from that last night.' He had to explain to her the truths so new to his awareness.

'Even if he'd not appeared, however, I would have been freed of constraints caused by feelings towards him,' he said. 'Because my actions were mine alone and I had completed the process I'd set out for myself. I didn't know he would respond to my invitation. I half guessed he had tossed it away. Two days before he arrived, I received a message from a footman that the Duke had accepted and the time he would be here.'

In fact, he'd expected none of the events of the night. Not his father's invitation. Or approval. Nor the exquisiteness of holding Sophia.

Her splendour awed him more than anything else, yet he feared their bodies were misleading them. And the changes in their lives.

He'd merely planned to repay the Duke and wanted to hand him the note himself. A way of erasing the feeling of powerlessness he'd had when he'd depended on his father's name to free him from his own foolish choices. His father had refused to touch it and that had somehow pleased Addison more.

And if he admitted the truth to himself, he'd hoped to see acceptance in his father. He hadn't seen it in the countenance, but he'd heard it and seen it in the crimped handwriting of the Duchess. He was certain he had her to thank for the invitation.

Now he was with Sophia. His world hadn't merely tilted in a different direction again, it had whirled at lightning-bolt speed into a different realm. And he didn't know what location he was hurtling towards.

If not for his father's visit and the acceptance, he doubted he would have made love to Sophia, but he'd been so stunned by the Duke being in his home and

that his father hadn't flared into indignation at the untrained butler.

'Talbot called my father a grape.'

Sophia jerked upright. 'A grape?'

'A slip of the tongue. I would have wagered that my
father would have left at that moment, but he didn't.'

'I am so sorry.' She twisted to study him in the darkness.

He put a finger to her lips, tracing the fullness before pulling her close. 'Don't be. It helped me see my
father differently. And it made me understand that he
came here to see his son—even if he had to brave an
untrained servant, he was willing to make the sacrifice.'

'I was a fool to think Humphrey could do such a
simple task. I should have known.'

'The visit went well. I was forgiven. I had to do the
same for Humphrey.'

He waited, relishing her movements. The femininity
he could see and imagine. The beauty of life.

Sadness tugged at him with just the awareness of
leaving the room, but it was for the best. He forced
himself to his feet.

He retrieved her dress and corset from the side of
the bed and helped her dress, finishing the task with a
hug. 'You need to forgive Humphrey also. He helped me
with my father's acceptance and that is a boon to me.'

'I suppose I do. He's never let me down before.'

'But I think it would be best for you not to do my
valet duties any more.'

She stopped her movement.

'It will be fine,' he insisted. 'You've taken on too
much for yourself.'

'I'm content with it.'

'But I'm not. You've Merry to train and you're both learning and I want the duties to proceed as smoothly as possible. A valet will be able to iron my clothing and save you time.'

'Are you certain?' She hesitated again.

'Yes.' He hugged her close, knowing she wasn't confident. Not wanting to undermine her but to help her step into her role, although it had refashioned itself in those moments before. It was impossible for it not to.

He could not let Sophia do the duties of his manservant. That had helped him with the decision to offer Humphrey a temporary position of his valet. It would help while Sophia was grappling with the changes in her life and the new employees. He had no choice and it was for the best.

'Sweeting,' he said, another kiss to taste her lips, lingering long enough before leaving her room to reassure her and himself. 'I would much rather prefer to help you dress in the morning than have you assisting me.'

Sophia heard the bell sound from her room, but it wasn't the one for her. Not the same ring.

She stepped outside and raised her eyes in time to see Humphrey marching down the hallway towards Addison's sitting room, answering the bell, his chin high.

He was supposed to be leaving.

'Humphrey?' she gasped.

He kept walking. 'I will speak with you later. Now the master is summoning.'

She scrambled after him, stopping as she caught his arm. 'Humphrey... You can't.'

'Miss Sophia. I have requested to stay until a permanent butler is hired. I asked the master as soon as the Duke left.'

'Addison will be furious if he catches you drinking to excess and you've never been moderate. You have to leave. You will not be able to stay away from the liquor.'

He shook her hand free. 'That is my choice, Miss Sophia. Now, pardon me as I have a duty to attend.'

'You've... You'll not...'

'Miss Sophia, as a friend, I would think you would wish me well. I did that for you.'

Then he sniffed and marched away.

Sophia waited for her chance to talk to Addison alone, then she rushed up the servants' stairway, her skirt bunched in her hands so she could run faster.

Then she gave three raps on the door.

'Enter.'

She dashed inside, then stilled when she saw him, momentarily arrested by the eyes, tousled hair and just plain masculinity given to him in abundance. The sight subdued her, yet strengthened and invigorated her at the same time.

He stepped forward when she came in, dropping his comb. 'What's wrong?'

'You're keeping Humphrey?'

'Yes. Is there a reason I shouldn't?'

She straightened the creases her hands had made in her skirt, composed herself and lifted the comb, placing it in Addison's grip and then letting their hands clasp. 'He has never been able, in the time I have known him, to keep from drinking to excess. He's tried. Over and over and over again. But it's never worked.'

Addison gave a deft movement, a dancing master's

joy, and she found herself against his chest and his gaze could have made any woman not in his arms envious.

'I understand. I'll see him daily and, if he is drunk, I will handle that.'

'He's…not the perfect butler you wanted.'

'I had an image in my mind of Wooten.' Words spoken against her skin. 'The butler from my childhood. But when I saw Humphrey and he asked, almost begging, for a chance, it's easy enough for me to give it.'

'He's shaky. He could never shave you. His own jaw is always nicked.'

Addison released her, moved to place his comb on the table and lifted the razor. 'If he keeps it sharpened, I can do the rest.'

She regretted not keeping her silence when she was in his arms. So many better things they could have discussed or forgotten about while letting their senses explore each other.

She moved to his dressing table, reaching out again and savouring the closeness when he put a kiss on her nose.

'Do you think you are taking him in out of pity? To give him a roof over his head?' she asked.

'What would be wrong with that?'

'I guess…nothing.' She couldn't have disagreed with him no matter what he could have said. 'That's why you took in me.'

'It doesn't concern me the reason of it. It matters that you're here. A group is always made of different people with different histories. At least, it seems that way. Either of the first two butlers might have worked, or might not have. Humphrey will be easy to let go if he doesn't work out.'

'What if he works long enough to be in your heart and then he missteps?' She was thinking more of herself than Humphrey. She straightened the cloth on his dressing table.

'Then I'll have a decision.' He placed a hand over her fist where she'd straightened the cloth. 'I'm good at making choices, Soph. I make them so many times a day, with so many fortunes at stake. I'm not always correct. I try to be, but I can't concern myself if I'm not. If a person needs to be right all the time, they've made the biggest error of their life.'

'I've made countless decisions, too.' And she feared she was making another. Falling in love with a duke's son could only lead to a broken heart. She truly didn't want to go to Broomer's household, but she saw it looming in her future.

'How can you say that? If you believe it, then you believe it's a mistake for you to be here. Those avenues brought you to me.'

'Could you let me go easily?' In those moments, she discovered that was the question she'd wondered about. The query that had lingered inside her.

'No. I could not.'

Her fingers slipped around his thumb. He pulled the loose clasp to his lips and touched them to her skin, before rubbing her hand over his jaw which was bristly. 'Don't look to the future or to the past. Our connection is too new to be dissected like every assurance of a speech. Right now, the most important thing is that we go forward. We've no idea of the depths we may find in each other. Or how time will treat us.'

He took her cheeks in both his hands.

'We need to concentrate on each other. On being

ourselves and making our own path. We're an investment. And you can never see how an investment will truly end until it has had time to grow. If everything were written in stone and laid out before us, then we would follow the granite ledger and do as it is written. We'd have no pride in what we did. No surprises. No feeling of joy.'

'I would have liked to have had a granite ledger. A list to read when I woke in the morning to tell me where to go and what I should do and say.'

'When we look back and say we should have done it differently, then maybe we're not taking reward for the amount we've learned. This might be the last opportunity Humphrey has to make something of himself. I am willing to give it to him and let him go on his way if it doesn't work out.'

'What if he falls asleep and perhaps there's a lamp he knocks over and it's too late to do anything but run?'

'Let's hope that doesn't happen. But it could have happened with the cat on the stairs.'

She'd brought Merry into the fold and now Humphrey was staying. Her old life seemed to be forming around her.

And she was the cause of it. But this time, Addison could be hurt. 'You're correct,' she said, giving him a kiss and backing away. 'I'm going to go make sure he is doing well.' With that, she bustled down the stairs, hoping Humphrey didn't ignite another flame, or drink Addison's best wine, or call her Ophelia.

Chapter Fifteen

After her supper that night, she knew how miserably she'd failed at keeping Addison from her senses. He was at the Duke's dinner party and she could see the gulf between them. Her, sitting alone in the housekeeper's room, stitching, while he was fêted at the finest events.

She'd once acted against her instincts and agreed to wed. Now those same feelings were telling her she neared a crevasse. She should have listened to the warning her senses gave her when she shoved them aside and married her husband. They only had her best interests at heart.

Her husband had been endearing, sweet, during their brief courtship. Then they'd married and he'd considered his duty to her to have ended with the ceremony.

She'd endured the rocky start and hoped things would improve, especially after he landed his dream role of Hamlet. He'd perceived himself a foremost actor, too grand to listen to anyone. Except the theatre owner had fumed while her husband was onstage during opening night. When the play ended, the owner said he would be let go after the next performance if he didn't follow the suggestions he'd agreed to. Hamlet did not need to bounce about and dance onstage.

After the performance, they'd arrived home. He'd been disgruntled. He'd given the best speech of his life, a dramatic soliloquy about being misunderstood, unloved and unappreciated. In a grand gesture, he'd dived through the window. He'd done it before, rolled and landed on his feet with arms outstretched, or pretending injury so she would be concerned.

In truth, he'd been excellent at taking a fall.

This time, the fall had taken him. Again, he'd proved he could jump through the window, but on this occasion he'd not survived.

What if Addison wanted to prove to her that the financial world and his heritage wasn't what he needed, but she was?

And he lived to regret it and her.

She tossed her sewing aside, wanting to escape the visions that hounded her from the past.

Addison wasn't home, but she couldn't wait any longer. The aroma of Cook's treats wafted along on the air. Perhaps berries this time. She wasn't sure, but Cook could make dried berries taste fresh from the bush.

Her stomach rumbled and, if she'd been able to translate, she would have said it was swearing at her most viciously for not moving faster to see if she could manage a pastry from Cook.

She peeked her head around the kitchen door.

'Can't sleep?' Cook asked.

'I'm being held hostage by my stomach.'

'I couldn't sleep,' Cook said. 'Fixing a treat soothes me.'

'Does it always work?'

She shook her head. 'Usually, I don't care whether it does or not because staying awake eating is a nice way to live. Sit. I'll take them out of the oven and you can tell me.'

Sophia did as she was told.

Then they heard Addison's carriage and Humphrey hurried through the hallway to open the main entrance door.

Cook observed the kitchen doorway. 'I've been worried because you didn't heed my warning. Worried about the master taking a fancy to you. If I didn't think you was worth half a keg, I wouldn't care. I don't think you really want to keep him from the life he should have been born into.'

She twisted the oven handle and used her towel to prevent her hands from burning as she removed the delicacies. She put the tray on to the table, found plates and took her chair.

Humphrey appeared at the doorway, peered in and Cook handed him a plate with a pastry on it. He did a pantomime of love towards Cook with his heart being pulled away by the food and left without speaking, holding the plate near his heart.

Cook gave Sophia a pastry and put others on a plate.

'Too late for me to wake the scullery girl to wash the dishes, but I won't have to. She'll wander in soon. And I do not leave dirty dishes waiting,' she admitted. 'Unless it is the middle of the night and the master is hungry.'

One ring sounded, the call for Sophia. Both the women stilled. A second one.

'Save yourself a trip to find out what he wants,' Cook said. 'Give me a second to dress them up.' Then she examined Sophia. 'One ring, and I might have been wrong. Two rings and it's definite, particularly after the pause. He waited, thinking. You waited. Hoping for that second ring.'

'I did not wait.'

'You did.'

'Perhaps I did. Is it so wrong?'

'If you can live with him marrying someone else right under your nose. He's a duke's son. Plus, he has the ear of one of the wealthiest men in London. One who wants to see his protégé succeed. The best thing for him is to marry a society woman and all she has to be is breathing. He'll move closer to the heart of London. Find a bigger house. He will possibly be knighted.'

'You believe that.'

'He knows it. It has been an adventure for him and he has been moving as he sees fit. The men in power will feel they are more successful if Addison succeeds. It is as if they can prove their true worth to the world by his success. Both the Duke, his father, and Burroughs, who made Addison a protégé at the bank. But he could walk away from it all. Distracted by you. Giving up the birthright that should have been his.'

She lifted the salver and put it on a tray.

'Addison was born under a lucky star. He won't get the dukedom. But he'll get everything else he's ever dreamed of,' Cook added. 'If he continues to want it.'

Cook put the tray in Sophia's hands. 'Tread carefully. These are fresh and light. A treat for the senses. But they could tumble off in an instant and become nothing but crumbs.'

Sophia hurried up the servants' stairs, Cook's warnings simmering in her like a pot left too long on the stove. She didn't want to slow Addison. To take from him what he should have. But surely he would not alter because of her.

The door was open when she reached the top. Addison waited, as precisely dressed as if he might be leaving for a night of entertainments, not at the end of the festivities.

To Sophia, he suddenly stood out of place, overpowering the room, but he took the tray and placed it on a table, putting an arm around her waist and twirling her in a half-spin and closer to him.

Awareness flared and a comfort that they were together.

He put her on her feet, but the swirling giddiness remained inside her.

'Did you enjoy the event?' she asked.

He reached up to rub the back of his neck and smiled. 'It was rather grand and I didn't want to overstay my welcome.'

'Did you feel comfortable?' What she wondered was if he'd felt among family. A trickle of fear warned her that he was further from her than she'd appreciated at first, but she let warmth override the disquiet.

'The new Duchess is hardly older than I am and she treated me like the guest of honour, and the Duke had to follow suit, but he seemed more pleasant than I'd imagined possible without his life being on the line. More genial than when he visited here, or than I ever remembered him being when I was a child.'

'Did you notice fatted calf being served?'

He laughed. 'I must have missed that.'

She secured the plate and held it out, offering the treats to him, mainly for a chance to hide from Addison how much she wanted to stay in his arms. She wanted him to be accepted, but it could shorten their time together. He belonged in his family circle and she would never be suitable for such an event.

He fastened his attention on Sophia. 'You're awfully quiet.' He waved away the suggestion of more food, but she didn't release the platter.

'Did it feel odd? As if you were on display?'

'Not really. But accepted for the most part. That's all I needed. Two couples were there that weren't of the Duke's family. His closest confidants and their wives. He insisted we meet.'

'He has other children, doesn't he? You've mentioned brothers.'

'Yes, two sons and me. I'm his lone child of a liaison, at least, as the boy said, *"that he knows of"*. In fairness to my parents, I believe they were sincerely devoted to each other, even if they couldn't tolerate much togetherness. The Duke is a moral man by all accounts…except my mother's.'

He frowned. 'The Duke's first wife was ill and my mother had been the Duchess's companion. I would say she never forgave herself, or him. From the angry comments I gathered they consoled each other on the loss of his wife—it led to something more—and she didn't get over the feeling of betrayal to the ill Duchess. He possibly was the same.'

He stood closer to her, a caress from his proximity. 'From what my mother claimed once the liaison began it was as if they were powder kegs meeting, both trying to create angry sparks, but not truly wanting an explosion. I recall their meetings as fraught with tension and drama.'

'But the current Duchess welcomed you. And the Duke. That is tremendous.'

'The Duke's other sons were on edge,' Addison admitted, 'and I can't say I blamed them. Someone had spread the word that I might be there, but I don't think the heir received the notice by the way he choked when he saw me.'

'Why shouldn't he welcome you? You're the youngest. You can't give him any grief.'

'Perhaps he felt resentful when my mother took his father's notice. Or perhaps…we didn't get along that well when I was a child. Father brought him several times to Mother's town house. But I don't want enemies now. I have to make as many people in London as happy as I can. It will be my fiduciary duty, just as it is my duty to keep Cook happy.'

'It's her duty to keep you pleased.'

'I want her content and happy to stay. Her skills are another open secret.' His shoulder brushed hers as his head dipped closer. 'She is the best cook in London. My first butler's duty was to read to her as requested after she'd told me her regret was that she couldn't read cooking manuals. After about a year of that, she told me she was satisfied that she'd learned all she could from the books. I even managed to get her a meeting with a renowned chef.'

She noticed his hand beside hers. So close and yet not touching.

'She took a chance leaving her old employer, but she was often the undercook.' He tapped the back of her hand with his forefinger. 'And then it was *quid pro quo.* I needed to reward her for becoming such a grand cook and she'd mentioned the great French chef. I could arrange for her to meet her hero. Why not? The driver said she cried all the carriage ride from happiness that she had met the great Carême.' His shoulder brushed hers again. 'Her cooking was off for the next few days as she worked to try new things, but she surpassed herself and reached new heights.'

'Many employers would not have taken the time.'

'Many employers have families and simply spend their efforts on them.'

'Or themselves.'

She stared at their fingers, so close and not touching, and returned the plate to the tray. 'You're the nicest man I've ever met.'

'That is a sad state on mankind.' He waited and she moved closer.

'The night lasted for ever,' he said. 'I smiled in the right places, but was bereft, because I was thinking of you and wasn't with you.'

'I felt the same.'

He pulled her close, lips meeting in a kiss of tingling sensations between them. A moment instantly heightening awareness.

She held his chin, the bristles on his beard crisp under the pressure of her hands. Both stopped moving, until his head bent and a whisper of his breath touched her lips. She parted them the merest amount, aware of the flavour of wine and the even better scent that was Addison.

'Soph—sweetest,' he said. 'Can you stay the night, or at least most of it?' he asked, whispering against her skin.

'Don't you have plenty of work to do?' she asked.

'Not tonight.' The lamplight reflected a hunger in his eyes and warmth tingled in response.

'I've missed you.'

'You don't have to,' he said, taking the lamp and placing an arm around her, pulling her flush to him. Her body lit as intensely as the flame. 'My room. The bed holds us both easier.'

She followed him out of the room and he paused, letting her precede him, staying connected with a gentle touch at her side. When they entered the other room, with his foot, he tapped the door closed.

She didn't just feel like a couple, she felt like a princess, adorned in silk with gold threads and pearls, leading her prince to their assignation.

He embraced her, walking backwards, moving with her to the bed, then pulling back so he could remove his waistcoat and shirt. Then he scooped her close again to bury his face against her neck.

Starched linen, wool and leather scents surrounded them and the textures of his clothing were more alluring than any royal robes because the awareness of Addison eliminated everything else. She marvelled how he could be so much larger, yet the exact right size for her embrace, and she fitted so perfectly into the haven he created.

He held himself at arm's length so that he could read her expression. 'Tonight, I was among the world of my father. The pinnacle of my dreams was in front of me. But my mind kept returning to the vision of you.'

The pinnacle of his dreams?

She stepped away and tried to quell the rush of awareness. She could not destroy Addison's future.

Cook had told her how important it was for him to find a wife in society.

And Cook didn't exaggerate.

Sophia could feel the truth. He did not need a woman who couldn't even find work as an actress in his life. He could have as much sway in society as Shakespeare had had in the theatre. She couldn't be an Ophelia who destroyed both Hamlet and then the bard.

'I don't want our connection to make it more difficult for you to have all your dreams.' Her fingers trailed his coat.

'You believe I will have to choose?'

'When I wed my husband, I moved into the world around him and it was more of an adjustment than I ever expected.'

'You already live in my home. It only took you hours to fit in here.'

'My husband struggled because he believed he should be in a world where he didn't belong. And drank more.'

'The problem was within him.'

'And a similar concern is within me.' She'd never been able to act the part of anyone convincingly and moving into Addison's world would be like acting a part that was too grand for her. She tried to explain without revealing too much, then she hesitated. How deep was their connection if she couldn't even tell him of her past?

'You will have to believe me when I say that this is a grand house and it's the best home I've ever lived in, and—'

And she needed to tell him about her husband and the night he died, and the constable.

He watched her. Addison, the banker, watched her. 'You are telling me there are things in your past you've not confessed to me?'

'Yes.'

'Do you mistrust me because I've been in gaol?'

'Of course not.'

The banker inside him faded away. 'Sophia, many things I've not told you. Because they were the sins of the man I once was and the man I am now knows them, but I don't want to speak of them, and I don't want them to be any part of my life. I don't want to hear the words from my mouth. If someone else begins to discuss it with me, and they may, I do not feel a lesser person and I will acknowledge it, and I won't linger in that conversation.'

'Truly, I didn't do anything terrible, but still—'

'You don't have to tell me if it causes you sadness, particularly now. I want you to experience happiness with me, and what you want to share. We can talk about it later.'

His forehead touched hers. 'Remember how I've taken risks in the past. I've also reaped the rewards. And to hold you, tonight, would make this the best night of my life.'

Then he kissed her and her thoughts dissolved into a consciousness of his lips.

He cupped the side of her jaw, lips closing over hers with a softness unimaginable, and her senses blotted out everything but the heated wine taste of Addison.

Unfastening each pin from her hair, he deposited them on to his night table, letting her locks cloak her shoulders and he gently brushed the strands, his fingers trailing the curve of her neck, never leaving her skin, but caressing even as he moved the tresses to let them rest against the ribbons on the front of her clothing. The strands had never felt so glossy, rich and luxurious as they did with his fingers intertwined.

She shivered when he pulled away, but even though he increased the physical distance between them, he held her connected with his eyes.

He turned her, undoing each hook, and caressed the back of her neck as the dress fell to the floor. He kissed above her shift. The corset followed, freeing her, and the chemise which had been held against her body, billowed out as he rotated her.

He took her hand, his own folding over it into a clasp, which he held to his lips.

This time, no urgency guided him, but gentle sweeps of his mouth brushed over her, stoking her feelings of being treasured.

The touch of his lips caressed her as he whispered her name against her knuckles. 'I cannot think how my life would be if I'd not found you that moment. All I can wish is that our paths could have crossed sooner so we might have met earlier. Call it fate, the heavens or my life of fortune.'

The rest of their clothing slid to the floor as he undressed them. Neither stood alone and they were clasped together by awareness of each other.

The warm night, or the intensity of his movements, caused a moistened sheen where their bodies met and she understood the pause, the moment of future awareness, their kisses a rush to make up for the long seconds they'd not touched.

She pulled him into bed and he lay beside her, and kissed her shoulder. His hair brushed against her cheek and chin and his touch brushed over her, with the reverence of touching pricelessness. He rose enough to see her better and their eyes locked—it was as if they could see as one. She was aware of her own body and now she could sense his with all her awareness. With the lightest grasp, she guided him closer.

Again, his lips moved over her shoulders again, this time leaving behind a trail of blazing need inside her. She clasped the back of his head, her fingers nestled in the locks.

He moved to kiss and hold her breasts and, the moment his lips touched her nipples, she gasped.

'Soph…' she heard him whisper and the emotion in the word made it a caress.

Stirred by the sensations, she drew him snug against her, pulling him closer so that they could join. A flurry of intensity, a combination of pleasures.

When he rose above her, he paused and rocked against her, giving her sensation after sensation, until she reached her pleasure and she pulled him deeper into her heated depths, satisfied with the knowledge that they'd been made to fit as one and he was sensitive to her needs, though she had none left, as he assuaged every one.

He held her against him, letting her catch her breath, his arms a secure haven, the silence a caring end to the encounter.

Addison awoke her with a kiss as a glimmer of light seeped in the window. He was already dressed in trousers.

'Have you been awake long?' She propped herself up on one elbow.

He moved closer, reaching out, putting a hand at her waist. She felt treasured.

'I've been writing some notes for my day. It helps me plan,' he said.

She touched his cheek and made sure her voice was bright. 'It's almost daybreak. I should leave. You made me so happy.'

'Please stay. I had to wake you,' he said. 'No one will disturb us and, in truth, there are few secrets inside any household,' he said, lightly running fingertips over her arm.

'I know. You have so much work to finish. When it is your time to relax from your day with your employer, your man of affairs is scheduled to visit to help you with your personal investments. When you arrive late from work, the library desk is clean and when you leave in the morning, the paper stacks have been altered and the ink needs refilling from the hours you work late into the night.'

He held up a finger and thumb, spread apart, smiling. 'I must work this much harder than the hardest-working person around me every day. And I must plan more than they. I visualise all I can about the details of the end result and work to get it. It is a game. A gamble. A test. Of myself.' He went to the other room and fetched his shirt before returning.

'My employer has no mercy on people who do not give him their whole effort.' He held his chin up and laughter sparked. 'He pretends to be similar to the Regent in enjoying the finer things he can have. He hires the same people as the royals do and insists that he must have the quality of a palace around him, but in truth, it is the frame for his life. He says he likes to live well, but he lives to make money.'

'You have been fortunate to have worked yourself into such a position that a banker can depend on you so.'

'Trust. Loyalty. Persistence.'

He pulled the cloth of the shirt through his spread fingers as if straightening wrinkles. 'I arrived where I am by persistence, but not with others. With myself. I kept pushing and pushing and pushing until I ended up where I wanted to be.'

He draped the shirt over a chair, strode back to her and settled close. 'I am a fool for talking about such a thing when you are in my room.'

'It reminds me that we are on such different paths. Wasn't that why you spoke of it? So I wouldn't forget.'

'No. My goals push me. Give me a reason to go forward. I don't expect you or anyone else to embrace them as I do. After you spoke with me earlier, I wanted you to comprehend that success in my family is my ambition, but I don't expect you or anyone else to feel the same as I do.'

She could embrace the goal for him. That was her concern. She could grasp it and see him obtaining it, but not with her at his side. Cook had told Sophia she would make it impossible for Addison and, even though she didn't want to, she believed it. She'd not been able to act on stage and she'd not be able to appear comfortable in a ducal world. But she wouldn't ruin his happiness now. He'd see it for himself. Cook would likely tell him again. Or the banker. Or his father. Or even Humphrey…who'd seen her act. But it didn't matter, because she couldn't share a future in society. It was an invisible law passed down from generations.

He might be able to make rude gestures at his brothers and society would understand. But they would not take less than a submissive bow from her. And if his brothers didn't respect him, they'd never truly accept her deference. She'd always be the housekeeper in the room.

She could take the happiness in the room now and not concern herself with tomorrow because it only decreased her joy.

He had accepted his past, but to have an unsteady presence at his side—her—it would hurt his future.

She didn't want to wed again and to be his lover would give her the happiness of her dreams, but it would rob him of his. And she could never, ever wed him. It would pull him even further from his ambitions.

She could not bear thinking of it any longer.

Addison moved, restless.

'It's hard for you to be still, isn't it?'

'Yes. Everyone else seems to sleep so many hours, and I don't need that much sleep. It's almost as if I have two days to work, when everyone else has one. That has been a boon.' He moved away, letting her slip through his fingers. 'I have wondered how people can spend so much of their life asleep, but my steward told me that without it, he has no life inside him to get things done.'

'I should be on my way.' She moved out of his bed, dropped the chemise over her head and he stood transfixed as the fabric slid down her body, whispering in the early light, creating a vision of shadows and softness.

'Don't leave. Please. Stay longer,' he said. He whispered closer, 'We can have breakfast together. I crept downstairs and I've food waiting in the sitting room. You don't have to leave.'

He took her hand, sat and tugged her down beside him, her eyes sparkling as he looked at her. 'I would prefer to get a late start on today and a glorious start on my morning, with you.'

'But you can't.' She pushed at his chest. 'I care for you and want you to have your dreams.'

The kisses they savoured sated him for a few seconds, before he had to speak.

He rolled on to his back, bringing her to rest on his chest in a hug. 'You were so frightened the first night we met and terrified when I told you your duties and yet— brave.'

He stopped. 'I didn't notice before how many times you've been in a fright since we met.' He paused. 'Are you sure you're feeling something for me and not a lack of distress?'

'You could be right, but I don't believe you are.' She embraced him. 'It's true. I've more than I ever envisioned here. Others share the duties. Funds are available to purchase what is needed. It's amazing. Thank you.'

'So are you. Amazing,' he said. 'Thank you.'

She whispered. 'I didn't think myself ever to experience this closeness…like love almost, but better.'

'Rather a sombre way of considering it.'

'Like you do with numbers, I suppose. The finances have been first in your life for a very long time. You're close to getting all your dreams.'

His answer was a grumble, but he agreed with her.

'Numbers are not often compliant, but they're precise. You know where you stand with a number and there's no argument. It is what it is. But people fill something else in us. Something vital.'

'Or they empty it. That's what happened when I wed.'

'My mother and father found plenty to disagree about and they had different residences. They couldn't even agree on whether a day was warm or cold.'

'Sounds as if they were married.'

'Perhaps—just—as the manservant said, not on paper.'

'Do you regret that they didn't marry because you would have grown up as a duke's son?'

'I grew up as a duke's son, particularly if I annoyed him.'

He recalled one cold, turbulent day.

'Once my mother decided that he should punish me for being outdoors, because I hadn't come in when I should. He sent the butler, Wooten, to fetch me. My parents were both enraged about my misbehaviour, but barely spoke a harsh word to me when I returned because they were shouting at each other.'

He shut his eyes and shook his head. 'I would have taken any punishment but the one I received. I had to wait in the room while my mother and father reached agreement on my penance. I remember Mother calling Father an ogre. I didn't know what one was and expected it must be tremendously bad.' He laughed. 'He called her an ogress. I was probably twelve before I learned what an ogre was. I expected it to be much worse.'

'What was your punishment?'

'I never found out. I fell asleep in the room while

they were deciding, and I woke up in bed the next morning. Mother said Father was not coming back. Ever.'

He reached out, gave her a hug and pulled her close. 'A few days later, Mother sent me to the estate with a note I was to deliver personally to him and no one else, but it didn't work because the butler informed me that His Grace was not in. The servant said he would deliver the missive. I wouldn't give it to him and took it back to my mother and she shredded it into the tiniest pieces you could imagine. The Duke showed up the next day and he didn't knock. A window broke before he left. I heard the crash. I never knew how it happened or who did it.'

He rubbed her shoulder. 'But then he visited with my brothers in the carriage and took me with him to see one of his friends, the current Earl of Warrington's father. Mother didn't like that. She feared Father was introducing me into his world and taking me from hers. That was an eventful day. Father reprimanded my brother Edward for trying to trip me and I stood behind Father and made faces at Edward. Edward called me a name under his breath and Father heard, and told Edward that if he had to choose at that moment, I would have been the heir.'

He shrugged. 'I wanted to belong to the stable-master's family. His son got to feed the horses when I had lessons. But I assure you, later I discovered I was luckier than any human has a right to be.'

'I would have considered you prosperous if I'd seen you in the carriage. I'd not ridden in a vehicle until my husband courted me. I felt so grand in the carriage, a beau at my side. He proposed that day. How could I say no? But I should have. He could be so happy one moment and upset the next, blaming the whole world for his problems.'

'My mother would have agreed with you concerning marriage. She said they were shams.'

'I should get to my room. I don't want Humphrey to discover me here.'

He stood, moving to the wardrobe. 'Take my dressing gown. It'll save you from getting dressed.'

He retrieved it from the wardrobe and wrapped her in it, encasing her in the feeling of being surrounded by him. She clasped the front, and pulled it tight around her, the hem of it dragging the floor.

He adjusted the collar, moving her hair free, his knuckles brushing her jaw and igniting a spark of togetherness.

'Let me see you down the servants' stairs.'

'Others will know.' She rushed out the words.

His brows rose and lips upturned. But then he reconsidered her and how it might reflect on her reputation. 'I understand.'

Instead of the pleasant feelings she was used to when Addison spoke, this time it was as if a pebble bounced around in a deep well, clinking at the beginning, but falling down and no reassuring splash at the end, the feeling of endless dropping, rather like a woman relegated to the servants' quarters in a man's heart.

She didn't think it would bother her and it didn't really, but an awareness tumbled inside her, one she doubted she would have experienced had she not told him of her feelings.

Before he led her out the door, she stopped. 'It was

a response to the lovemaking. The sweetness, I said. I meant it, but not—'

'Soph—' He held her close. 'I know. Completely. Our emotions arise to the front when our bodies are so intense. We've awakened to each other physically and it is a natural reaction for the heart to feel included. And it is. For that moment. Maybe for longer.' He kissed her.

'We have something special between us. I don't know if it's that we met at the right time in our lives to have such an awareness or it's nature rearing up, but whatever it is, I am thankful for it.'

She draped her dress over her arm, fearing he would turn his back on his heritage.

He moved. 'Wait and let me go first with the light and make sure no one is about. Those stairs are narrow.'

She lifted the hem so her feet wouldn't get tangled in it and trod down the stairs, escorted by Addison.

'Do you want me to light a lamp in your room?' he asked.

'No. I'll be getting dressed straight away,' she said, but knew she'd linger. She was wrapped in his dressing gown, and that would be almost the same as being held in his arms.

Addison perused the stale treats by the library door from the night before and added the uneaten food he'd expected to share with her.

He'd never been intimate with a woman living under his roof. It hadn't seemed right, but it did with Sophia.

A bit of unease flitted inside him. He'd been introduced to someone's niece the night before. A woman he'd never seen, a shy innocent who would make the perfect society wife and yet bore him to tears. A nice enough person, easy to smile at, a caring mother for children, but remembering the moment jarred him.

He saw the portent in it now. He was being told it was time for him to marry, and he had no interest in the young woman.

He didn't need anyone to hold a mirror to him. Without comprehending what he was doing, and as certainly as two plus two equalled four, he'd installed a woman near him who could act the part of wife behind his walls.

But he couldn't have the society functions without a wife at his side. He'd not cared in the past, but the girl's father at the supper the night before had mentioned it less in passing and more up front.

It would be like the Duke to plan Addison's life if he thought it possible.

He had not expected to consider alterations in his life, but his father's acceptance had shifted his view of the future.

Just like with any project he started, obstacles appeared from nowhere and he had to sort them out. Sometimes he had to make concessions, adapt as he progressed forward and adjust to have the results needed.

He'd grasped from the beginning that his father's acceptance would make his plans easier to accomplish and he'd known, even without Cook telling him, that a wife could help his respectability, but Sophia hadn't been in his home then. It hadn't mattered, particularly.

But he'd touched her. And her hair had brushed his face. He'd comforted her when she'd been terrified. And she'd looked like a siren in his robe. He was growing hard just thinking about how she'd appeared in his robe.

He rang for Humphrey, knowing the man's nonsense would distract him.

Sophia kept lingering in his mind while Humphrey appeared and scrambled around, sloshing the water, then trying to find a shirt for Addison, a waistcoat and matching cravat. He staggered so much Addison feared he'd take a tumble. Addison took him by the shoulders and positioned him at the edge of the dressing table, suggesting he'd like to hear about Humphrey's early days in service.

The tale continued after Addison had finished shaving. Standing and removing his towel, he studied Humphrey.

Humphrey had remembered another story about an actor he'd known and had lost himself in the tale.

The man was now blissfully unaware of his duties and standing, weaving about and going on about a particular woman the performer had courted. Then he delivered the last line of his story, a humorous moment when the woman put him in his place, and he raised an arm, addressed the space beyond Addison and gave a shudder.

Addison laughed, entertained. Then it dawned on Addison. He'd seen that arm movement, and the shudder. Heard the voice from a distance. But he couldn't place it.

'Time for you to leave,' Addison said. If he didn't, Humphrey would still be talking with him an hour later.

'Of course. Will there be anything else after I remove the water?' Humphrey asked, ever so serious.

They both heard it at the same time. Carriage wheels.

'Well,' Humphrey said. 'I suppose it's time to go

onstage again.' He caught what he'd said. 'I meant—assuming my role as a butler. Not my valet duties.'

Humphrey was from the theatre.

No wonder he wasn't the best butler.

In truth, he'd not been the best of actors, but he'd been interesting to watch. And definitely the best at overacting.

Addison couldn't remember if he'd ever heard the performer's name. He'd been wearing a wig and a robe with a green slash across the front, but the man underneath had been Humphrey. It wasn't the features Addison recognised, but the movements. And when he listened closely, he could recollect that the voice was the same.

He'd been at someone's soirée and they'd brought in several people from the theatre to act out a farce. Humphrey had been one of the performers dressed in an outlandish costume. Perhaps a fake beard.

No, he would never have been able to recognise the actor.

Well, Humphrey had said he'd had other jobs before this post.

'Likely it's bank business,' Addison said, pretending not to notice the error. In truth, he liked Humphrey. The man could hardly be quiet and Addison had to tell him the valet duties were over in the morning or Humphrey might be so caught up in a story that Addison would never get to work. 'If so, show them to the library. I'll be waiting.'

He started to ask if Sophia knew about Humphrey's history, but then he realised Sophia knew whom she'd hired.

He would talk about it with her later. He wondered

why she wouldn't tell him such a simple thing, particularly as she'd told him about Talbot's fondness for drink.

A few minutes later Humphrey brought the guest to the library.

Addison lifted his head, but he didn't see someone from the bank. He recognised the man despite all the years that had passed.

The man smiled. 'I suppose this will be better for you than a hanging.'

'Did you get my banknote?'

'Oh, yes. I took care of that. But I have some other business the Duke asked me to see to.'

Addison waited and surmised that after all the years of working for his father, the man had taken on some of the supercilious airs his father had.

Addison braced himself.

Sophia had heard the vehicle and heard Humphrey rushing to the door.

'Who is it?' Merry asked, peering out the window after the man was inside.

Sophia didn't recognise the phaeton, but sensed the visitor was important.

They went to Humphrey's post. Humphrey had returned, yawning. 'I believe I will take a respite.' Then he paused, shoulders defeated. 'Oh, no. I must let the man out the door.' He sighed. 'As if the man couldn't open the door himself.' He rolled his eyes, changing direction. 'But I'm temporary. And I would like to be that permanently.'

'Who is visiting Addison?' she asked, quietly. 'The banker or Addison's steward?'

'I don't know. Addison wasn't expecting anyone and

the visitor had that puckering scowl that said he thinks himself important.' Humphrey touched his chest. 'I had on that *"I am but a door latch for you"* smile. We got on so well. A lasting moment in neither of our lives.'

Sophia touched her lips, feeling certain that whatever was being said would have a consequence on Addison's life and her own.

Chapter Sixteen

With the subtlety of a tree crashing at the edge of a glen, Oldston had put plans in place for Addison to reach the heights of society.

'Why did you ask me to visit with you?' Sophia twisted in the carriage seat.

'Because I'm considering moving my household. More than considering it.'

'Relocating? All of us?' Sophia's head lowered.

'Yes. Of course.' He could not leave her, or Cook, or the stableman behind. 'My household. Everyone.'

'Oh…'

'Don't look so dismayed,' Addison said, interlocking their fingers. 'It's little bigger than the space we live in now and the garden suffers by comparison. I was pleased to leave the town house behind, but after my father offered me a chance to return and said I could the use the money I'd given him to repay the debt for my education as the cost… He said he and I both would benefit from the transaction.'

When the man of affairs had informed Addison that his father had decreed his son would conduct business better from the lavish town house, Addison had been surprised, but then pride had invaded his body. And a sense of power. Acceptance.

The carriage ride with Sophia would be brief compared to the steps home from the gaol with the offal scent he'd worn, trapped in his nostrils. His clothing did not reflect the short time they'd been unwashed, but the years of trapped people within the walls.

The garments had been cleaned, but he'd never been able to wear them again. He'd not even wanted the buttons kept. A coat made by the finest tailor in London and he'd demanded it destroyed.

'This time, when I return to the town house, I'll be arriving in my carriage, specifically invited by Oldston. A first for me.'

A town house his father was going to sell since his wife's aunt had vacated it—or he claimed he might let Addison have it...if he would live in it.

In the past few days his father had, for all intents and purposes, put an arm around Addison's shoulders and introduced him to the upper reaches of society, and said he trusted Addison with all his funds.

'I am going where I belong. The world I was born into.'

'I like the world you live in now.'

'But you've not seen this one. Not from the inside.'

She didn't answer, but he could sense her trepidation.

He took her other hand. 'Wait until you see it to form an opinion. And you'll like it just as well. Even better.'

Cook had said Sophia would never be comfortable among the society world Addison needed to reach the height of success, but he would prove her wrong.

Then the carriage stopped and he appraised everything with a fresh perception. He would have to get a grander vehicle. The one he had wouldn't do now. Caldwell would be pleased.

He led Sophia from the coach and kept a hand on her arm. 'It's fine,' he reassured her, sensing her unease, but then his own apprehension invaded him when he studied the familiar façade. He'd not before considered how stately it appeared.

He remembered his first view of the house he lived in now and how decrepit it had been— with the only thing agreeable being the size and price. But over time he'd altered it to suit him and the changes made it a comfortable home.

Yet, it was not the structure rising in front of him.

He told himself it was just a home. Walls. Windows. Doors.

He squared his jaw. Years had passed and he had changed and everything was different—but not. The house spoke of grandeur he'd taken for granted.

'Do not let it intimidate you,' he said to Sophia when he saw her face. 'It's only my childhood home.'

The instant he said the words, he knew he'd made a mistake in speaking them.

She stared at him as if she'd never seen him before.

The door opened and the butler, Wooten, greeted him and his stoic expression gave away nothing. Wooten hadn't changed except the creases in his face were deeper. Addison imagined the man had so perfected his station in life that he didn't feel emotions until he was alone, if then.

Addison paused and introduced Sophia as his housekeeper, and the word was bitter in his mouth. She stepped away from him. He could not introduce her as such ever again.

Quickly, he continued speaking, wanting to erase the moment.

'Are you the solitary person remaining?' Addison asked. 'Of Mother's servants.'

'Yes.'

'If I were to live here again, would you stay?' Addison braced himself for an unfavourable response.

Wooten was the perfect butler. He would never err on addressing a duke, but he'd been able to convey a duke-like displeasure over Addison's indiscretions without ever once losing his demeanour of servitude.

Addison hadn't returned easily past Wooten when he'd arrived at the town house after the gaol. He would have let his father see him in the filth and somehow conveyed to his father that he was to blame for the stench, though he'd not been.

But Wooten—that had been more difficult than peering in a mirror.

'Of course. I could not leave your father's employment,' Wooten said.

'What if it were my employment?'

'If your father asked me to stay on with you, I would do so happily.'

'It would be an honour for me,' Addison said and continued into the home, leading Sophia to the upper rooms in silence.

They stopped at the dining room.

She increased the distance between them. 'Humphrey would not be at home here,' she said, studying a gilded mirror framed by two matching sconces.

'He might. And as a valet, he could keep to the background.'

'It would be hard for him to stay hidden away. And how could that help your advancement? To have people in residence who did not fit their surroundings?'

'It appears grand here, but it is only better paint.'

'You can't paint everything.'

He took her arm. Kissed her fingertips. 'Not everything needs to be painted.'

She didn't speak.

He walked to his father's room and heard his own footsteps in a way he'd not noticed before. And Sophia's timid ones.

His father's room held the basic furniture he remembered. Ducal to the last carving on the bed frame.

He stopped in the room that had been his, but he'd not stayed in it long after he'd discovered wine, women and song.

'Your room?' she asked.

He nodded. 'Yes. If you look out the window, you can almost see the roof of my father's estate. You can view the chimneys for the fireplaces.'

'How nice,' she said, but she didn't stroll to the curtains.

Then he led her to the solitary room of importance he'd not entered. The library where his father had often worked.

Once inside the door, he stilled at the sight of the painting across from the mantel in order to keep it further from possible soot. The one piece of art in the home. One familiar to him. He blocked it from his awareness.

'This was the room where they had their loudest words.'

His mind latched on to scenes of his mother sewing and his father striding back and forth, gesticulating about this or that.

A silent laugh escaped Addison's lips.

Not all the recollections of his parents were of their true disagreements, but they were often spirited. He could remember avoiding the room, preferring the steadiness of his own domain. Sometimes he would be aware of strident tones, but it usually didn't mean anything more to him than the patter of rain on rooftops. It was volume and frustration. Not hatred and not always anger.

His mother had overacted as much as Humphrey did.

His brothers had had his father's name and title, but their lives likely had little of the Duke in it. A man could be divided in just so many portions and, in Addison's younger years, his mother's town house got the largest measure of the Duke, he suspected. Not that it mattered to him then. But perhaps it should have. His half-brothers surely noticed, although he doubted Benedict cared any more than he had. Edward, the heir, possibly felt differently.

'I was happy to be the bastard child. My father came here to see me, or so my mother sometimes shouted,' he mused. 'And her greatest fear was that he would take me. Because of that, she had to watch her step. She truly burst into a rage at herself one night when he left, angry she would have to placate him, or risk losing me.'

'He would have had all rights to you *if* they'd been married when you were born. But she was your mother and your only rightful parent because they weren't wed.'

His brows rose. 'He had friends in Chancery Court. In Parliament. Among royalty. And he had funds. And since he recognised me as his son, Mother feared the Duke could take me. He could have.'

He watched as realisation dawned in her eyes.

'But there were instances my father reassured her, stridently, that he would not separate me from her. Never, he claimed. But many times, in a temper, he would retort he only came here because of me and then he would take me for a short trip. At first, he would be furious with her, but we would see a menagerie or purchase a treat, or he would show me where Parliament sat, and he would talk, and then his anger would fade and we'd return here.'

'Perhaps, because they fought so easily, it's best they didn't wed.'

He firmed his jaw. Staring overhead, and shaking his head, he said, with a hint of false incredulity in the words. 'But if they married, what would they have fought about then?'

His dry laugh bounced back at him from the empty shelves where his mother's vase collection had rested. He moved closer, running a hand over the wood on the mantel, making three distinct circles in the dust, unhappy to see the indication of emptiness. He brushed his hands together to clean them.

She stepped to his side, opened her reticule and took out a folded handkerchief, giving it to him to wipe the dirt from his fingers. 'My husband and I never argued. I did all I could to appease him. He—himself—wasn't mean. But I wanted to avoid the petulance, the conflict and the feeling of being cornered. I didn't own the house, either, and I didn't even feel I had the option to argue with him if I disagreed.'

'My mother never questioned her right to disagree and my father would give gifts to appease her. I sold them, later. He had to know. He'd taken me to the shop once when he'd purchased a gift for Mother and I tended to sell them back to the best tradesmen.'

He pointed to the circles he'd made. 'The Meissen. The Sèvres. The ormolu clock.'

If he could find the valuables he'd sold to support his rakehell lifestyle, he wondered if he'd try to purchase them again, but doubted he'd be successful. Besides, he wasn't certain he'd be able to afford it.

He'd sold them, but he'd retained her favourite vase, which he no longer had. He'd sold his mother's treasures, except the one. The one Crisp had explained as broken. Perhaps it had been. He had kept the inferior, worthless trinket which Crisp had used to replace it. The memento of his mother's that he'd treasured had likely been stolen from him, explained away as shattered. A justice only fate could deliver.

The recollection sent a shard into his midsection.

His father knew. Knew when he'd visited and he'd tapped the ugly little pot that sat on the shelf, the true artwork not in Addison's dwelling. Not left behind in the town house.

Addison had felt the slap, accepted it and remained standing.

He again recalled his mother saying the Duke treated her better than if their positions had been reversed. He suspected he could have said the same thing.

'She should have been his wife. Who knows if it was guilt, or stubbornness, or perhaps she didn't truly love him? *She* preferred to be his *mistress.*' He jerked his head sideways.

'Am I not—?'

'Don't say it,' he commanded. 'Sometimes my brothers and I crossed paths without my father there. They called my mother names and that enraged me. They settled on *mistress*. The ugly word. The one my parents used in fights. The one most profane to me. They were older than me, but not as swift on their feet.'

Addison walked away from the mantel and fought back his emotions, staring at the one painting in the house. He'd once sold the artwork directly in front of him. A gift his father had given his mother. The dealer had likely contacted his father and his father had purchased it a second time.

He owed his life to his father and his loyalty.

Chapter Seventeen

Sophia stood in the doorway, watching Addison standing transfixed by a painting. She suspected he saw the past in it and didn't dare interrupt his perusals.

'Please go to the carriage if you wish, Sophia. I'll catch up with you later.' He spoke—terse—his mind on some faraway place.

It meant going past the butler.

She did and the butler opened the door for her as if she were a queen, but they both knew she wasn't.

She strode to the carriage, feeling like a pauper, choked by her awareness of the gulf between her station and his. She would have felt much better entering and exiting through the servants' entrance.

His childhood home.

The driver of the carriage opened the door for her and the nod he gave her was friendly, more of a recognition of one servant to another.

'I never realised the master came from such high steps,' the driver said, awe in his voice.

'Neither did I,' she said, staring back at the façade.

She settled herself inside and viewed the other

houses. She didn't think she'd ever been on this street in her life.

Carriages moved past. And not one with a ducal crest, so she wasn't necessarily in the most affluent part of Addison's life.

Likely she was surrounded by earls and viscounts and bankers and didn't even know it. More vehicles sped along than she'd ever seen on the streets in front of Addison's house.

Addison moved into the conveyance, his lips firm as he sat beside her, and his hand casually taking hers. But he wasn't relaxed. Not with the tension in his face.

But then, he'd been where his mother had lived. The reminder of the life where his father had visited. A duke.

She'd never seen his father, but when she caught a glimpse of Addison's profile, she could easily see him as a duke's son.

She would have felt so much better if he'd been a banker's son, but even that was rather elevated.

Her husband had been a carpenter whose mother had taken residence in Humphrey Talbot's upstairs rooms. Then, after the theatre had hired her husband to make some repairs, he'd decided the actor's life was for him. And Sophia had not suspected him of being in a performance during their short courtship. It had been the best performance of his life.

She faced straight ahead.

'Can we take a different direction?' she asked. 'I'd like to see where I grew up.'

He agreed and she gave the driver instructions, but she admitted to him that she wasn't sure how reliable they would be. Travelling by carriage, instead of walking, made all the distances different.

Addison squeezed her fingers, supportive, and she didn't know if it was to be close or if it was a way of combining his past and present.

The driver took them to West Lane and then turned to a familiar area. A light rain pelted the top of the vehicle. She wished the rain would have held off longer, because the thunder and raindrops had turned the day dreary and colder.

After directing the driver again, Sophia found where the structure stood, but loomed like a bad dream, except for the memories of her mother. Just rooms for different families.

She'd shared rooms with her parents and Merry. The winters were to be endured and summers could be escaped somewhat, but being with her family had made it all easier.

'I mostly had a happy life when I was a child,' she said, finding it hard to remember herself as content in those surroundings, but she had been. Her father had been forceful with his fists, but he'd mostly stayed away, working or drinking, arriving late at night. Her mother had always tried to make sure Sophia and Merry were asleep during those times and she'd often taken them for walks to keep the peace around them. 'Everything seems smaller now than it did.' And older. And tired. And hardly standing. 'It was a long walk for us to go anywhere, but it was always an adventure.'

Then they switched direction and proceeded to the place she'd lived when she was married, except it had burned to the ground. Humphrey had lived on the first floor. She, her husband and her mother-in-law had lived above. She couldn't summon any happy recollections. Her mother-in-law had been such a wretch. They'd not spoken again after the woman had tried to get Sophia imprisoned, but it had always been like a conversation with a hungry vulture holding a scythe. Sophia had moved out the day after her husband's death because there had been no alternative. She'd had to leave everything behind except what she could fit in her portmanteau, but she'd not left much.

She feared she would have followed her husband out of the window if his mother had had an opportunity and it would have been claimed suicide. Grief. An impossible scenario.

But she'd done as well as she could, which her own mother once said was what everyone always did.

'Do you think people always do the best they can?' she asked Addison.

'No,' he said. 'I did what I wanted to when I got out of my parents' vision and sometimes in their view. I wouldn't listen to them. Then it stopped being an adventure and became an experience where foolishness becomes clear.'

He still held her hand and she wondered if he noticed her roughened skin from the mopping and cleaning.

'Some people are consumed by drink before they feel its tentacles and then, when they grasp that they are there, it's too late. It has them hugged too close.' He rubbed his jaw. 'I was pulled into risk much the same. And I took it and almost perished for it.'

'But you escaped.'

'Yes. Though I am doing a similar adventure now, except within the bounds of utmost propriety. I take chances with properties and livelihoods. Perhaps the steadiness I had when I risked my own life makes this tame to me. And I'm able to distance myself and judge everything based on merit. The height of the peril it-self doesn't concern me. The chance for success fac-tors does.'

'Will you move back into the town house?'

'My father asked it of me. Not demanded. But asked. I doubt he's asked more than half a dozen things of any-one in his whole life.'

'It would be like living inside a royal castle.' But she wasn't a princess. She'd never be accepted among these people. Doubtless even the other servants would stare down their noses at her. She was fairly certain of that. It would take years to earn a spot in their good graces.

He had no idea that the servants would slight her, or she would think they did. Wooten stood so correct and stonelike. She'd never know what he truly felt and it would always make her wonder. She would feel like a mouse encircled by hungry cats, licking their whiskers and watching for a mistake so they could pounce, rather like living with her mother-in-law had been.

'The town house is for the wealthiest of people.'

'If riches didn't matter to us...' he studied the scene outside the window '...then we might have no desire to better ourselves. As someone who lived a good many years completely without such yearnings, maybe it's for the best to have them.'

'The town house is more lavish than what I knew existed. But being content with what you have is good, too. I had so little when I was a child. But I had a mother who cared for me and our little, drab abode seemed so fanciful some nights when we were falling asleep and telling stories and entertaining ourselves with quiet songs or rhymes. And sometimes, we'd act out stories we made up. I always enjoyed that.'

'Walls, roofs, windows,' he said, 'but some are results of a craftsman's art and some are walls, roofs, and windows. A place to keep dry and warm.'

'You belong among the art. I could tell as you walked around the rooms, reacquainting yourself with them, that you were comfortable there.' She forced the sentence to end on a smile.

If she'd understood who Addison was when she first saw him, she would have bolted for the brothel door and put her hopes in a child. The place with oars and a man who hid under the bed.

Addison belonged in the town house.

She did not.

To let him go of her own volition seemed harder than she could manage, but she had the opportunity to move to Broomer's.

The oars at the door didn't make her feel intimidated. True, it was in a respectable area, but not one so deeply entrenched in perfection. One closer to the docks and the oars seemed to be a message telling the neighbours to accept them as they were.

Perhaps she could find a way to do the same, but when she searched inside herself, she doubted it. She'd never been a person who'd been able to stick out her jaw and barge forward. That wasn't how she'd survived. If she'd been brave enough to lead with the chin, she would have been knocked, head first, into the nearest wall.

She wasn't sure about living among the best. Addison's true world, not the one he lived in. That was the error for him. The plain residence with ordinary people who went about their lives. Well, in truth, his plain world was a grand one to her and she was pleased to live in it.

'It is a glorious home.' She wished she'd never seen it. 'In a world full of important people.'

Addison's laughter rumbled in the coach. 'Important people? I suppose. But normal people. Ones who have enough funds to purchase a bit of distance from others. The staff helps build a barrier, hiding the routine moments. My mother could afford to purchase things that cloaked her differently, giving her the appearance of a swan among crows Because our life was not always grand when glass was breaking,' he mused to himself. 'Mother never, ever broke the expensive porcelain or glassware. The anger was drama, not rage.'

'There is a divide between the master and the staff in most houses. You do not see it.'

'I do.' Quietly spoken. Almost too soft. 'I won over Cook easily enough. With Beldon and Crisp and her niece, I was an intruder below stairs.' His lips firmed. 'Under my roof. But they were right.'

'You let them go. At least Crisp and Beldon. And I gathered you wanted Ina gone, which was a good decision.'

'I would not have if I could have trusted them. I saw errors. Mistakes in bookkeeping that they didn't know I ever watched. After the first butler, the ledgers were stored in a closet near the entrance. An easy place for me to inspect them when I visited the kitchen late at night. I insisted. My house. My rules.'

When the coach stopped at Addison's, Sophia stepped out of the carriage, and saw the front door. With the firm pressure of his hand, Addison pushed her forward.

His house. His rules.

True, she could enter by the front door here, but she would be relegating him to the servants' entrance in his life if she did the same elsewhere. She would have tentacles in him and be holding him from the opulence he'd been born into. He didn't even see the obstacle growing around him.

Addison took Sophia's arm after he escorted her from the vehicle. Humphrey opened the door, then greeted them.

She slipped from his grasp, following Talbot to the servants' quarters.

'Sophia, would you please follow me as I'd like to speak with you privately,' Addison said.

She hesitated. Humphrey stopped, studied the situation and continued on his way.

'We can talk in your room if you'd prefer,' Addison said.

They seemed to be at a stalemate.

Sophia gathered her skirts in a grip which would leave wrinkles in the clothing, and hurried up the stairs in front of Addison. But he had a feeling she was keeping something from him and he wasn't certain of what it was. And he didn't think Sophia was particularly good at evading questions. They needed to talk. They'd done too little of it.

The knowledge slapped him across the face…the only thing that had done so in his life.

He'd been intimate with Sophia, close with her. But how much of himself had he truly shared? And how much of herself had she revealed?

In his library, he saw a tray had been left for him

and he moved to it, and cut an apricot tart in half. But he put it down before handing it to her.

'Are you thinking of going to Broomer's?'

She released her grip on her skirt and the crumpled cloth fell into place—so many steps past the top of the stairs.

'I may be.'

'Please don't, Sophia.'

'Can you not see where you are going?' she asked. 'Can you not see where you belong? Where I belong? And what if I were to fall in love with you?'

She walked over and rested her forehead on his shoulder. He didn't embrace her, still hearing her words.

'I could not do that to you. I could not jeopardise your future. I could not stay with you if I felt more for you than you felt for me. I could not move into such a grand residence without feeling inferior. I could not live like I did before with a sense of circling vultures all around me.'

'You are overreacting.'

'If it were five years ago, perhaps I would be naive enough to think I could. But that innocence died in me fairly quickly.'

'I will not have a *mistress* in that house, Sophia.'

'I understand that. And I don't think you realise how flawed my past is. Society would not accept me. And if they found out who you had as a housekeeper they would talk. And I can't raise a single finger to the world in a rude gesture like you can. I. Am. A. Housekeeper. And in truth, that is far more than I ever expected.'

He took her shoulders. 'We have time to think this through. We don't have to make any decisions today. Please don't go to Broomer's.'

He saw her uncertainty.

'Please.' He kissed her forehead. 'Please.'

Before she could answer, he heard a vehicle's wheels screeching as a brake was applied.

A cacophony of shouts and noises erupted at the entrance. Humphrey's voice reached them.

Footsteps pounded up the stairs. He stepped in front of Sophia, moving her behind him for protection, wishing now she'd not stayed.

The library was the room with the open door and the footsteps ran to it first. Two men burst inside, dishevelled in their haste, and he recognised them instantly.

'Father told us,' the future Duke shouted.

'I'm sorry, sir. These heathens rushed past me.' Humphrey ran in last, a broom in his hand, ready to swing. 'I'll escort them down the stairs.'

'I'm not a heathen. I'm *the* heir.' His brother whirled to Humphrey, then jumped back when he saw the broom.

'Pity.' Humphrey sniffed, giving a wide, slow swing. 'They let anyone inherit these days.'

'Not if he has anything to do with it.' His brother addressed Addison. 'You traitor. Once a bastard always a bastard. Never forget that.'

Addison shrugged. 'I don't have a problem with it.'

His eldest brother rushed forward, flinging a punch. Addison ducked, caught the fist, clasped it and used it to push the heir back into his younger brother Benedict.

'I will escort them out,' Humphrey said. 'If you will start them down the stairs, face first.'

'They're my brothers,' Addison said, resignation in his voice.

'We all have family members we'd like to hide,' Humphrey mumbled.

'I know you! I saw you at Drury Lane. You were in some comedy that put me to sleep,' Edward said.

Humphrey gripped the handle tighter. '"*There be madness in my broom, but there is a method to it. God gave you one face, but I will happily make you another.*" As Shakespeare would have said if he'd met you.'

'Down, Humphrey,' Addison ordered. Then he spoke to his brothers. 'If you wish to stay, you will treat my butler politely.'

'Did you realise you have an actor for a butler? And not a good actor either,' Edward asked.

'He's a fine butler and I will keep him,' Addison answered, knowing Humphrey could never reach the heights of service, but it wasn't his brother's decision. 'As I have to do with my brothers.'

Addison stepped closer to Humphrey, took the broom and commanded him with his eyes.

Humphrey left, the essence of high dudgeon. Addison tossed the broom near the wall.

'When this *servant* leaves, we have a discussion to attend to.' Edward shot a glance at Sophia.

He'd be damned if he'd let his brother dismiss Sophia.

Addison heard her moving away. He reached out, caught her arm and pulled her close, taking her hand to his lips for a kiss, meeting her eyes and imploring her not to resist. She didn't. He stood at her side. 'She is welcome to hear any discussion between us.'

'Your *mistress*?' Edward said the words as an oath.

All the years of his mother being the Duke's mistress resurfaced, and Addison stared at his brother. And he could not introduce her as his housekeeper as he had to Wooten.

'Betrothed.' He spoke softly. It would have carried more weight had not Sophia gurgled. He shot her an exasperated look.

He could not let his brothers relegate her to the status of a mistress and she could end the betrothal at any time she wanted.

Her lips firmed, but she managed to get the edges of them up.

'Father has told us nothing about this,' Edward said.

'It's recent,' Addison answered. 'I have yet to inform Father. And she has yet to decide.'

'Well, now that you've got your paws on *His Grace's* funds, I can understand this woman accepting your offer of marriage.'

'She didn't know about Father's lease.' Addison kept Sophia close, speaking with his brothers, yet really paying more attention to her. 'Now you've done it. You ruined the surprise.' He would have preferred her to have given a semblance of happiness, but then perhaps she'd not really heard what he said.

'You're stealing Oldston's funds. My inheritance.'

Edward was ready to charge again, but Addison held out a palm, stopping him.

What he wasn't stealing was Sophia's heart. He could see it on her face. No pleasure shone through at being introduced as his betrothed. She appeared more choked than ecstatic. A splinter of coldness pierced him. She was serious about her dislike of marriage and it didn't only brush the surface. He knew she found him appealing, knew she enjoyed his presence, their moments together, and yet, at the merest hint of a betrothal, she appeared to have been plunged in a cold vat of seawater.

His brother's shouts captured his attention and he had to glare at Edward to keep him from rushing forward with his fists. But blast it, he wanted to reassure Sophia.

'We're not—' she said.

'Let's discuss it in private, Sweeting. I misspoke.' Addison tried to soothe her and he would beg her forgiveness later.

'Oh, you misspeak all the time,' Edward shouted. 'And end up in gaol and everyone thinks you a saint for it.'

'Are you already married?' Benedict inserted, moving closer to his brother. 'He could do it, Edward. He could get a Special Licence and likely keep it a secret so Father wouldn't find out.'

'We are not wed,' Addison said, more to comfort Sophia than anything else. 'And are not likely to wed soon as she is still undecided.'

That seemed to bring life into her eyes.

'It doesn't matter,' Edward said, a growl after the words. 'You're trying to control my inheritance. You cannot expect me to believe it wasn't your idea. You came to the estate during the anniversary celebration and acted as if you owned it.'

'My father's estate. I've agreed to nothing. And have you ever known the Duke to do anything he did not decide to do on his own?'

Neither brother spoke.

'Father never could think regarding your mother, or you.' Edward's hands fisted at his sides. 'Our mother died and within days we couldn't find him. He set up his mistress in a house nearby and off he ran. Then when you were born—'

Benedict nodded. 'He called us in and told us we had a brother, but that we must keep it among family for the time being.'

'He did?'

'Yes. The same thing he told half of London,' Edward said, his lips twisted into a snarl. '"I have a son. I have *another* son. But keep it among yourselves. It's not something to talk about." Then he took me on a carriage ride to Uncle's house and said, "My Vera had a boy." He said he'd wanted you named after Grandfather, but Vera insisted against it.'

Addison hadn't known that.

'Then when you were every bit the hellion and a disgrace, I told Father how you were acting,' Edward said. 'And he told me not to mention it again and then I had to listen to an hour of instruction about pious behaviours that befit the future Duke. And I was a perfect son. Perfect, but never good enough for him. You nearly got strung up for all to see and it hurt Father, yet he welcomed you with open arms.'

'I could tell when Father heard of your indiscretions. We got the sermon,' Benedict muttered. 'It's a wonder any of us survived.'

Addison mused. 'One year must have been particularly rough for you.'

'We were sent to a tenant's farm and had to pick up rocks in the fields,' Benedict agreed. 'But that was the last time we received your punishment.'

'I apologise that you were chastised for my errors.' He went to the pull. 'I'll have the maid bring us some wine. I've some good vintages that may help make up for the sermons.'

'Nothing will,' Edward said.

'You've not tasted this wine…' Addison took the pull and tugged it. 'The major renovation I made here was to see that the wine could be stored properly.'

'We could listen, Edward. You know His Grace can be strong-willed. And you're usually thirsty.'

Edward glared, unspeaking.

Addison released the pull. 'The proposal is to lease everything to me—the houses and the estates—for twenty-five years. I make the decisions regarding major purchases and make sure invoices are paid, and the profits are to be divided among the two of you, the Duke or Duchess, and me. He wants to protect his wife in the event that he should pass on. If I die in advance of him, the lease becomes void and reverts to him. I would also agree to let tenancy of the ducal estate remain in his domain, his wife's and the two of you.'

'That does have some merit,' Benedict said. 'And Father does care for Her Grace and she does treat him well. And Addison is our half-brother.'

Edward sneered in response. Addison knew that it would be almost impossible to divide the properties should his father pass on, even the unentailed ones. Benedict and the Duchess would likely get nothing but a pittance. Edward, as a duke, would get the total amount of the entailed.

'It's said you've done well with investments,' Benedict said. 'So it's possible Edward's inheritance could be more.'

'It's possible.'

The room quietened as Edward pondered that.

In a few moments, Merry arrived, answering the bell, her cap askew.

'You!' Edward shouted, jumping to the wall behind him, fingers splayed. 'Thief!' he sputtered, voice shrilling as he spoke to Addison and pointed at Merry. 'She picked my pocket.'

'I never picked your pocket,' Merry gasped, eyes wide. 'I never took one penny from you I didn't earn.' Her voice firmed. 'And trust me, I earned it, by just giving you a smile.'

'I will see justice done.' Edward glared at them all.

'I will refund any money taken from you,' Addison said.

'That's not enough. I want her arrested. Transported.'

'Drawn and quartered?' Addison asked.

Edward gave him the ducal scowl and Addison shot it back to him, and if his mother had been correct, no one could give that particular glower better than him or his father.

'Then let's get someone here who knows what punishments might be merited.' Addison said, knowing his neighbour would be gracious. 'There is an official nearby who can help us. Fetch him and he'll help sort this out.' He gave his eldest brother direction.

Edward left. Benedict shrugged and followed after him.

'Did you know my brother?' Addison asked Merry.

She nodded. 'Before Mrs Wilson's. A private arrangement.'

He glanced at Sophia. 'Amazing. A woman with good morals from the brothel.'

'I do have good morals.' Merry straightened her cap.

'I don't always use them. But they can be exemplary on occasion.'

Addison spoke to Merry. 'Did you pick his pocket?'

'It's possible.' She stared at a corner of the ceiling. 'You'd think he would have had more funds than that.'

'How much? Err on the high side. He will be repaid.'

'A few pence. I took it to let him know I could and to get rid of him.'

'A few pence?'

'Yes. I didn't want to see him again.'

'Leave me to sort this.' Addison shut his eyes. When he opened them Merry was gone.

His eyes raked Sophia. 'Were you an actress?'

Sophia gasped, much louder than any he'd heard before. He braced himself.

'No. The newsprint lied. The theatre didn't hire me.'

He put one hand to his temple and tensed. 'The newsprint? Is there anything else I should know?'

'I did not murder my husband,' Sophia near shouted. 'No matter what his mother claims.'

He stared at her.

'I didn't kill my husband,' she said, softly this time. 'I didn't. He jumped out of the window on his own.'

Addison swore under his breath, imagining his future. All the respectability. Gone. 'If the bankers find out— If the Duke does—'

'His mother wasn't there. But she claimed to be. She said I pushed him and she saw it.'

He reassessed what he'd heard, considered it again and knew he'd not made a mistake.

He saw the respect swirling away. He'd worked so hard since gaol to live a pristine life. He'd been careful of drink, of women and not been to a gambling hell once. Blast it, on most Sundays he went to services and stayed awake. And he was careful to appear appropriately interested at the service and be discreet. If he had a business idea, he pencilled a note on the paper he kept in his prayer book.

'I didn't mean for this to happen,' Sophia said.

He could have said the same. His brothers could spread tales faster than newspapers could be printed. This would not sit well with his father or the banker.

A clattering came again from the front door. They both waited.

Edward and Benedict rushed in again, with a third man. Sophia gasped.

'I found your constable friend,' Edward said. 'Where's the lightskirt? I want her arrested. Now.'

'Ophelia is the pickpocket?' The constable shook his head, speaking to Sophia. He'd obviously recognised her. 'And that actor who opened the door? He swore you didn't kill your husband, but it would have been hard for him to see you from the stage floor where he spent the night.'

'I did not kill my husband,' Sophia said. 'I assure you of that. And I believe my mother-in-law burned down Humphrey's home.'

Edward and Benedict stared.

'Well, that has a ring of truth,' the constable said. 'I told his mother no court would sentence you guilty and she threatened to burn my residence if I didn't arrest Ophelia.'

'Ophelia?' Edward gasped, suddenly picking up on the name, eyes gleeful. 'This is the murdered Hamlet's wife?'

'He only played Hamlet the one time,' Sophia said.

'And I had to answer to the name Ophelia since our betrothal or he would go into a rage. And all his friends called me that. Everyone in the theatre did. They didn't know my real name.'

'I'll pay you,' Edward said to the constable, clapping his hands. 'To arrest Ophelia and—the other one.'

Benedict chuckled. 'I'm going to be the favourite son.'

'No, you won't,' Edward snapped. 'But Father will hear about this.'

'Please see that he does,' Addison agreed. There was no way this would not find its way back to the Duke with both his brothers present. And the constable, too.

Benedict slapped his brother on the back. 'I think you should tell Father about Addison,' he said, grinning at Edward. His laughter erupted. 'And I will tell him about your funds getting stolen. That way, he doesn't get too much upsetting news at once.'

'No one will be arrested under my roof.' Addison's command slashed into the air.

'Come on, Benedict,' snapped Edward. 'It doesn't matter if she's arrested as long as Father knows she should have been.'

His brothers left, clattering down the stairs.

'Tell me what happened,' Addison commanded Sophia.

She gulped in a breath. 'It was terrible.'

'Let me,' the constable said. 'It was my most interesting job. I remember it like it was yesterday. The theatre owner said the man was always dancing off chairs and heights, trying to prove he could act, but he couldn't. Apparently, he couldn't land that well either.'

'Humphrey lived in the rooms below us,' she explained. 'He rented the ones above to my mother-in-law as she wanted her son to be near the actors.'

Addison recalled the story. 'I remember reading that Ophelia pushed Hamlet out the window and his mother had tried to stop it, but feared for her own life.'

The constable agreed. 'The mother went to the newspapers with her side of the story. They printed it without verifying a word.'

'My husband was upset that night because the theatre owner had threatened to let him go if he didn't remain in character onstage. Hamlet was to die a still death. Not a tumbling one. He jumped out of the window to show just how he thought Hamlet should die. He'd done it before, many times. He could fall and roll. But I heard a cat screech on the roof. I thought he rolled over it on the rooftop and it caused him not to alight as he usually did.'

'That's likely the way it was,' the constable said. 'He'd not amounted to much, but people said he could tie himself up almost like a worm. All the actors said he was a right fine acrobat. Learned it from moving around on the boards when he was a carpenter.'

'Is that the truth?' Addison asked Sophia. 'About the death?'

She nodded. 'I didn't kill him. His mother said she was there. She'd been to the theatre with us, but went to the tavern afterward with a male friend.'

'True. The mother did say you pushed him, but he was bigger'n you. I couldn't find you later, Mrs Marland, but when I was working on another case, I found someone who said the older Mrs Marland was in the tavern until someone arrived to tell her there'd been an accident. I found the man who'd left the theatre with her. Turns out the tavern owner didn't want her to burn his place, so he kept his mouth shut about her being there, 'specially since you didn't end up in Newgate. He said he would have shoved both the mother and son out of the window if he'd had a chance so he figured you might have. But she's died of drink and meanness now so he's not worried.'

'I didn't push him,' she answered.

'Didn't think you did,' the constable added. 'Didn't then. Don't now. That man who told me the mother died informed me the old Mrs Marland grumbled all the time about her son's wife and wanted to make her suffer.'

'If anyone pays you to say anything else, you will answer to me,' Addison said.

'I'm on the side of the truth.' The constable held his hat, nodded to her. As he left, he grumbled, 'And if the son was a worm, the old woman was a snake.'

Addison watched her after the constable left. 'No one you brought here was what they seemed. Even the cat was a villain. He attacked you on the stairs.'

Chapter Eighteen

Sophia waited. Expecting the rage he'd never exhibited before. The wrath.

Then she worried that he might be in some sort of locked anger. Perhaps he'd lost his senses. He would surely storm at her in an uncontrollable fury.

Then he picked up papers that hadn't been on his desk when she'd cleaned it last, examined them and shook his head. He tossed the papers back to the stack. 'Was the cat that attacked you on the stairs the one at your house on the night your husband died?'

'Yes.'

She watched as he digested the information, a sad smile fleeting across his lips.

Goodness, was he going to take for ever to toss her out? Perhaps he'd meant it when he said he'd never raise his fist. But he wasn't acting normally.

'If it is acceptable, I will gather my things now.'

He seemed to remember she was in the room at that moment. 'Why?'

Oh, he had lost his senses. 'To leave.'

'You'd go to that Broomer's?'

'I have nowhere else.'

'Yes, you do. Here.'

'You would let me stay? Continue working?'

'Yes.'

'But what of Merry?'

'I should send her away. But, still, she has nowhere else to go except Mrs Wilson's.' His upper body didn't move, but his glance did. One brow rose before he spoke to her. 'The maid…has good morals?'

'She's working on them.'

'I can't send her back.'

'We could both go to Broomer's.'

'Please don't. None of you has your sea legs and neither do I apparently. You seem to get on better with Cook than the previous housekeeper and butler, although I think she's going to be upset for a few days. Keep your distance and give her a chance to get over this…when she finds out what happened. I'll smooth things over after she has a chance to accept it.'

'You're willing to let us stay?'

He nodded. 'I was willing to consider you my betrothed to my family.'

'You didn't ask.'

'No. That was wrong of me. Very wrong. I wanted them to see your importance in my life.'

He touched the ink bottle, making sure the stopper was set. 'Did you not trust me to believe people could transform their ways? Could start over?'

'You were so particular about the butler. About clothing.'

'Yes. And dear Humphrey Talbot Bonette, who gave me a false name, I let stay. With possibly a new tale for every morning the rest of his life. A valet who…' He paused, gaining speed. 'Who shakes so much I would not let touch a razor to my neck for any sum. But he is amusing. And he near begged for the job.'

He shook his head.

Running his fingers through his hair, he said. 'I never guessed at what you might be hiding from me. I first saw you in front of a brothel so I thought any confessions would be of former lovers.'

'But you introduced me as your betrothed.'

'Again, I apologise for that. I didn't want my brothers to think less of you. My mother had been a mistress all my life. I didn't want that for you. Until that second, I didn't grasp that my mother's status had mattered so much to me. I didn't think it did because I knew it irked my brothers that I was base-born. My mother didn't want to wed, but I suspect it was a corner she'd argued herself into and refused to leave.'

'You could have said I was your housekeeper.'

'Edward would never have believed that. Never. And I didn't think of it because that was not how I was seeing you. I was seeing you as a mistress.' He beheld her and spoke sincerely. 'I apologise for that, Sophia.'

Silence lingered.

He puffed out a breath. 'In the last years of my life, I have done all possible to maintain the appearance of trustworthiness and integrity. That has been foremost in my every movement. I didn't want my family to think me as even having a sweetheart. A beloved. I couldn't deny you and I couldn't introduce you as my beloved.'

'You do have a decent life.'

'But I wanted nothing less than the most upstanding life. Not after being locked away. It isn't you I'm critical of. It's myself.'

She couldn't speak. Addison hadn't kept secrets. She had. And he was worthy of achieving all his dreams and he would never do so with a housekeeper or a mistress by his side.

'If we are together, you will never have the respect due to you. I cannot be accepted as a young woman from the soirées you attend would.'

'Are you not even willing to try?'

'I don't have the family lineage. It's not there. Nor do I have the glittering ways of a person who finds herself at ease in social situations.'

'How do you know for certain?'

'You are the one who considers the situation and makes the decisions. If you think that is me, then you are not seeing the woman standing in front of you.'

He examined her and she couldn't tell what perceptions were behind his eyes.

'If you'll pardon me,' he said. 'I have to visit my employer. I have to explain what is going on under my roof. I need to tell him Ophelia did not murder Hamlet. He was done in by overacting and that Hamlet's mother was rotten in London.' He studied her. 'That sums it up, doesn't it?'

She didn't answer.

He left the room.

She would have preferred him to have shouted at her.

Before he went to see Burroughs, Addison instructed the driver to take a detour.

Addison tried to think logically about the way his world had turned upside down. He'd known the romance would change things between him and Sophia. But he'd expected it would be in the future.

That they had all the time in the present to learn about each other. That they could slowly come to know the deepest truths of each other. Not the frippery-type truths of what dance each preferred at a soirée, or what businesses he was pursuing and who had purchased what and lost money or gained wealth.

Whether they could be happy together the rest of their lives. Perhaps they'd have a disagreement about the length of time he worked or the old friends she had.

Until he'd heard himself introduce her as his betrothed, he'd not known his own mind where Sophia was concerned, and he understood her reluctance with marriage.

He had his own burdens to bear in that regard.

He suspected both his mother and his father had always been troubled in some part of their soul that their attraction had begun while his wife—her friend—was ill. And it wasn't that neither had forgiven the other. They'd not forgiven themselves.

He'd once, in a moment that was foreign to him, contacted the Duke's younger brother, a man he'd met briefly. And he'd asked, simply, if the Duke had been the same when his first wife was alive. If her death had altered him.

Oldston's brother had answered that the Duke had always been supercilious, but yet he'd had the exuberance of youth when he'd married his first wife and her illness and death had taken a part of him as well.

The man had considered carefully after that. He said at first Vera saved the Duke's life by being there for him after he'd lost his reason to live. But then he'd seemed drained and that, because they'd not married, the Duke felt she'd done a grave injustice to Addison and the Duke had had a great deal of trouble with that.

The Duke's brother said when Addison had been wayward, the Duke had blamed himself and Vera. But Oldston had known that no matter who'd caused the problems, only Addison could correct them.

And now Addison did not want to take a wrong path again.

He knew Sophia didn't want to live in the town house. He'd sensed it in her every movement. In her downtrodden face on the return trip to his home.

While in the past, it had been his own life he was to pilot, this time it was more than that. He was responsible for the people around him.

And he wasn't sure of the outcome.

The town house his father had offered him, and the percentage of the profits from his father's holdings, would take him further than he ever believed he could go. It would be as if all of London were helping him and, in a sense, they would be. His father and his friends, and Burroughs and his associates. The influential people around him.

He would have exceeded his dreams and been accepted in the house his father once visited. No longer would it hold the arguments of the day, but he would be the head of his household, close to his father, and they could visit as needed.

The notion touched him that his father had probably always planned for Addison to return to the town house. He'd not tossed Addison out when he was dissolute, nor had he sold it afterwards. But now that Addison had the responsible ways to care for it, he'd invited him to return. He'd never seen his father as a man devoted to family, but now Addison wondered if he'd been the distant one.

Perhaps his father wanted them close.

He stared at the exterior for a moment as the carriage slowed when it trundled by. The structure was little more than a shadow in the night, except for the dim lights Wooten used, yet the view flourished inside him.

Yes, his father wanted him to return. To be a part of the ducal family.

That evening, before time to eat, the new scullery girl, gaze lowered, found Sophia and told her that she'd placed cold vegetables in her room at Cook's request. She said the light repast was all Cook would have time to prepare that night as she was busy with other things. Humphrey and Merry fared the same. Humphrey's soliloquy about a Romeo who'd once tasted the foods of the gods and later had it denied it by Juliet carried through the walls.

The night ended with the aroma of baking wafting in the air, followed by a scorched scent that would likely linger for days. Sophia didn't believe the burning aroma was accidental.

Then, she heard it. The carriage stopped in front of the house. Humphrey's feet thumped as they hit the floor and he rushed to the door.

Not long after he returned to his room at a normal pace.

The world was quiet. Deceptively peaceful.

But perhaps not so deceptive in its peacefulness. All of them were there, in their beds, under the same roof.

And she suspected that they all loved each other in the way family members care. Addison was in his quarters and he could have been across town from her. But, no, he was near enough that she might see him if he strode into the kitchen, or hear his laughter, or be summoned.

To live under his roof and see him daily. To be aware when he arrived and left, even if she didn't want to know would tear at her, especially if he wed.

No one in London would consider *Ophelia* a suitable match for him.

She couldn't continue to hurt herself by staying, nor could she hurt him by moving with him, and she doubted he would even consider the possibility of her moving with him now that he'd discovered her past.

Then she heard a carriage, which was odd because Addison was at home.

Chapter Nineteen

The cooling garden breeze touched Addison's face, giving him a respite from the unusually warm night, and he heard the horses moving at a fast trot and the carriage wheels.

Likely half the neighbours would be peeking out their windows, even in the darkness, and they would guess whom the coach belonged to. He already had an idea. He didn't know why it had taken his brothers so long to locate the Duke, but then Oldston never felt obligated to let his sons know his plans.

He unlatched the side gate and strode to the front door just as his father banged a fist on it. One of the coachmen scurried behind him with a lantern. Another lantern did a nice job of lighting up the ducal crest.

The door opened and Humphrey stood behind it, silver hair sticking every which way, and a lamp in hand, peering into the night.

'Your Grace,' Addison greeted his father before Humphrey could speak.

The Duke whirled to Addison, but his voice was soft enough that the neighbours wouldn't hear. His teeth clenched around the words. 'You're betrothed to the murderess actress Ophelia. Have you lost your senses?'

Humphrey took a step forward, His lamp high. 'She is not a murderer,' Humphrey lashed out, almost hurting Addison's ears. 'I told the constable. She wouldn't hurt anyone and she didn't kill her husband. Hamlet always dies at the end. Everyone knows that. And her name is not Ophelia.'

Addison stared at his manservant who had apparently learned the ability to cast his voice to every patron in a loud theatre.

'We're not betrothed,' a tiny feminine voice from behind Humphrey said.

'And she's not in your home,' the Duke muttered, raising his hands.

'Sophia is my housekeeper.' Addison shrugged, trying to imagine how many neighbours were listening.

The Duke spoke softly. 'You will not be getting your mother's town house to entertain your *friends*.'

'I am content with that.'

'With all due respect, Your Grace, that is so unfair.' Now Sophia's voice rose and she pushed past Humphrey, stopping in the light, and she stood there, in Addison's oversized dressing gown, the sleeves rolled up and still billowing about her hands. 'Mr Addison has worked for all he has accomplished and he should not be punished because of—because of anyone else.'

The Duke turned to Addison, his words soft but distinct. 'You must pay your housekeeper well as she can afford to visit my tailor.'

'With all due respect, Your Grace, Mr Addison does not buy my clothing.'

'I suspect he purchased what you are wearing now.'

'I don't believe much else needs to be said tonight.' Addison directed his words to his father.

'You're right,' Oldston said and turned on his heel, the coachman following with the lantern. Then the Duke stopped, rotated and stepped in front of Addison, nose to nose, speaking softly. 'I still will not attend your hanging.'

Sophia lunged forward and her voice reached a crescendo and if there was a man in the moon he would have awoken to watch and listen. 'That is a horrible, horrible thing to say to your son,' she called out. 'Especially someone as well respected as Oliver Addison. You should be ashamed of yourself. You cannot know what it is like to live in fear of gaol when you are innocent. No one should have to survive like that.'

'I stand corrected.' Sarcasm dripped from his father's voice.

Addison walked over, put an arm at Sophia's back and spoke to his father. 'She turned me down.' He nodded several times, lips pressed together before adding, 'Yes. Doesn't want to wed me. Possibly because I'm illegitimate.'

His father's mouth moved, but a rumble issued from his throat and the jab he gave towards the carriage was enough to send the coachman running to the vehicle.

'Shall we go inside?' Addison asked her.

When the door shut behind them, Humphrey shook his head and lowered the lamp. 'I cannot believe a duke would stand in the street and raise such a rumpus.'

Addison noticed Sophia was trembling. He pulled her close. 'Sweeting, you do not have to defend me to my father.'

She sniffled. 'I could not bear it if you hanged. That is horrible to even speak about.'

'I know. He doesn't mean it. He'd likely attend.'

He felt her shoulders heaving and patted her. 'I'm jesting. Don't take it so hard. The Duke has a temper. He's my father. And I care for him, though I sometimes wish I didn't. He's not a bad person, just an opinionated one.'

'You're ten times the person he is. A hundred.'

'And you didn't want to be introduced as my betrothed.'

She stilled. 'It wasn't true.'

'You're right,' he admitted.

He stepped back and brushed a kiss across her forehead. 'Do you think you will be able to sleep?'

'No.'

'Try,' he said. 'Don't let my father upset you.'

A voice came from the doorway. Cook. 'Come along, Sophia. Mr Addison needs his rest and I'll sit with you until you feel better.'

She took Sophia's arm and led her away.

Addison watched Sophia leave. She'd likely been wearing his dressing gown in her room. And it was a warm night.

Chapter Twenty

The sun would be rising soon on an uncertain day.

His mother had been a natural duchess, yet she'd refused a marriage which would have put her into the true ducal estate.

He couldn't imagine Sophia daring to throw anything in a rage, yet she'd surprised him by answering his father.

In his fury, his father had removed the offer, which Addison wasn't sure how he felt about.

It solved the problem of Sophia being uncomfortable there, but it didn't solve the true difficulty.

He'd had few significant setbacks since he'd changed. None, truth be told. Oh, he'd had minor business failings and a few bobbles to sort out, but for each misstep, he'd still managed to jump three steps ahead.

He'd not even had to make true decisions, but only follow the best choice in front of him.

Perhaps he wasn't that experienced at making a true decision. Now he had one facing him.

In the past, each consideration had been completed

based on the possible consequences to the future. If the chance to increase his holdings was greatest by selecting one path, then that was the path he took.

His forward momentum would stop with Sophia at his side.

True, he didn't see his livelihood fading. But continuing along, not rising.

His jaw clenched, certain his father would agree to their previous agreement if Addison left Sophia, Humphrey and Merry behind. Within weeks Addison could be squiring some young lady on his arm and the past would again fade behind him.

He'd once left all his friends behind, only to discover that truly none of them had been more than someone he caroused with.

Then he'd left the town house in his past, but he'd not had much time to reflect on his immediate surroundings. In fact, it hadn't seemed like he'd been living in a home, but more similar to his university days.

Then, Beldon had improved the appearance of his current dwelling and Caldwell had created a magnificent garden. The greenery had reminded him of the beauty of the well-tended gardens of his youth, not just the one at his mother's home, but the lush one at the ducal estate.

He missed the art. The treasures. Fragile glassware. Clothes pressed to perfection.

Meeting the Duke the night before had not been what she'd expected. No wonder Addison's mother had called him an ogre.

Addison favoured his father in stature, but Addison

had a heart to go along with the outward appearance. If the Duke had one, he'd purchased it somewhere and kept it in a safe place.

It was another example of Addison's mettle that he'd done so well in life after having such a parent.

Sophia heard Humphrey taking Addison the shaving water and she wished she could still be the one visiting his room in the mornings.

Her feelings stormed inside her. One moment, it was as if the wind blew achingly and the next a gale from the other side peppered her with ice.

She pushed the sorrow away, aware of the many times she could have told Addison the truth, but how she'd not wanted to relive the worst moments of her life. How she'd not wanted him to know she was the one they called *Ophelia*.

When she'd been poor, she would have envied anyone working in such a fine house. And once she had the position, she'd been fearful of losing everything.

Entering the elaborate town house had been like walking into a palace too fancy for her to even work as someone who emptied the chamber pots.

She still didn't believe the grandness of it. He'd lived there. And he'd attended university. And he had a carriage. And a duke for a father.

If he'd been just a plain base-born man, that would have been easier. But instead he was a duke's son.

Then the ringing bell shattered her reverie and she was halfway to the door before she grasped what she was doing. She forced herself to stop and the pain invaded her again.

Moving forward, she entered the library.

Addison was at his desk and he raised tired eyes.

His hair had been trimmed. By Humphrey most likely. It was uneven in places in a tousled way, which didn't harm him at all because he was so particular about the rest of his attire. It made him more endearing.

She yearned to comfort him, but could feel enough frost not to move forward. She had to break the silence. 'Did Humphrey cut your hair?'

Their eyes met, and he half smiled, reaching to touch the uneven spot. 'It shows, doesn't it?'

'But I like it.'

He held her with a glance. 'That is solicitous of you to say.'

He stretched and covered a yawn.

'We have some mending to do and not of the sewing variety. Can you please have Merry compose a brief, very brief, note to be sent to my brother? Perhaps a simple sentence of apology without admission of what for. Write it for her if needed and send it with Humphrey for my perusal. Humphrey has a bottle of wine selected that I've approved and Cook is preparing treats. If you could get that arranged in a basket after Cook is finished with her part and leave it in the vestibule.'

'Will the coachman deliver it?'

'I will because if Edward is in a temper, I'll be able to defuse it.'

She bit the inside of her lip.

He studied her, sitting at his table, pen in hand.

'I should have told you everything,' she admitted. 'I apologise that I didn't. In part, I was ashamed that I didn't stand up for myself. I hid instead of risking the consequences.'

'Well, perhaps it was best you didn't assert yourself when accused. Sometimes the truth gets lost among others' lies and vehemence.'

'I'm sorry.' She reached out, offering solace without touch but the movement of her hand.

'Don't concern yourself, Sophia.' He shrugged.

'You angered your father. A duke. Because of my actions. And he removed the offer of the house. Did he rescind the offer of letting you handle his finances as well?'

'No. He's not daft,' Addison muttered.

Sophia gulped.

'Don't be dismayed. I'm not. And I don't think my father is. He demands deference in public from his family and from me, he expects grit in private.' He shook his head. 'I suppose it makes the observed respect more valuable to him as he knows it is a charade we must play. But I appreciate the things he did for me.'

Addison's voice softened. 'I think he grasps he is getting older and wants us to be a family again. The location is so close to his own and his wife would be pleased to have me near.'

The town house. The place where she would never fit.

Her heart plunged, along with the hope she'd not known existed.

'Soph—'

Her hand on the door, she stopped.

'I've missed you.'

He could have said ten thousand things that would have affected her less. 'I've missed you, too.'

She heard it. All the longing in her voice softly blaring into the room.

'It'll get easier.' He spoke softly.

'Are you sure?'

'No.'

She reached out and put a hand flat on the door to keep herself steady. She shut her eyes briefly. 'I know that I should have told you. I had lost everything once, then twice. It had been impossible not to believe it would all vanish. I wanted to save every coin I made in case we were tossed out again. Humphrey's home had been burned and he had no place either. Merry hated her life. We were doing what we could with what we had.'

She glanced down. 'Except Humphrey did drink a bit too much. And Merry shouldn't have taken the money from your brother. And I shouldn't have hidden from the constable. But my mother-in-law would likely have lit a flame to the older lady's house if she'd found me. I apologise, but I can't say for certain I wouldn't do it all again.'

She went through the doorway and dared not stop on the other side. He might hear.

She could not live where he'd grown up. No. She would always be less than all of her neighbours. Less than their staff.

Waiting until she reached her room, the loss flooded inside her, unable to be contained any longer. He'd said it might not get easier. Perhaps it would. But it could have meant he hadn't felt the same way she had.

Then she realised. If he moved and sold everything... she, Humphrey and Merry would all be homeless. Not only had she endangered her future, her friends would be hurt as well. Best for her to leave and give them a chance.

She had Broomer's. All she would have to do was go

there and ask for employment. But she couldn't. She'd lost all her strength because she'd needed it to keep her heart beating.

True, she'd been married before. But he was her first love.

Chapter Twenty-One

Addison stepped out of the carriage, the basket in one hand and Oldston's family home in front of him.

He was part of that family.

He walked up, and the butler opened the door. The man had been there the night of the anniversary dinner.

'Is Oldston here? Or Her Grace?'

'No. They are out for the evening. I don't expect them to return soon.'

'Benedict or Edward?'

'I would not know. They use a separate entrance.'

'Could you have someone show me to Edward's chambers?' he asked.

Within moments, a maid had taken him to his brother's rooms, and he deposited the basket inside the door and turned to the woman. 'I would like to see Benedict.'

Off on another walk through the house he went and this time Benedict responded to the knock.

When Addison came inside, his brother, dressed for a formal event, greeted him. 'Never seen you here before. Are you moving in?'

'No,' Addison said. 'Edward might cry if he had to see me more often.'

Benedict laughed. 'In that case, please stay.'

'I've never considered it.'

'The guest room is to your left. The Duchess likes everyone to gather at breakfast and I wouldn't mind seeing the Duke's face when you stepped in.'

'You've inherited Father's charm.'

'Of course. I just hide it better than everyone else.' Then, Benedict squinted. 'Was your valet asleep when he cut your hair?'

'He was telling a good story and got diverted. I wasn't sure I wanted him to continue.'

'Well,' his brother said, moving to a pull. 'I've got a valet who can assist you with a good haircut and whatever else you may need here. I'm on my way out, but I hope you stay, particularly for breakfast in the morning. Father always behaves in front of the Duchess, and, if you can believe it, so does Edward.'

'I will see you at breakfast then.'

Sophia stitched in her room, unaware of the bright threads of her embroidery, her mind only seeing fibres, not the colours.

Humphrey had said Addison left with the basket.

Now everyone was talking after dinner, and she'd left the table first, unable to taste the food. She didn't want to be around her friends.

Cook and Merry had watched her, and Merry had tried to tell humorous stories, but they'd all fallen flat. Humphrey kept quoting verse from Shakespeare, but only the tragedies.

She remembered the tragedy of her marriage, a disaster for both of them.

She'd felt her husband had trapped her, but he hadn't. Her mother-in-law would have carried her portmanteau away for her if Sophia had requested to leave. With no way to support herself, the unknown outside her door had been more frightening, unpredictable and unsafe than the unhappiness inside.

Then she'd needed help again and went in search of Merry. Merry would have seen that Sophia had enough food to hold her until work had been found.

With the people she knew, she could survive. They'd helped each other on good days and through the worst. And now she could see they would always be there for her.

Someone rapped on the door and she jumped to her feet, and rushed to pull it open. Cook stood there. Sophia slumped, expecting Addison.

The older woman held a tray with a pastry on it.

'The carriage driver returned,' Cook said, putting the tray on the small side table. 'But without Addison. Humphrey is gathering some of Addison's clothing to send back with the driver.' Cook spoke as if she were delivering a eulogy. 'At the Duke's estate.'

'The estate?'

'Yes. I'm afraid he's going to leave us, Sophia.' Cook's eyes were downcast. 'I'll find another post, but…' She sighed. 'It's right that Mr Addison should be with his relations. His world. His mother did wrong by him and his father is righting it.'

'They don't get on that well.'

'They won't have to get on at all in the ducal estate. They won't even have to see each other, from what I hear.' A tear rolled down her cheek and she wiped it away with the towel tucked in her apron. 'I had my hopes set on that town house and didn't even think of Addison moving into the estate. The new Duchess thinks the world of him.'

Cook gulped and her voice wavered. 'The carriage driver believes Addison will keep the house for now and let us stay until we find new employment.'

She trudged away, her towel fluttering in her hand.

Sophia sat on her bed and studied the dressing gown lying beside her. Addison's soap lingered on the cloth and she touched it to her cheek.

She'd known not to succumb to her feelings. Known she would eventually have to lose him. But she'd hoped for more instances to hold dear.

But there could never be enough memories.

Chapter Twenty-Two

Sophia took the midday treat Cook had prepared for her to her room. She didn't want to be around anyone.

A rap at her door. Not soft. Firm. Assured.

Her heart flip-flopped and she braced herself before answering. She pulled the door wide.

Addison. A tower of a man, with clothing suitable for any ducal event, and the haircut Humphrey had given him had been evened out. His clear blue eyes locked with hers.

She touched her fingers to her lips.

He took her hand from her face and held it. 'I want you to go with me to see my past. Afterwards, I want to speak about the future.'

Her feet didn't want to move. She didn't want to hear the words Addison would say. The words telling her about how wonderful it was to have the Duke in his life again and he didn't need the town house because he could stay at the ducal estate where she wasn't welcome.

'I borrowed the Duke's carriage to take us,' he said.

Her mouth dried. 'Certainly.'

She didn't even gather her reticule, but went with him outside. A cat scurried across the path in front of them.

Addison led her to the town coach. She hesitated at the steps, but the driver smiled, and Addison took her elbow and nudged her forward.

Inside, she realised leather could smell new and when the vehicle moved, she didn't know if it was the horses or the coach, but it travelled more smoothly than she'd believed possible.

Addison sat beside her, not touching. He stretched his legs. 'Father had this coach specially made,' he said. 'And it will be the first time it's ever stopped in front of a gaol, I'm sure. I didn't tell Father where I would be taking it. And he didn't ask.'

When the wheels stopped rolling, he helped her out of the carriage and waved the driver on. 'We'll get a hackney to return.'

The coachman doffed his hat and snapped the ribbons.

Addison stared at the cold stone structure as if he'd never seen it before, determined to seal the image into his mind. Next, he secured her arm and trod a few steps from the entrance.

'This is the exact place where I spoke with my father's steward, but inside is where I changed my life.'

He tucked her hand over his arm and began the walk. 'Even now, I can get a whiff of the stench inside. I always do when I'm near. Always.'

He rubbed the back of his neck. 'It makes my hair stand on end to be here. I cannot believe the banker Burroughs trusted me afterward with funds.'

'What did he think when you told him you had Ophelia living in the household?'

'Burroughs said he has an actor in his family and it is what it is. He told me not to sleep with any windows open and laughed.'

He shrugged away his next words. 'I'm sure the constable has informed everyone of your being in my home, and also, when my father arrived at night, they surely paid attention. I did notice when I left the house yesterday that everyone who saw me grinned and waved. For someone who hasn't appeared onstage, I feel more celebrated than David Garrick was.'

'I didn't mean for this to happen.'

'I know,' he reassured her. 'That was nothing compared to when I was on this walk before.' He took her hand. 'Imagine. This time, I stepped out of a vehicle with a crest on the side. And now I have a beautiful woman strolling in the sunshine with me.'

Over the last few days, he'd considered his past, his present and where he wanted his future to be. And he'd not wanted to leave the world behind that he had around him. It meant too much.

To move into the sphere of his father, and step into that environment, would mean more servants would be needed. More things to be polished and more visitors to impress and more of everything. Everything.

And he'd have less of the closeness he had with the people in his life now. He hardly had time to eat some nights and the kitchen always welcomed him. He slowed when he moved into that room. Sometimes, he lingered and decided that work had finished for the night and could wait.

In the morning, Humphrey made the day brighter

with his nonsensical stories, though someone else would need to be hired soon for the true valet duties.

The coachman's wife had sisters nearby. The new scullery maid's parents were close. A caring family had formed around Addison without him noticing. A family he'd chosen for the most part and who'd brought their own lives into his. And he didn't know how a move would uproot their lives.

'I've lent a few neighbours my vehicle over the years. I hardly know them and yet I do. The carriage driver is acquainted with everyone up and down the street. He's the one who's given me direction when help is needed because of a funeral, an illness or a marriage. He's even warned me away from a few places I've planned to go, telling me it will do me no favours in the long run.'

Addison had even discussed a few investments he'd been uncertain of and the man had listened with an impartial ear while Addison relayed his concerns.

'The neighbours here don't eat with the peers, but they accept me as a prince. No one dares disparage me because of my birth.' He clasped his hands behind his back. 'Everyone sees me as Addison, a man who lives among them and belongs on my own merit.'

'I don't want you to stay behind on my account.'

'I'm not. I was ambitious until I paid my father back and then I took a moment to observe around the world I have now. You are a part of that world.'

'Am I? You have no word you can use for my place in it.'

He acknowledged her statement with a nod.

'If I spend time with you as we live now, we will make love and then I will go back to my work. And

you will go back down the stairs and we will go along our own paths. Mostly alone.'

He'd decided he didn't want that life.

'I want someone who tells me she is my wife and that I must spend time with her and not go on about my way. That was something my parents never had together. They loved each other until her death, but the door was always there for both of them. I don't want someone in my life who always has a foot towards the exit.'

'I've been trapped before. I don't want to be trapped again.'

'Is that truly it? Do you believe me like your husband? Or is it what you tell yourself, so you do not have to trust me. And why should you not trust me? You see around me the life I have.'

He took her hand. 'If you need a position away from me, I will see that you have one. My father's wife can help. The banker. I can find you employment. Perhaps not as a housekeeper, but the finances will be as good. You aren't imprisoned. You will never be confined under my roof by anyone except yourself. And if you wish for time to find other work on your own, you will have as much time as needed.'

The wind blew a lock of hair across her face and he took her arm, stilling her and brushing the wisp from her gaze.

'Last night, I stayed at the ducal estate. Everything gleams. It's longer to walk to the breakfast room than it is to walk from my house to the coachman's.'

When Addison had stepped into the room, it had been no surprise at all to his father and the Duchess. Their house. Their rules. Their servants.

Seeing Edward spit out the egg had been worth it.

'Did you enjoy it?'

He let his lungs fill with air before speaking, considering. 'Yes. The meal with the Duke and Duchess was nice.'

'Your father wasn't angry with you?'

'No more than usual. He asked how you were doing and I said you were well. He also told me it was kind of you to say you wouldn't wed me because my parents weren't married and obviously you meant to spare my feelings, as he was certain I was where the fault lay. He likes to get in the last word. The Duchess shushed him.'

He didn't tell her that the Duchess and the Duke had both given his brother a direct glare when Edward asked if Ophelia had taken any new ventures at the theatre recently.

It had been easy enough to respond politely.

He continued walking with Sophia.

'Sitting with only my relatives around me was odd at first, but pleasant. I've never lived in a true family. I think it's time.'

'But your father said you couldn't have the town house if I was in your life. He doesn't feel I'm right for you.' She clutched his sleeve long enough for him to stop briefly, then released the garment and they continued on.

'Doesn't matter. I believe he wants me closer in any event. If I lived there, I would be in his daily path. Now, he has to acknowledge that he planned to visit. At my mother's, it would be a coincidence.'

His boots crunched on the road. 'Sophia, if you think a marriage to me would be worse than the one you had, then you truly are not thinking. You're not opening your eyes. I've never been this lonely in my life, except for the moments I was locked in with criminals. Now my room feels almost as alone.'

'I can't walk among the people you know. And I don't know I will change. If I disagree with you, I may not have the courage to speak my mind.'

'Oh, you will. I have no doubt of that.'

'How can you be so certain?'

'My father assures me that once the new has worn off the vows, a wife will make her opinion known. And truly, Sophia, you have made your choices evident. You searched Broomer out for other employment. Think of all you've seen. You're not the same person you were at eighteen. You couldn't be. If we wed, everything will cease to be mine and it will be ours. Our house. Our rules.'

'But I don't know that you will continue to keep that promise. Promises are easy to give before the wedding. After, they're words. Figments of hopes that evaporated.'

'Not with me. I made a promise once to alter my life and I carried it through with a vengeance. Once, I swore to the man who gave me a chance at the bank that I would not let him down. Wedding vows would be the third promise of my life and I will keep them.'

He strode along and she would have guessed him unaware of her at his side if she'd not known better.

'But I suppose the true question is a different one.' Again he didn't gaze at her. 'What do you want?'

'What I want can't happen. I want our lives to return to the way they were when Oldston first visited. I acted the part of your wife in my imagination. When your father arrived, it was as vital to me as it was to you that you appear successful. It was grand and I felt so close to you. But we can't go back because you have the opportunity to return to your world and achieve your dreams.'

Grit flared in his voice. 'My dreams are achieved,' he said. 'I am where I am, in this world and in this town, by my actions after I changed my life. I worked hard. I work hard. Every night I work harder and I go among society on nights knowing I will need to work longer into the morning because I am at an event.'

'A wife could help you. She would fit in with the bankers and peers.'

'When I told you before that Merry hadn't left one brothel to move into another one, I meant it. Not only does that apply to the women who work for me, but everyone under the roof. I am not selling my body for a position in society. I put up with such nonsense from Cook because she feels herself my mother and I fob her off with a smile and a laugh. From you, it is different.'

'I didn't like marriage. It's true, I didn't murder my husband, but when I realised his neck was broken, I wasn't as sad as you'd expect a wife to be. I wasn't half as sad as you'd expect a wife to be.'

'I'm not like your husband was. I know that.'

'No. You're not.'

She watched the movement as her shoes peeked out from under her skirts as she strode forward. 'But what do you want? Is it that you have reached a position in your life where you've decided it's time for a wife and I'm the person who happened to be in front of you?'

He saw a hackney and waved it to them.

She swallowed, gathering her courage. 'You're of society now. If you wed the right person, it could help you advance.'

He stared directly into her eyes. 'If I wed the *wrong* person, it could help me advance.'

He let the silence linger between them in the vehicle.

When it stopped at his home, he took her into his room. Inside the doorway, he clasped her close. He kissed her with a lifetime of hunger for her, more want in his body than he believed possible.

Her mouth opened; their tongues touched. He leaned into her, his body holding hers upright against the wall.

He could not breathe or think of anything but asking her to marry him.

His father and his mother had loved each other. He knew that now. But love wasn't enough to make happiness. And needing each other wasn't enough to create peace. She'd experienced that.

He held her face in his hands, her cheeks in his palms. Addison let her breath mingle with his, savouring the garden scent of her.

'Hearts and flowers won't sustain two people.'

He waited. 'Will you listen, listen with your mind, not your heart? Don't let your heart mislead you into believing your past is happening again.'

'I will try.'

He lifted her and carried her to his bed.

Instead of lowering her to the bed, he meant to give her a soft kiss, the kind he expected a woman would want who liked tender words, but her arm reached around his neck, pressing close, their breathing combining into a taste of sweetness, hunger and desire from the depths of their bodies.

He pulled back and studied her. 'My parents loved each other, but possibly no one truly knew it. Even them. Until the end. I want the statement to the world to be that we are in love. We care about each other. And we are each half of a whole. I want that statement to be between us as well. I don't want to leave that to chance.'

He lowered her to the bed and moved above her.

'You're so much, Sophia. You're a woman who made a place for the people she cared about. Who stayed with a man who was worthless because she had made a commitment to him. Who found a place in my life and made it her own.'

She reached out, putting her arms around his neck and pulling him close for another kiss.

He angled his mouth against hers, but it would never be satisfying enough. Only marriage. A commitment of a lifetime together would satisfy the longing in him.

He rolled to her, his elbow on the bed, and propped his jaw on his fist. His free hand traced a heart above hers.

'Soph,' he said, 'you remind me of wildflowers. Unexpected, yet miraculous. All of them. Every flower I've ever seen and all those I haven't, and they've never been as beautiful to me as you. Beside you, they're simply greenery and one fleck of colour in your eye is more radiant.'

His movements stopped and he beheld her. 'The first time I saw you, I couldn't let you go. I knew you needed someone. It wasn't that I comprehended I wanted you with me, but I did. I wanted to protect you in those first few seconds that we met. I judged you a possible lightskirt, but there was something in your eyes that called to me. You were the woman I wanted to discover. To learn more about.'

He rolled on to his back and gazed at the ceiling.

'Soft words don't do you justice and you should never listen to them. Because they can't paint the picture of the true you. You should experience them always, though, inside yourself. You should have them floating about your memories all day, hearing them whisper, a reminder that you are a woman who survived a terrible time and didn't give up. Who had nothing to eat, but managed. A quiet warrior. A woman of strength and courage. I want to say to the world, this is my wife. My life. This is the woman at my side. She's not a guest in my life. She's in my life. To stay.'

Epilogue

Before the wedding, Sophia heard Addison tell the bishop how happy he was to have found her. Then after the vows, he kissed her hand and held it close to his heart, and gazed at her.

She wasn't certain the bishop didn't shed a tear.

Then, Stubby sneezed into the flowers he held and Broomer used one handkerchief in each hand to wipe his tears.

The Duke grumbled. 'I came because if I didn't see it myself, I wouldn't have believed it. But the town house is empty if she needs a place to get away from you,' Oldston said to Addison. 'If you won't live in it, she might.' He glared at his son. 'As a matter of fact, I think I'll give it to her for a wedding present.'

'Come along for the breakfast,' Addison said. 'That's a discussion for another day.'

'That woman you have cooking for you refused to prepare the meal at my estate,' the Duke mumbled. 'The ducal estate. She told my staff she could not trust the ovens. The ducal ovens.'

'Well, we've not prepared a fatted calf for you, Father, but you'll have one of the best meals you've ever had.'

'If you insist. You've always been difficult. Even your staff is. I expect no different from your wife.'

His voice could have broken nails, but Sophia knew by the glimmer of a smile he gave her that he welcomed her into the family.

'What'd you do with the painting I gave you? The one you didn't like well enough to keep the first time?' the Duke asked.

'It's in the library,' Addison said. 'And I purchased a vase that reminded me of my mother to go with it. I expect them to always remain in my family.'

'Your mother would have cried at the sight of that urn you had.'

'I got rid of it.'

Sophia held out her left hand. 'The gold coins inside were melted to make my wedding ring.'

'Well,' the Duke muttered. 'If it had gold inside, your mother might have tolerated it.'

Benedict spoke to Sophia. 'It's nice to have a sister. Edward will accept you some day. As soon as he sees the profits. Father has convinced him that financially this will be in his best interest and he's shopping for a new carriage. He noticed Addison's was bigger.'

The Duke cleared his throat. 'Seeing Addison wed made me want to see all three of my sons married.'

'You'll have to drag Edward to the altar with a chain if you want him wed,' Addison said.

'I can do that,' the Duke said. 'Chain… Funds… Whatever works…'

When they arrived at Addison's and stepped inside, a woman was waiting with Humphrey. He'd stayed behind because he said weddings were for the loving couple and he didn't want his fame to overshadow their day.

'How can I assist you?' Addison asked.

'Mrs Wilson told me to come here,' she said. 'I'm Delilah August. I'm here to see my son,' she said.

'Well, that be me,' Stubby said, popping around Addison. 'I got hair as pretty as you do, too.'

She sniffled and put a hand to her throat. 'You've beautiful hair.'

'Think I need fattenin' up?' he asked. 'Most people do.'

'I think you're handsome just as you are.'

'Well, you could use some fattenin' up. And we be about to have a weddin' breakfast.'

'Would you like to join us?' Addison asked.

'I'd like that,' she said. 'And thank you for assisting my son. I know Mrs Wilson didn't help you find me, but it was to protect me. She's as near a saint as you can be without following a single commandment.'

Stubby hooked a thumb to Sophia. 'And this woman here is my sister, but we got different parents as you'd know 'cause you be my mother. You'll like her, though. And her husband there, used to be a duke's son and I guess he still is 'cause that man there's the Duke. And we's about to have some new babies and if you want one, I'll save one for you.'

'We are?' Addison asked, questioning Sophia.

'Rufflestiltskin is Mrs Rufflestiltskin,' she answered. 'Merry is taking care of the midwife duties,' she answered. 'By the end of the day, we should be able to visit the kittens.'

'I be keepin' one,' Stubby said. 'But I don't know what I'm goin' do with all this family and a cat, too.

Guess I'm settlin' down. It's gonna' take some gettin' used to. I think Addison's my brother now since he married my sister and then he's got two brothers, and then he's got His Grace.' He shook his head. 'I got more family than I know what to do with.' Then he smiled at his mother. 'But I be keepin' you close cause us with pretty hair got to stick together. Broomer always said if he ever saw a woman with hair like mine, he'd marry her so I'm figuring I'll be gettin' a new father.'

'Food's getting cold,' Cook said, peering around the doorway, ladle in her hand. 'And I made some peas for the little fellow. I've heard that sailors couldn't exist without them.'

Stubby's face changed. He threw up his hands. 'A starvin' fish won't even eat peas.'

'Come along, everyone,' Humphrey said. 'We will have a most delicious repast as prepared by my darling Juliet.'

'It's Cook,' she muttered. 'I told you plain and clear. I am not your Juliet. Where you are concerned, I'm one of Shakespeare's witches at the kettle.'

'She says that now,' Humphrey said, putting a hand at his heart. 'But only because she never saw me on the stage. Her love would have been instant could she have seen me as Romeo.'

'Oh, hush up, Humphrey,' she muttered. 'Let's eat. That'll keep you quiet for a while.'

Sophia and Addison waited as everyone gathered for the meal.

'I forgot to carry you over the threshold,' he said.

'It doesn't matter.' She took both his hands. 'You'll have many opportunities.'

After a kiss, they followed everyone to the wedding

breakfast. When Sophia looked in the dining room, she realised how large her family had become.

'Are you comfortable with this?' Addison asked.

'Like Stubby, I wanted a big family.'

'So did I, but I didn't grasp it until you arrived and I understood how important it can be to belong to others. Not just to yourself, but to be a part of someone who cares about you. That's the true lifeblood of having a family. Being a part of their lives.'

'You don't mind that you won't live in the town house and have a life among the peers and royals.'

He shook his head. 'I plan to see my father more. Much more. But this is my life. And the best place for me to have a family. Merry is the housekeeper now and she'll need guidance, and so will Humphrey. The coachman is happiest here and I believe we all will be because we've lived here longer. Shakespeare said, *"To thine own self be true"*,' he added. 'And this is the true me. A part of you. A life with you is the only one that will make me happy and this family is the one for me. I love them all, but you are the one I love most and always will.'

He gazed at her. '*"To thine own self be true, and to thy wife."* That's how he should have written it. That's how I feel.'

She put her arms around him, secure in the knowledge that she'd found the other half of her heart in Addison.

* * * * *

If you enjoyed this story, why not check out these other great reads by Liz Tyner?

To Win a Wallflower
It's Marriage or Ruin
Compromised into Marriage
The Governess's Guide to Marriage
A Cinderella for the Viscount